Playing With Fire

Playing With Fire

Cho Chong-Rae

Translated by
Chun Kyung-Ja

East Asia Program
Cornell University
Ithaca, New York 14853

The Cornell East Asia Series is published by the Cornell University East Asia Program and is not affiliated with Cornell University Press. We are a small, non-profit press, publishing reasonably-priced books on a wide variety of scholarly topics relating to East Asia as a service to the academic community and the general public. We accept standing orders which may be cancelled at any time and which provide for automatic billing and shipping of each title in the series upon publication.

If after review by internal and external readers a manuscript is accepted for publication, it is published on the basis of camera-ready copy provided by the volume author. Each author is thus responsible for any necessary copy-editing and for manuscript formatting. Submission inquiries should be addressed to Editorial Board, East Asia Program, Cornell University, Ithaca, New York 14853-7601.

Number 85 in the Cornell East Asia Series.
© 1997 by Chun Kyung-Ja. All rights reserved
ISSN 1050-2955
ISBN 1-885445-65-2 cloth
ISBN 1-885445-85-7 paper
Printed in the United States of America

Acknowledgments

The translator, on behalf of herself and the author, wishes to express thanks to Dong-Ah Publishing Company for its kind and generous support of the translation and editing for this project. The Korean Culture and Arts Founddation provided a subvention in support of publication, which also was much appreciated. An anonymous reader designated by Cornell East Asia Series made some useful suggestions for improvements to the English text. Finally, thanks are due to Professor David McCann and Ms. Karen Smith of Cornell East Asia Series for their part in making this text available.

PLAYING WITH FIRE

Human Practice

1

Like a bolt from the blue, the incident unfolded without the slightest warning, shattering mundane routines.

In the heart of the city, the day was waning toward twilight. Each afternoon at this hour, as sunbeams slip down between tall buildings to the narrow streets, he reclines his armchair to the second notch. As darkness descends, his gaze turns to the world twelve floors beneath his window.

"Another day safely passed."

So he mutters to himself, peering contentedly at the crowds squirming aimlessly on the streets. It means, for him, that his business has prospered and his wealth increased for one more day. His success must go on flourishing, he muses, and in no time he'll be looking down not from the twelfth floor, but from the fiftieth, the hundredth.

It is his favorite hour of the day, a moment of relaxation, like lighting up a cigarette after a satisfying meal or receiving a massage at the gates of sleep, not from your hag-wife, but from the soft hands of a woman still in the bloom of youth. What he feels is a kind of triumph, and each day he feels an urge to shout his victory to the world. But he stays silent, like a Buddhist monk tirelessly rolling prayer beads.

Forty minutes before office hours end, his secretary, Miss Kang, serves him ginseng tea seasoned with walnuts, pine nuts and dates. This signals that no one is to bother him in his office, the president's suite. He takes no calls, unless the company's survival is imperiled.

But then, his phone rang at that exact hour.

Miss Kang said it was the president of Sun Corporation calling, and he'd picked up the receiver in the best of moods. For earlier that same day he'd closed a four hundred thousand dollar contract with Sun Corporation for a simple construction job.

With an affected laugh, he began, "Ah, it's you, President Park, Hwang here."

There was no response, but the line didn't seem to be disconnected.

"Hello, hel-lo?" Just as he relaxed his voice, those unbelievable words had rolled into his ear:

"How do you do, Mr. Bae Jomsu?"

Like a child just learning to read, or a judge pronouncing sentence in a grave tone, the caller crisply enunciated "mis," "ter," "bae," "jom," "su." Each distinct syllable was a spike penetrating into his heart, brain, lungs, eyes, tongue. . . . That single sentence left him tottering on the brink of unconsciousness.

For a moment he struggled to reply, but he couldn't manage to utter a word.

"Mr. Bae Jomsu, don't even think about hanging up! Only a fool would do that."

He wanted to scream "Who the hell are you?!" but couldn't reply.

"Mr. Bae Jomsu, I am very happy to have this chance to make your acquaintance."

By this time Hwang was shaking like a leaf. "Bae Jomsu, Bae Jomsu"— the speaker deliberately prefaced each sentence with that name. He seemed to relish driving the spike deeper. The name itself was uttered as a cold-blooded threat: "The jig is up, you're caught," or "You're a dead man." With each merciless repetition the listener shuddered.

"Mr. Bae Jomsu, I'll stop here for today."

"No, no, you, you, who are . . . ?" Out of breath, unable to finish, he was reduced to a miserable wretch.

"Mr. Bae Jomsu, no need to be in such a hurry. This is only the beginning. Anyway, I might as well let you know who I am for future reference. My name is Shin Bomho."

That was the end of the conversation.

Head in hands, he rose halfway out of the chair. He was too distraught to figure out who the caller could be, or how he could have dredged up his distant past.

"Miss Kang, Miss Kaaang!" he shrieked with the receiver still in hand. His voice, normally dignified, was imbued instead with sheer terror.

"You called, sir?"

Like a mechanical doll, Miss Kang swiftly stepped into the office.

"Miss Kang, that, that call, who'd you say it was?"

"Sir, are you not well?"

Normally she wouldn't have dared to respond to a question from the president with an inquiry of her own, but Miss Kang was concerned at his suddenly pale, bloodless countenance and the pathetic quaking of his hands.

"Office Supervisor, Office Supervisor!" she shouted, turning around. Her boss rushed in, short of breath, repeating, "What, what's the matter, what's the matter?"

"Quiet, everyone, be quiet . . ." the president said feebly, his strength drained.

"You seem in a dreadful state, sir. Please put the phone back and sit down."

The president handed the receiver over to the supervisor and collapsed into his chair.

"Miss Kang . . . ?"

"Yes, sir, that call was from Sun Corporation. They said their president had something urgent to talk over with you about today's contract."

Miss Kang sensed something had gone terribly wrong, so after the interruption her reply gushed out and she emphasized the word "urgent" lest his anger fall on her.

"Sun Corporation . . ."

He felt engulfed in darkness. Putting his elbows on the desk, he pressed his head tightly between his hands. He felt a chill. No use trying to dodge that son of a bitch, he told himself.

"See here, from now on, if any calls come from Shin Bomho . . . a guy by the name of Shin Bomho, put him through to me immediately, regardless of the time."

He had almost said "a bastard by the name of Shin," but somehow he'd managed to say "a guy" instead.

"Sir, since you're not feeling well, why not . . ."

"Get out!"

He yelled for them to leave in his usual coarse manner. Once they were gone, he fumbled around for his pills. His chronic high blood pressure had flared up. His aching head felt like an overinflated balloon that was about to burst. He imagined all the blood in his body rushing into his head and was overcome by a panic, terrified that without medication his head would explode.

"Why now, after all these years?" he asked himself.

Then, all at once, he was flooded with memories he dreaded to face even in dreams. He moaned and, clutching at the table, gulped down the pills. A balloon in the mouth of that damned caller—he tried to repress this ominous image. Who did he think Hwang Bokman was? But against that voice, such a question was pointless.

"How do you do, Mr. Bae Jomsu?"

Bae Jomsu was a name that had vanished from the face of the earth. He had cast that name into the flames and incinerated it so thoroughly that not a speck of ash remained. But now, to his horror, it had returned to haunt him, resurrected by a stranger he had no way to identify.

The ghost had come back after twenty-nine years.

"Twenty-nine years," he muttered, moaning from the splitting pain in his head. So very long ago. He had been thirty when he took "Hwang" as his new name, and now he was fifty-nine. He shuddered to recall he had lived the first half of his life as Bae Jomsu and the other half as Hwang Bokman, successful businessman. Since he had laid to rest the name Bae Jomsu, not even once had he thought of Hwang Bokman as identical to Bae Jomsu, until now, at least. To do so would've been fruitless, like opening your own veins. Once in a while memories from those days erupted to torment him, but each time he'd been able to calm himself by repeating, "You're Hwang Bokman, not Bae Jomsu."

"Sir, are you feeling better, now?"

Slowly he opened his eyes. He felt irritated that the others had seen him stretched out there on the sofa, helpless. But he couldn't vent this anger. The pain in his head had not abated in the least. Those wonderfully effective pills seemed of no help on this occasion.

"About your appointment this evening, should I . . . ?"

The office supervisor was tentative, prepared for an outburst of screaming.

"Cancel it. I'm going home."

President Hwang's voice was mild and his eyelids drooped.

"How do you do, Mr. Bae Jomsu?"

He shuddered yet again, each syllable falling like a drop of icy water into his eardrum. No, they were not falling from without, it was more as though they were surging up from deep inside him.

Shin Bomho . . .

Suddenly he was hit with a shattering realization. Until then, he'd been so shocked by the recognition of his past identity he'd failed to notice that the bastard's family name was Shin. Since leaving behind his identity as Bae Jomsu, Hwang had carefully avoided contact with all Shins. His company employed over five hundred, but there was not a single Shin on the payroll. Down to the most menial janitors and laborers, he screened each résumé himself before hiring. Anybody named Shin was eliminated, the name crossed out in red ink.

Precautions went beyond hiring. Even for big contracts promising ample profits, Hwang avoided any business that would entail dealings with anyone named Shin. Nobody seemed to have noticed these idiosyncracies. He concealed what he was doing and it was easy to come up with a pretext of some kind.

This systematic avoidance of Shins was not motivated by any instinct of revenge on his part. Rather, such measures were to protect himself against possible retaliation by them, the Shins. It was a key part of his strategy for burying Bae Jomsu once and for all, to secure a safe life for Hwang Bokman.

And now, what should happen but this Shin Bomho pops up right under his nose? Far worse, this bastard appearing from nowhere seems to know everything inside out. How in hell could he have found out about the contract with Sun Corporation? From his use of that information to reach him by phone at that hour, it seemed Shin had been keeping a close watch on him. He felt a sudden dread, as if an unseen weapon was aimed at him.

Then he exclaimed, "That's it!"

The agony of his aching head began to subside. That son of a bitch must work in some section of Sun Corporation.

"Mr. Chang, Mr. Chang!"

He summoned the supervisor in his usual haughty tone.

"Yes, yes, sir. Your car is ready."

"Wait. Listen carefully. Tomorrow morning, go yourself to Sun Corporation and find out which section has a staff member named Shin Bomho."

"Certainly, sir."

"I'll be going home, now."

Although he had to be assisted to his car by the supervisor, Hwang was in considerably better spirits.

Once in the car, more composed and breathing easily, Hwang told himself that the most urgent thing was to locate the bastard. Then steps could be taken to solve the problem. The solution was obvious: Gorge the guy with money. A mouth full of money doesn't chatter. Now, how big a mouth would this son of a bitch have? A hundred thousand dollars? Two hundred? Suddenly, he had a fleeting thought of murder. Two hundred thousand dollars was an impossible sum. At the prospect of being stripped of such a huge amount, premeditated malice coldly raised its head. He shut his eyes, feeling a surge of self-loathing. That he so readily could contemplate murder made him bitter. Besides, this bastard who was threatening revelation of his secret past would not be an easy customer to deal with. If things were handled rashly, a worse catastrophe might follow.

The Shin clan—he shut his eyes and conjured up a vivid image of three peaks. The mountain was known as *Sambongsan*—Three Brother Peaks. Literati of the Shin clan were said to have chosen this name centuries ago, and the triple-peaked mountain was still revered by the Shins as an ancestral shrine. They believed the spot had special powers and over the years legends about the place had been passed down from one generation of Shins to the next.

Long ago, a high-ranking magistrate, a leader of the Shin clan, was said to have been banished from the capitol due to a conspiracy of despicable courtiers. On his way to his place of exile, he stopped for the night at a village tavern not far from the mountain with three peaks. That night, he dreamt of an old man who commanded him to go to that spot and build an estate once his sentence of exile was over. The old man claimed that the veins of minerals were in harmony with the Shin blood, and he prophesied that Shin descendants who settled in the shadows of the mountain would enjoy perennial prosperity. The exiled magistrate's future was uncertain, but so uncanny was the dream that, as a token of obedience to the elder's injunction, he had dug up a sapling and transplanted it to a weed-filled field on the slope of the mountain.

Then, before the year was out, the magistrate was released from exile in apparent fulfillment of the dream. He declined to resume his former post, deciding instead to heed the portent of the dream and to resettle his family near *Sambongsan*. His wife soon dreamed of a phoenix soaring out of the center peak, darkening the sky with its wings, a sign of pregnancy. Nine months later, she gave birth to a son. A second time, from the right peak, the phoenix soared, and a third time, from the left peak. And so, according to the legend, there came three sons and the mountain was named "*Sambongsan*" in memory of these three Shin brothers.

The Shins always recounted that story when boasting of their noble ancestry. They repeated it to their offspring, who bragged of their heritage to the other children and beamed with pride even more than when they paraded their fancy rice cakes.

None dared to dismiss the legend as mere fantasy. For, as had been foretold, many Shins enjoyed high government posts over the generations, and their offspring bloomed with such prosperity that the Shins became landlords over three towns: Chungokri, Hoejongri and Tongchonri. In that part of Korea, other families had to eke out a living beneath the shadow of the Shins. Their lives were miserable beyond description. The mountains, the rice paddies and the vegetable farms all belonged to the Shins. Outsiders were reduced to being serfs or tenants working the Shin lands. True, there had been a few who strove for independence from the Shins, but they always faced ruin in the end. Not even one tiny plot of hillside land could be had for ten miles in any direction from the old dangsan tree in the center of Hoejongri. Within that domain the Shins owned all the land, and they never allowed outsiders to buy any portion of their estates.

"Sir, you're home now."

The chauffeur opened the car door. Slowly he opened his eyes, feeling almost unbearably exhausted.

"Oh, my goodness, what's happened to send your blood pressure up again, dear?"

His wife made a fuss as she came running down the steps from the door. The office must have notified her. He was about to lift one leg out of the car, but paused, looking up blankly at his wife. For an instant another face, the face of an entirely different person, was superimposed on his wife's. It was the face of Sangnimdaek, his first wife, who had been stoned to death many years before. He clutched at the window frame of the car door.

"What's wrong, dear? Get a grip on yourself, please."

All at once he was irritated by his wife's fuss.

"Shut up, I'm not dead yet!"

He fiercely barked, trying to stave off her overreaction. It was the only way to stop her.

He took another batch of medication and went straight to bed. His headache lingered and he felt nauseous. The symptoms were consistent with a rapid rise in blood pressure. He tossed about in bed, choking back the pain. Blood surged into his head, as from the jets of a fountain, and he worried that his nervous exhaustion might set off a seizure of diabetic shock.

He was terrified.

Shin Bomho . . .

He cursed and moaned. He knew perfectly well the cause of his maladies. They were not just conditions commonly afflicting people as they age. Neither were they mainly attributable to the overwork necessary for an un-schooled man to build his business to its present stature. Those were second-ary causes. His ailments really were due to the nerve-rending task of sustaining a life as Hwang Bokman after Bae Jomsu had been annihilated. Others could never understand how debilitating the constant stress had been. Not even sleep brought any relief. There was not a soul to whom he could open his heart and confess his dread. He'd endured the slow self-immolation all alone, and with each passing day his nerves, strand by strand, were reduced to ash. After thirty years of incessant trepidation, his flesh was bruised and broken.

A year before the Korean War erupted, Jomsu already was a Red through and through.

"Mr. Bae Jomsu, see that flame burning there? And see that metal melting, helpless in the heat? That's just it. The so-called nobles and land-lords are the metal, and we are the flame that can mold the metal any way we choose."

Pointing at the flame dancing bluer and bluer under the bellows, Pang's voice had a vehement rasp. On such occasions, the normally soft-spoken teacher Pang became a completely different person. His thin lips turned hard as iron, and his calm voice resounded deeply, imbued with a power to lift the weight of oppression from his listener's chest.

"You can't remain a blacksmith forever, abused and downtrodden. Just as you forge molten iron into a knife, a sickle or a scythe, the day will come when you and I will mold these creatures called capitalists and landlords into any form we wish."

Whatever the topic, the schoolteacher had a way of saying things simply. None of the pretension or condescension of the intellectual could be detected in Pang's manner. At school or on the street, he carried himself like a gentle maiden. That was why the students had nicknamed him "The Bride." Yet this very man, perched beside the forge, could metamorphose into a figure as hard as stone. Jomsu trusted him, was entirely dependent on him. Even though Pang was younger by five years, Jomsu held him in the highest esteem and each conversation made him feel his spirit had been immersed in clear light.

At the beginning, of course, he had not trusted Pang. He'd been very cautious when Pang first approached him with talk about the proletariat and the peasants. In the first place, he didn't understand the big words, and later when he began to catch Pang's drift, he grew still more wary. After all, Pang was a school teacher, a calling remote from the lives of the peasants and workers he so often extolled.

Each night, like clockwork, Pang paid a call at the smithy. At last Jomsu ran out of patience and spat out sentiments that long had been boiling within him.

"Mr. Pang, seems you think I'm a fool of some kind, but you'd better stop. See here, you're a teacher, no? And there's nothing here you need, so how's it you got to be on the side of farmers and smiths like me?"

Mr. Pang glared fiercely as if he might pluck out Jomsu's eyes at any moment.

"My father was a serf," Mr. Pang said in a serene voice.

"Wha'd you say?"

"My father was a serf, I said."

"Teacher's father was?"

"That's right. And my grandfather before him was a serf, too."

"You're tellin' me some kind of ghost stories? I don't know."

Jomsu was too astonished to know what to say.

"Why don't you ask me how a serf's son got to be a school teacher? Care to hear it?"

"Well, that's just what I was gonna ask," Jomsu murmured, his indignation waning.

For generations, Pang's ancestors had been slaves and serfs on the estates of a certain rich landlord Kim, who was a high government official as well. The eldest grandson of the Kim family kept on philandering after he married, as befits the scion of such a clan. Admonitions and reprimands hurled his way by his own father had no effect. Then one day, he committed a murder. He had been lusting after a recently arrived courtesan. When she scorned his advances, he thrashed his fists about and inadvertently killed her. Pang's tale actually commenced with his arrest. To save the grandson, pressure was applied to Pang's father. Six acres of prime rice fields, emancipation from serfdom, and bribes to the witnesses and the magistrate to mitigate the sentence as far as possible—these were the inducements. The master himself extended the offer in person. To reject it would have meant facing unpredictable retaliation. Pang's father had no choice but to accept being cast in the role of murderer. There was only fate to blame. Before being bound over he was given the papers drawn up for the transfer of the land and for his emancipation.

"Six acres of good land was always beyond my dreams. While I'm gone, work hard and send the children to school. No longer will we be serfs. Don't forget my words." Then he went out into the night, leaving the rest to Providence.

Before dawn the substitution for the perpetrator was accomplished, and not a soul knew the whereabouts of the grandson. Due to the Kim clan's intercessions, the punishment was not death or life imprisonment, but a sentence of ten years. At that time, Pang had been ten years old and his father was twenty-nine. He started school late. Pang's father contracted some grave disease and died in prison. His last words were again an injunction to educate the children.

"Jomsu, I'm curious, did you ever learn to read and write?" Pang asked, once Jomsu was more comfortable in his presence.

"No, can't do that."

"I see. To live, a man doesn't need a lot of knowledge. But you should at least know how to read and write."

"Sure, everybody knows that. But I was lowborn, y'know."

"It's not too late."

"What do you mean? You can't mean I should go to school old as I am? Why, next year I'll be thirty."

"It's up to you. I can come by in the evenings to teach you."

Pang visited the smithy every night, never missing a lesson, and Jomsu chased his sleepiness away by striking himself with his fists. Within six months, Jomsu had mastered reading and writing. Without realizing it, he'd been saturated with Pang's Red ideology, too.

Like bats out hunting, they met only at night. Jomsu's smithy, far from town, was ideal for clandestine meetings. As time went by, their group grew in number. All newcomers were screened by Pang with the utmost caution. His incandescent eyes drew the group tightly together as if they were linked by an invisible wire.

"Soon the day will arrive when our heroic struggle will shine in the light of day. Until then, we must unite with a bond like iron, and never relax from our preparations for that coming day."

Pang irrigated the seeds of vengeance in the hearts of all present. Seeds sown in generations past sprouted and grew day by day. In all they were eight, including one woman, another teacher at the same school where Pang taught.

"My life stems from a noble's frustrated longing for a male heir," the woman teacher casually remarked one night. Then, she had laughed until the corners of her mouth sagged. The chilling sound of that laugh was enough to shrink a man's balls, like a snake rubbing against your skin. It was more jarring than Pang's "My father was a serf."

This schoolteacher's mother had served as a surrogate wife to a noble who was a second-generation only son. After several sexual encounters, she became pregnant, all right, but gave birth to a daughter. All that was left for this woman of humble descent who'd failed to bear a son was endless sorrow and redoubled poverty. Her daughter was seven years old when the noble died, leaving her fifty bags of rice. With this bequest the woman had purchased a plot of farmland and sent her daughter to school. That was how she came to be a schoolteacher.

"Three inches of loose tongue can ruin the party and all of us as well. Like one weighted and cast into deep water, our secrets must never see the light of day."

These dagger-like words were from Chun Sukja, the female teacher. No one dared to slight her because she was not a man. Apart from her skirt, there was nothing feminine about her. She was as smart as Pang, and sly as a fox.

"Jomsu, you can make spears, can't you?" Pang asked one night in a hushed voice.

"The kind to kill people with, you mean?"

"Shhh . . ." Pang quickly pressed his finger to his lips, surveying the surrounding darkness. "You can forge spears with wooden or bamboo grips, can't you?"

"Like the police used in the old days, you mean?"

"Exactly."

"Sure, did you really need to ask? It's no different from making hoes. Fact is, making spears is simpler. Hoes got a curve but spears are straight. Don't have much faith in me to ask such a thing, eh?"

"I didn't doubt your skill. I was only a little concerned because spears aren't made these days."

"What you gonna use spears for, anyway?"

"The time is coming. We have to be ready. From tomorrow, begin making spears, secretly."

Jomsu felt his blood heat up. From the following evening, they started secretly bringing axe heads, hoes and sickles to Jomsu's forge to be melted down and reworked.

2

In vain he tried to sleep. The headache lingered, but more unbearable still were the horrible memories haunting him.

Around ten o'clock, he got up and dipped a spoon into a bowl of pine-nut gruel. Not good to take pills on an empty stomach. Then the phone rang. His heart thumping, he could hardly resist the impulse to rush out and answer it himself. He thought: what the hell is wrong with me, the children get calls all the time.

"Hello. Who?" It was the husky voice of the maid. "Who did you say this is? Mr. Shin Bomho?"

Immediately he leapt out of bed and rushed into the living room. Mustn't get excited now. Have to cast out a nice big chunk of bait, then slowly, slowly, reel it back in. He took a deep breath as he picked up the receiver.

"Hello, Hwang Bokman speaking." He used the official manner he used with his employees.

"Heh, heh, heh . . . don't delude yourself. Call yourself Bae Jomsu, at least to me."

He nearly dropped the phone. Just as before, the voice enunciated each syllable slowly, distinctly, coldly. And the horrid laugh on the other end sent a graveyard chill through him. His composure was already gone.

"Mr. Bae Jomsu, I'm calling to let you know that from tomorrow I'll be contacting you at home. Your office is a nuisance, besides, calling during the day interferes with my work."

"No, not at home. Call at my office," he said in confusion.

"That's your problem. Answer the phone yourself if you're afraid of your family finding out. Well . . . enough for the moment."

"Wait, listen. I must see you. Immediately, tomorrow."

"I have no such intention."

"Please, let me discuss this with you. I'll satisfy whatever conditions you may have."

"You think fast, just like Bae Jomsu. But I am so sorry. I have no demands."

"What do you want, then?"

"Wait and see, you'll find out in due time."

"What do you mean, 'wait and see,' what harm have I done to you?"

"You've done nothing to me, precisely, but you've been a mortal enemy of my father and mother."

"Who the hell are you?"

"Calm down. Excitement's not good for your blood pressure."

He bit his tongue and swallowed his rage.

"Forgive me for losing my temper. For God's sake, let me meet with you to talk. Once we meet I'm sure we can reach some understanding. If you won't meet me, what is it you intend to do?"

". . . ."

"Hello, young man, hello?"

"Mr. Bae Jomsu, don't you think you've lived too long?"

"Wh-what, you son of a bitch!"

He screamed at the top of his voice, but the line was already dead. His wife and the maid rushed in. He dropped the receiver, staggering as if he would collapse at any moment. The two women half-dragged him into the other room to lay him on the bed.

For almost two hours, he writhed in pain, only half-conscious. He wasn't aware the doctor had come and gone. He gradually came back to his senses near midnight, but was sleepless the rest of the night.

"Mr. Bae Jomsu, don't you think you've lived too long?"

Those words were not uttered by a human. They were poison, ingested and already swallowed so that it couldn't be spit back out—a deliberately designed torture.

That insipid chilling voice, the laughter that made your hair stand on end. The bastard couldn't be human; it could only be a vengeful ghost of the Shin clan.

Who could've fathered that son of a bitch? Which Shin's whelp could he be? How did he uncover everything?

No intention to see me? What'll he do? I mean, how can I get ready for his next move?

Twenty-nine years of constant dread and fear at being unmasked. Everything he had achieved was about to go up in smoke.

What is a crime? Even after so many years was it still the same crime?

"Mr. Bae Jomsu, don't you think you've lived too long?"

"Bae Jomsu is a fine exemplar of the proletarian revolution and a heroic figure. His birth shows it, and his life up to now itself has been a brilliant struggle."

Holding Jomsu by the arm, Pang spoke forcefully, explaining in detail what made Jomsu's life such a great one, focusing on exemplary incidents.

At the tender age of thirteen, Jomsu had beaten a son of the Shin clan almost to death. This, according to Pang, was a battle against the landlord class at the risk of his own life. Furthermore, his sweat-soaked labor as a blacksmith was a manifestation of the spirit of unrelenting struggle against the bourgeoisie. That wasn't all. At liberation in 1945, his denunciation of the Shin clan as Japanese collaborators was, in Pang's opinion, proof of his heroic qualities.

At first, Jomsu had been puzzled as he listened to the same story over and over, but eventually he came to a firm belief that in fact he'd done grand and heroic deeds. Things he had done out of rage, for revenge, or merely to survive, suddenly had been recast as heroic struggles that made him into a paragon of revolution. Jomsu felt a mysterious strength surging within. His shoulders, which had always been stooped out of timidity, became broader, and for the first time in his life he relished living.

That the Shin boys had been different was only natural. In their presence, even his father had been subservient. One day, as his father was lugging a bucket brimming with excrement, he fell head over heels after stepping in a hole dug by the Shin children to trip him. The shit flew everywhere and showered back down on his father. The Shin brats jumped out from their hiding place and danced around his father, laughing hysterically. "Why'd you do that, it ain't nice," was all his father could manage to say as he staggered to his feet.

Unable to bear this spectacle, Jomsu had run away from there as fast as he could. "Father's an idiot, a fool, gotta wring those little bastards' necks." He himself had dug the hole at the command of the Shin kids. And as his father came nearer, he'd wanted to run out and warn him. But the fierce stares of those little devils had stopped him cold and gagged his mouth.

Jomsu always behaved like a frightened mutt around the Shin boys. They ate rice cakes until their belly buttons protruded, but Jomsu didn't even have a lousy barley cake. He went around with his tail between his legs and accepted it all as natural. His humble birth accounted for everything. But deep down inside Jomsu was burning. When wronged, he exacted retribution in his dreams. He swore to himself that he'd never live a life like his father's when he grew up. In Jomsu's mind, his father was no better than a ragged scarecrow standing in a rice field.

"Always live like the dead. Don't fight back, that's like hitting a stone wall with a raw egg. You hear me?"

Father often issued such warnings to Jomsu. His father never looked more hideously foolish than at such moments. Still, it wasn't his father's warnings, it was the Shins who forced Jomsu into living death.

Once Jomsu had been trudging along the side of a hill around twilight with a load of firewood on his back. During the days the summerish cry of cicadas droned loudly, but mornings and evenings already exuded the mystic fragrance of autumn.

"Hurry, hurry, carry down that wood. Thirteen's old enough to marry, so the least you can do is earn your keep."

Mercilessly, his mother had sent her son up the hill as if he were a mule. No food for lunch, straining under the firewood on his back, Jomsu felt dizzy. If living meant more hunger, it'd be better to die, he told himself. To be a dog in the Shin house would be better. At least a dog could eat to its heart's content. Jomsu plodded down the hill, dwelling on the usual resentments.

"Ay, ayee! It hurts, ayee . . . Mommy!"

It was the voice of a little girl crying and then,

"Ha, ha, ha . . ."

"Heh, heh . . ."

So went the muted giggling of two boys. Jomsu abruptly halted. The sounds were coming from the shrubs behind a large rock alongside the path.

"Ayee! Mommy! It hurts . . . Mommy!"

Jomsu took the A-frame full of wood down from his back. Stealthily, he approached the rock. He slowly craned his neck around to look and then froze. A little girl was lying down on the ground. A boy was sitting on her stomach, with his back to her face. The little bastard was holding the girl's naked legs, forcing her bony knees apart while the other boy was holding a wooden stick. They were giggling and gleefully poking the girl between her legs as she let out smothered screams, writhing in agony.

At first, Jomsu was unable to believe his eyes. But there was no doubt. The girl was his little sister, Sunwol, and the bastard with the stick was Byongchul, one of the Shin sons. The one sitting on her belly was a son of the Ha family, neighbors.

"Goddamn sons o' bitches!"

Jomsu dashed forward, shrieking at the top of his voice. The two boys had no time to escape, and both fell to the ground, struck by stones. Jomsu stoned them again in turn. In an instant, their hands and clothes were covered with blood.

"Brother, stop now, enough! You'll kill them! Oh, Brother, you shouldn't have hit Byongchul so bad, now we're all in deep trouble," Sunwol said, sobbing miserably.

"Gotta kill 'em, all of 'em!" Jomsu mumbled incoherently, standing there in a daze as if his soul had flown.

At dusk the same day, a gang of sturdy male servants from the Shin estate came to Jomsu's place. They dragged him and his father before Master Shin.

"Such a unmannered pup, how dare a base thing like you lay a hand on . . . . Double up the beating the little bastard gave to my son, and teach him a good lesson."

Standing in the hall, Master Shin coldly spat out those words.

"No, master, no, I . . . it's my fault for bringing him up wrong. All my fault, mine only."

Kneeling in the yard with his hands bound behind him, Jomsu's father implored helplessly.

"Why do you tarry, off with him at once!" shouted Master Shin. Immediately, Jomsu was pulled up from the ground by the neck. The imminent peril was overwhelming.

"Byongchul and his friends had my sister Sunwol and they . . ."

"Silence!"

Jomsu was not allowed to speak. A servant's huge fist struck him in the mouth.

"Don't lay hands on my son. Kill me instead, kill me . . . !"

Then Jomsu was dragged away by the servants, leaving his wailing father behind. His father didn't follow, and must've been taken away by other men. Jomsu was hauled to a storagehouse, his mouth sealed shut, and then was beaten with a club. He lost count of the blows raining down on him. At first he tried to scream for his father, but later, as consciousness slipped away, he swore to himself that he would kill that bastard Byongchul without fail.

When he woke up, Jomsu found himself lying in a room back home. His whole body burned like fire. Dimly, he could see his mother sobbing and his father silently smoking. His mother wouldn't stop weeping, twisting and wringing Jomsu's clothes. At her side his father sat like a wooden statue.

Jomsu was unable to get out of his bed for over a fortnight. The nameless, bitter potion his mother kept feeding him seemed to do no good. His only thought was that one day he would surely pay them back for all they had done to him and more.

Two days after this incident the Ha family was driven from the village. On the morning they left, the Ha boy's father came to see Jomsu's father.

"I ain't got the face left to look you in the eye, brother. Guilty of having this bastard of a son, I wronged you and I don't know what'll become of us now."

Jomsu's father made no reply.

A few weeks after Jomsu was up and about, his father took him to live with a blacksmith as an apprentice.

"With a temper like yours, you'll end up getting beaten to death if you stay on the Shin lands. Now shut up and learn smithing till it's in your bones. Smithing's a real skill, and it'll put food in your mouth better'n farming, you hear me?"

"Yeah."

Jomsu answered in a nasal voice. His father had been speaking softly, but the "You hear me?" was tacked on in a loud voice, nearly a yell. This outburst wrenched Jomsu's heart and his eyes filled with tears.

Autumn had once more returned to the fields, its radiance glistening on the rice stalks. Unlike at home, at the smithy Jomsu had three meals a day, so no longer was he dogged by hunger. But the toil of an apprentice blacksmith was very hard. Three years on the bellows, five as a helper with the hammer, three as a journeyman, it took thirteen years in all before he could work the metal with ease. Sick and tired of the work, he often grew disgusted and had an impulse to run away, but each time he heard his father's voice. "With your temper . . ." Each time he stifled those urges.

After Liberation in August 1945, it was only natural for the Japanese to flee back to their homeland. Their departure was not enough to satisfy the liberated, however. All of Korea was like a beehive, buzzing for collaborators with the Japanese to be unmasked and punished. Amidst this helter skelter, many who had been oppressed regained self-respect, and some quickly rose in stature. On the other hand, those who previously wielded power were downcast and demoralized. Seizing the chance, Jomsu sank his teeth into the neck of Byongchul's father, Master Shin, who became the only Shin family member indicted as a Japanese collaborator. But this episode did not end as Jomsu had hoped.

"The time is at hand. Everybody stay alert. Let's conduct our drill one last time."

Pang must have been in communication with the higher command. He confirmed the tasks assigned to each member of their cell for the final day, and one last time he checked the stockpile of spears that recently had been completed.

It happened scarcely two weeks later. It seemed incredible, but they were sure the day had come on which the world would be turned upside down.

"Look, at last the workers and peasants are free, and the hour of revolution is upon us. We'll deal with the landlords and nobles. From now on, you, comrades, must carry out your orders thoroughly and completely."

Flushed a bloody red, schoolteacher Pang shouted to his heart's content. It was the first time he'd used the word "comrade."

Pang became Chairman of the local People's Committee, and Jomsu was made Vice-Chairman. Miss Chun Sukja became leader of the Women's League.

Jomsu couldn't believe the sudden change. Faced with razor-sharp spear-tips, glinting with a diabolical bluish light, the whole Shin clan was squirming like worms. Not even worms, they seemed mere ants or bedbugs.

The once-powerful men, young and old, of the Shin clan now kneeled too readily before his spear. He gave several little jabs into their thighs with the tip of his spear, but none of them resisted or even dared to cry aloud. Suspecting these spear pricks didn't bestow enough pain, he pounded several of them relentlessly with his fist. His formidable strength, gained from years of working iron at the anvil, was well-known. Still, their responses did not change after the blows. Eyes full of fear, every last one of them ignominiously begged for their lives.

So these were the oxen whose reins henceforth would be in the people's hands. The sudden recognition of this fact made Jomsu strangely exhilarated. To have been trodden under the feet of men who were now totally helpless before his strength . . . . Jomsu felt his muscles flex with indignation as a craving for revenge welled up within him.

"Well, Comrade Vice-Chairman, how do you like things, now that life is worth living?"

Even without Pang's prompting, Jomsu was now fully aware that the world's ways were not preordained to stay in the same stifling pattern. The same sunset did not always follow sunrise, it turned out. Even as he surreptitiously manufactured spears, he had not dared even dream of a day when the world so easily would turn upside down.

"Comrade Chairman, to dry up the seed of the Shin clan, we gotta sever the veins under *Sambongsan*."

"Comrade Vice-Chairman, that old fairy tale was conjured up by the landlord bastards to paint themselves as lofty nobles. It's nothing but lies, and to believe it is to be superstitious," replied Chairman Pang, a scornful grin on his lips.

"You're right, no doubt. But don't you see, the sight of that damn mountain makes me feel like fish bones are stuck in my throat. I ain't sayin' we dig up the whole mountain, I just think we gotta dig a hole and bury these reactionary Shin bastards there on the mountain. Then, with the vein cut, and the Shin corpses rotting away inside, at any rate the Shins'll never again . . ."

"All right, good. That's what I call killing two birds with one stone. Your idea, Vice-Chairman Bae Jomsu, is a good one indeed."

In July the forest was dark green and soundless. A myriad of hot needles of sunlight cascaded down through the branches. Up on *Sambongsan* the trees were so dense the grey darkness of dawn persisted through the calm daylight hours. Nearly every day, men of the Shin clan were taken in twos or threes up the mountain slope to die.

"Goddamned counterrevolutionaries, move! You're gonna cut the vein of this mountain with your own hands."

Jomsu thundered orders, flourishing his spear. His voice reverberated in the stillness, echoing far and wide. He felt ecstatic as he listened to his commands resound in the distance. The world before him was so clear and so cool. In an even louder voice he shouted,

"Goddamned reactionaries, hurry, dig! Faster!"

The spear was stroked across naked backs, and instantly blood flowed to mix with the dirt and sweat. After digging holes as deep as their waists, the men were forced to stand in their own graves.

"You gorged yourselves like hogs, suckin' the blood of farmers and workers, you reactionaries, do you know your crimes?!"

Jomsu howled at them, poking his spear right under their noses.

"Of course, of course, we know, we'll do anything, anything, just spare our lives, please."

"Yes, we're guilty, really. We confess. Just forgive us this once, just this once . . ."

"Sons of bitches! While you were gulping food till your bellies bloated up, did you know we went days on end with not a crumb, our bellies stuck to our spines? Do you even know what hunger is? When we couldn't make a thin soup, you bastards had your granaries spilling over, and you stuffed your faces with rice cakes. Know where that rice came from? It was the flesh and blood of people like me! Now do you know your crime?!"

Jomsu no longer was the Jomsu of old.

"We execute you in the name of the proletariat and the peasantry."

With those words, several spears swiftly split the air.

Death rattles echoed. As though the sunlight itself was swept away by the soul-shattering sound, the whole area seemed submerged into darkness.

Standing motionless, Jomsu listened for a long time to the sound, gazing vacantly into the distance. Rancor realized itself. How did such hateful resentment come to inhabit human hearts, and what are its forms? As one suffers unforgettable and mortifying injustices, with each incident another layer of bloodstained bruises accumulates in one's soul, and the sediment left behind in time hardens until it is like stone.

Perhaps that is the nature of rancor. Like a stone that will fracture, maybe a mass of rancor also forms many layers that break cleanly along cleavage lines. To Jomsu, the final shrieks of dying Shins had crawled inside him and somehow melted the layers of rancor in his heart. And it was no mere feeling. For was it not true that those who for generations had sown rancor in the hearts of his grandfather, his father, himself, had been dispatched one after another to the land of no return, by no other hands than his own?!

3

He was unable to go to work. For him, it was a very unusual occurrence. A man who hunts tigers must frequent their lairs. To be a consummate slavedriver, a company president himself has to be the first to reach and the last to leave the office. He seldom broke this rule he had laid down for himself twenty-five years before.

He telephoned the office and asked for the supervisor. He was told the supervisor had gone directly to Sun Corporation that morning. An efficient fellow. In the throes of suffering, he felt a fleeting tinge of satisfaction.

"Sir, I haven't heard that your company has been passed a worthless draft, so what sent your blood pressure soaring?"

The family doctor, who'd been summoned early that morning, wore a feigned grin as he joked, but he did not seem at all pleased.

"Sorry, Dr. Chun . . ." He heaved a long sigh.

"Well, well, you may crack the floor. That sigh, that's the culprit. What in the world is it that causes such a god-awful sigh?"

"Looks like my time is almost up, eh?"

"Hold on, that's nonsense. Hypertension is a disease, and at the same time, it is not. It can be treated easily enough if you just calm yourself and keep an even temper."

He shut his eyes. He wanted to avoid looking at the doctor, whose visage seemed to be pronouncing him an illiterate money grubber. Besides, he was distressed by such expressions as "calm yourself" and "even temper."

"Soon you'll feel a little better. But don't forget that the real remedy is your attitude and not the drugs I prescribe. There won't be any need, but in an emergency you can reach me at the University."

Immediately after the doctor left, a call came from the supervisor.

"Oh, it's you? Let me have your report, first!" he hurriedly huffed.

"Two Shins there, but neither was named Shin Bomho, sir."

"Neither one . . ."

In his heart he felt a thud like a pumpkin falling from its stem in the rainy season; then it occurred to him that the man was using a false name, that had to be it.

"Investigate the backgrounds of those two and report back to me at once. Birthplace, hometown, present address, got it?"

"Certainly, sir."

He felt his pulse gradually gaining speed. He had been almost sure he would find the man this way. But if neither of the two . . . . His pulse raced faster and faster. Must track him down. Whatever the cost, must meet him.

Within five minutes the supervisor called again.

"One was born and still lives here in Seoul . . ."

"Enough. The other, tell me about the other one." His voice was almost a squeal.

"Right, yes, the other was born in Chungch'ong province . . ."

"Stop. Enough!"

Screeching, he smashed the receiver down on the phone. Sweating like a dog, he collapsed onto the bed, moaning. He was in bed all day groaning with a high fever. Even drinking a little water nauseated him. The instant he fell asleep, he would reawaken fitfully with a shrill scream. The vision of his wide-open eyes grew blurred.

After two calls, the doctor rushed back to see him, though it wasn't easy for a university staff physician to make house calls during duty hours.

"Check into the hospital. Not that your condition is critical, but you need complete rest," said the doctor without smiling.

"It's unnecessary, I understand my illness." Wincing, he forced a smile.

"Sir, other times when your condition wasn't half this bad, you yourself insisted on hospitalization."

"He's right, dear. Please don't be stubborn."

"Out with you!" He yelled at his wife in a piercing pitch.

"Sir, what's bothering you?"

The doctor looked soberly into the eyes of his favorite patient as if to extract the source of his anguish to lessen the pain.

"Nothing, no, it's just my old age." But he longed to spill his guts and tell how he was being haunted. But this man was merely a physician for bodily ailments, not someone who could cure his past. In fact, if he learned everything about his history, he might decline to treat him at all. He was entombed in a terrible solitude.

"If I need to check in, I'll call you right away. Twice already today, I'm sorry, and thank you very much."

"Don't mention it, you should have several hours of sleep now."

Thanks to the sedative, he managed to sleep for a few hours. It was already dark outside when he awoke. Swiftly he cast a glance at the wall clock. It was nearly eight.

Ring. Rrring . . .

He shook all over. The sound was only in his head. A frosty chill penetrated from his chest to his groin. At once he shivered in a cold sweat.

Suddenly he was seized with dread. As though the darkness was encircling him, raining ice over his body, he felt his blood run cold. It was the first time in his life he had been consumed by such a bloodcurdling horror of darkness. Perhaps half of his whole life had been spent in darkness. Part in the darkness of night, the remainder in the blackness of a dark mind.

Chairman Pang and the others had become nocturnal creatures. As darkness crept up the slope of the mountain at twilight, they stretched themselves, together with the owls. Darkness was their guardian, protecting them with its warm caresses. As they grew accustomed to the dark, it bestowed upon them new eyes and legs. Darkness had become the most potent weapon at their disposal.

But then a messenger came into this darkness, reporting that Bae Jomsu's wife Sangnimdaek had been stoned to death.

Jomsu showed no sign of surprise at this news, but an awful tension gripped the group. Unable to bear the restless silence, the messenger offered unrequested details.

"They did her in beneath the dangsan tree, they say."

Bae Jomsu asked in a low voice,

"And my son, Chilsung, what's become of him?"

The murder in his voice registered at once in the ears of the others.

"Looks like Chilsung was spared and still lives."

"Where is he now?"

"I tried to find out, but Malbong didn't . . ."

"Shut up! Fool, you ain't got half the brains of a scarecrow!"

Shouting, Bae Jomsu knocked the messenger to the floor.

Chairman Pang stood up from his chair, peering out into the thick layers of darkness filling the valley, and said in a cold voice, "Comrade Vice-Chairman, don't get so excited, calm yourself. A mind chained to blood relatives can defeat great causes."

At these icy words, Jomsu wanted to yell back at Pang that he wouldn't say such things if he had a wife and children of his own. How could he ever understand what it meant to have your wife stoned to death? But he stifled the urge to grab Pang and throw him down, bit his lip and said calmly,

"I'll be taking care of this on my own, Comrade Chairman, so no need to worry."

"Impossible, too dangerous to go down there."

As the argument between Jomsu and Pang escalated, it drew the attention of the militia commander of their group, who asked, "Comrade Vice-Chairman, what do you mean to do?"

"Can't rest till I wring the necks of those counter-revolutionary bastards."

"Did you pause to consider that if you're caught, our hideout may be revealed?"

"If I'm caught, I'll stick this deep into my heart." Jomsu waved his sword, trembling.

"Comrade Vice-Chairman is a man of strong will, no doubt. Very well, go on, then."

Jomsu shot into the darkness all alone. The thought of his wife's death obsessed him—what had been her thoughts as she was stricken in unbearable agony? She was so good-hearted, most likely she didn't even blame him. At last he stopped and just wept, overtaken by grief. He had not expected any of this. They had not laid hands on women or children before. It was his fault for thinking these foes would spare the innocent.

"Please, dear, don't be so cruel. An ignorant woman like me knows little, but revenge breeds revenge, and there'll be no end to it." His wife's words came back to haunt him.

Jomsu crept into the house of Malbong, their informant.

"By God, who in the world is this? Ain't it Jomsu, no, I mean, Comrade Vice-Chairman?" Malbong was harried, his eyes heavy with sleep.

"Wake up!" Jomsu grasped him by the throat and shook him hard.

"What if someone saw you come in here? You think I got ten necks?" Malbong didn't conceal his displeasure.

"You're a damn ungrateful creature. Will you come to your senses if I stick your throat right now with this?" Jomsu unsheathed his knife and poked it under Malbong's chin.

"A worm in the shithouse, that's what you are. Now what's happened to Chilsung? Where is he now?"

Malbong, very much awake, gulped.

"I already told . . ."

"It been some time, but you made no effort to find him, instead, you're sleeping in peace?"

"I can't act recklessly and reveal my allegiance. I'd like to help, but for the greater cause . . ."

Jomsu felt all the strength oozing out of his anger. Faced with the primacy of duty to the party, he put the knife back into its sheath.

"Locate him by tomorrow without fail. Know where they put his mother?"

"Dumped with the other corpses next to the undertaker's shed."

"I see. Go back to sleep."

Jomsu left and again hid himself in the darkness. Malbong drew a long sigh, rubbing his throat where the tip of the knife had been. The image of his wife dying came vividly before Jomsu's eyes. Bound to the dangsan tree, stoned and clubbed to death, she never screamed out loud. Amidst the senseless and frenzied mob, Chilsung had fallen into a fit, kicking and thrashing.

At the end of the village, a big pit had been dug near the undertaker's shed. It was full of corpses strewn on top of each other. He checked every last body, pulling them out and laying them in a row on the ground. Then a difficulty arose. Altogether there were nine corpses. Judging from the hair, three seemed to be women. It was pitch dark and he had no way to tell his wife's body from the others. He mopped the sweat running over his face as he tried to recall anything by which he could identify his wife in the dark—but there was nothing like the protruding bean-sized mole under his own left eye. Her unblemished body had exuded a freshness like an evergreen sapling, but these three corpses all stank of rotting blood.

Jomsu was utterly exhausted when at last he crawled away from the pit. He could hear his wife reproaching him, "See, what did I say? Didn't I warn you not to be so cruel?"

"No, gotta dry up the seed of that family."

Grinding his teeth, he wiped the sweat and tears from his face. Then he bid goodbye to the dead, bowing twice in his imagination.

With his knife, Jomsu hacked through the darkness. The way he felt, he couldn't return without at least slitting the throats of a couple of those bastards, so he rushed on. Reaching the stream on the edge of the village, suddenly he felt goosebumps all over. An unexpected gust of wind pushed him back. He collected his senses and tried to stay alert. As he started to cross the stream, the wind whipped up, sending a cold shiver through him. He felt something wrap around his neck. Reflexively, he felt with his hand. Nothing. Yet something kept pulling him back. In his mind he was crossing the stream, but his feet were shuffling backwards and the cold wind shoved him farther and farther away from the water. He felt a terror that shrivelled his balls. Then suddenly it dawned on him. It was his wife's spirit. He turned back, walking carefully. Gradually his fear faded and there was no trace of the wind.

Not since that night long ago had he been frightened by the dark. Back then he had soon shaken the fear, but this time it only grew worse as time went by.

The telephone was ringing.

His heart sank, and he looked at the clock. Nearly ten. The ringing was real, not just in his mind. He lifted the receiver, drawing a deep breath.

"Hello."

"How do you do, Mr. Bae Jomsu?"

The voice on the other end had not changed at all.

"Look here, young man . . ."

"I gather you've been checking the backgrounds of Sun Corporation employees named Shin."

He was almost suffocating. Was he dealing with a man or a ghost? How could he possibly know that?

"You used your head, all right, but not quite well enough. After all, it's only the brain of a blacksmith, right?"

"What, what?"

"If you're so eager to identify me, why not send a man to our hometown and get the family register of the Shin clan. Then, you can trace and easily catch me."

"Look . . ."

"You're a hopeless idiot if you think Shin Bomho is my real name. To approach a man like you, a man with corrupt blood, a butcher who slaughters men like bugs, I had to disguise my identity, of course."

"Look here, please . . ."

"Calm down. Mr. Bae Jomsu, do you happen to recall how many people you nonchalantly murdered with that spear of yours?"

"Look, young man . . ."

"Answer me, how many? If you've forgotten, shall I remind you? Thirty-eight! You killed thirty-eight men!"

He was white as a sheet. "Please, let me meet you. Let me see you, please." He was almost howling.

"Mr. Bae Jomsu, don't you think you've lived too long?"

The call was over.

Screams . . . screams pulverizing the shafts of sunlight shining through the trees, drifting off in echoes through the ravines, and men dying before his eyes, slumping into graves dug with their own hands. No, instead now they were being resurrected, as in a film running in reverse. The blood spurting from their wounds was being sucked back in, the spear punctures were closing, and the echoes of their screams were floating back up the valleys and vanishing into their gaping mouths. Then the cords that bound them loosened by themselves, and the Shin men slowly were approaching him.

"No, no!" He thrashed about shrieking.

"Darling, what is it? Wake up, won't you! Who was on the phone, anyway? Who the hell is he to be tormenting you this way?"

With foggy vision, he looked up at his wife vacantly, frowned and waved her away.

"If he's blackmailing you or something, why not report him to the police right away?"

"Shut your damn mouth!"

He rose abruptly, his eyes ablaze.

"My goodness, what's come over you?"

His wife sat back and gazed at him, fear and suspicion on her face.

"Your health's being ruined, so why do you let him do this to you?"

"Out! Now!"

By sheer force he pushed his wife outside. His panic worsened. What if the bastard goes to the police? He could furnish irrefutable evidence and witnesses, too. A political criminal, a murderer, and, what would be the penalty for using a false name and fabricating a personal history? He recalled hearing there were statutes of limitations for crimes—how many years would have to pass for him to escape prosecution?

The bastard had said it was thirty-eight—a ghastly number. Not thirty-eight apples or fish, thirty-eight human beings. He had no clear recollection, but probably the count was accurate. Somehow the more he killed, the more bloodthirsty he became. Pang had said indiscriminate killing would serve no purpose. He warned that strong metal does not bend, it breaks—because it's too strong. Politics was the same way: if you went too far, it would cost you support. Even those who joined with us in the beginning would grow frightened and turn away. But these warnings had not swayed him back then.

"Mr. Bae Jomsu, don't you think you've lived too long?"

That he actually had considered having the guy murdered to save a hundred thousand dollars, that made him seem more pathetic to himself. What Shin Bomho wanted was not money but his life. Now, like an invisible virus, this caller had penetrated his flesh and was gnawing away at his life. And he had no way to stop it. If things went on like this, everything he had, his company and his family, would capsize like a ship with a gash below the waterline. Three children, his company. He felt he was losing his mind.

It was a mystery. How the hell did that bastard Shin Bomho, who had to be a descendant of one of the thirty-eight dead, find out he was Bae Jomsu? He had not just changed his name and birthplace. By plastic surgery, he had removed the bean-sized mole from his left cheek. He had taken to wearing glasses despite his perfect vision. By biting his tongue he had left behind his Cholla dialect. And twenty-eight years had safely passed. He could have understood if his true identity had been recognized soon after the war, but now, decades later?

In the grip of the desperate loneliness of a man tottering on a precipice, he struggled with physical pain. Not only had his blood pressure soared far too high, his urine also had taken on the ominous color of washwater.

4

Bae Jomsu never dreamt it would end so absurdly. He kicked the table, shouting,

"What d'you mean? You telling me our time is over and done?"

"Lower your voice. It's not the end, we're only retreating for a while. Hurry, time's short."

Unlike his usual self, Chairman Pang was flustered.

"Fuck, three months and we gotta run away in the dark? What the hell's next?"

Jomsu couldn't handle himself when it looked like the tables were turned and the old world was closing in on him again. He'd been so sure his new world, his bright day of plenty, would last forever.

"Get a grip on yourself, Comrade Vice-Chairman! What you're saying is an unpardonable breach of party spirit!"

The sharp voice of a woman rang out. The Women's League leader, schoolmistress Chun, was glaring at Jomsu with the eyes of a cobra. Jomsu felt himself soaked in a cold sweat. The predicament was too dangerous.

"This once we'll excuse it as a moment of excitement, but such slander must not be repeated."

"Understood, Comrade Chairwoman of the Women's League."

Like stray cats, they had to creep out of the village under the canopy of night. There was no time for families or anything else. There was not even time to muster all the party members. Walking in the dark, nobody dared to utter a word, but each felt the imminent peril, as if their own hair was about to burst into flames.

They camped in dense woods on the mountainside some miles off from the village. A spy who came up the next day reported that the ROK Army had retaken control of the area around noon, just a few hours after their departure.

"Sons of bitches!"

A communist militia officer in their group struck his boot with a stick and scowled. His curse ruptured the deep silence, but nobody else opened their mouth.

Jomsu vacantly watched a fire-ant crawl across a leaf. All the work of the past three months seemed as distant as in a dream. He felt limp; all his strength had been sapped. What now? Would the old days return? Absorbed in images as vague as clouds gliding above a distant horizon, slowly he sank into sleep, lying comfortably on his back with all four limbs stretched out.

His father appeared with his usual bloated face. "Son, however great your hatred, it can't be greater than mine. In spite of myself, I sent you off to become a blacksmith 'cause I wanted you to grow up without bitterness in your heart. But you turned out like this? Those you murdered, were they mortal enemies? Did they kill your parents? No, they were just lazy rich men, taking for granted a world where they always had things and the poor never did. Take a good look at yourself, slaughtering men like dogs, where'd you learn to treat men like that? Did you make tools for farmers? No, you made spears for killing. Foul, worthless murderer! You'll never sleep in peace."

Jomsu woke up from the dream, alarmed. Dusk had wrapped the surrounding area in shadows.

"Comrade Vice-Chairman, you're a tough one. How can you nap like a baby?" Chairman Pang said as if to himself, smiling bitterly.

"Really, I wh . . ."

Jomsu mumbled, wiping his face with his palm. His father had died two months ago, yet the dream-image of his face still lingered. Jomsu did not even know what the illness had been. Suddenly bedridden, his body rapidly bloated. A Chinese herb doctor came with medicine, saying it was some stomach ailment, but it was useless. Jomsu had been busy with many duties, and wasn't even there at the deathbed. At the funeral, people whispered behind his back:

"Like they always say, you reap what you sow. The ghosts of those Jomsu killed must've returned for his father."

Jomsu went through the motions of the mourning rituals, but he felt no great grief. Only later, upon reflection, did he begin to feel guilt for not having been at his father's side as he lay stricken and dying.

Jomsu's father had been disturbed by his son's conduct from the first. He had trembled for his daughter, Sunwol, who, as one of the Women's League, rampaged about as if possessed by a demon. The world had gone to the devil, and the household was turned inside out. There was no stopping Sunwol. Without so much as a lifted eyebrow, she took to calling her own father "Comrade."

From the day she killed Byongchul and his wife in a chillingly sadistic way, Jomsu had lost all affection for her. When Jomsu and the others fled the village, Sunwol hadn't been able to escape. They sent for her, but she couldn't be found. She must have been among the first to face retribution.

At dusk the militia officer summoned all of them to issue the orders.

"From now on, all-out struggle is our only choice. We're in dire straits, so much the more must we unite like an iron chain. A victory won against all odds is the greatest triumph. Our great People's Army soon will win a total victory."

The officer went on to announce strict orders. Unconditional obedience, with insubordination punished by summary execution. All command structures and ranks to remain as before. Nobody was permitted to carry matches or implements to make fires. No leaving camp without permission. Such were the rules laid down.

The same evening Jomsu had returned to camp after failing to find his wife's corpse, they had gone on the move. Their agents had reported that the army planned to comb through the mountains above the villages, so they had to retreat deeper into the wilderness. In his mind, Jomsu tied a silk thread to his son's wrist and unravelled the skein of paternal love as they crossed a ridge above the valley and headed up into the mountains.

Their days and nights were reversed. By day they hid in caves or other spots invisible from the air. Only with the fall of night did they stir into activity. Their most important nightly tasks were to contact superiors in other partisan units by signal fires and to forage for food.

Every week or so they had to raid an isolated hamlet to secure food. This business was like holding an armed hand grenade. To protect their sanctuary, they could not strike nearby villages and had to travel far. Once a likely target was marked, they had to double check for ROK garrisons or well-armed police contingents. They sought food, not battle, so they avoided confrontation whenever possible. Hounded by pursuers, they couldn't afford to waste a single life or even a single bullet.

For nearly all the raids, Jomsu acted as leader. There was one order Jomsu always gave before departing. Nobody was to kill anyone without his direct order. In wartime, people wouldn't be surprised to be robbed, and sparing lives would make the robbery victims grateful later. Wanton killing would swell the enemy's ranks. This logic sounded impeccable, but it was only a rationalization. Secretly, Jomsu realized he no longer was able to kill.

One night with six men he invaded a small hamlet of about a dozen dwellings. The occupants they rousted were helpless before the guns stuck under their noses. Jomsu's men swiftly and without hindrance seized the food.

"All done," one of his men reported.

"You, stay on your bellies and shut up. If you make a peep or light this place up after we're gone, you'll be shot on the spot."

Jomsu cried venomously, waving his gun barrel, then wheeled around to go out the door.

Someone screamed loudly, running out. Instantly, Jomsu tripped the fleeing shape, shouting, "Hold your fire!"

Jomsu drew his knife and pounced heavily upon the figure on the floor. It was a young woman who'd been trembling like a leaf in the corner. His edginess subsided for an instant, but as quickly he became enraged again,

"Dirty bitch!"

Jomsu raised the blade high above his head. But he couldn't slash down. A blast of icy wind pulled him back by the throat. He lowered his arm and replaced the knife in its sheath.

"Take the bitch back in."

Ever since that night, Jomsu knew he would never again be able to harm others.

Winter descended. They scaled many mountains. The new year came and still their trek continued.

"What in the world will become of us?" Jomsu asked one day.

"The war goes on. We must hold out a while longer."

Chairman Pang made the same reply as always. They had lost one man to disease, and another broke his leg in a fall and they just left him lying in the snow to die. Finally, spring arrived. By this time they had no idea how to find their way back to their home village.

Jomsu, on sentry duty one afternoon, was sitting in the crack of a rock idly listening to the birds when Chairman Pang walked up to him.

"Comrade Vice-Chairman, I have a favor to ask."

"What is it? Spit it out."

Intuitively, Jomsu knew he was not going to ask to bum a cigarette.

"I'll explain the details later and start with the favor first. On your next night raid, please bring back a woman or two."

"Women? Drag them up here to work and wash?"

As these words passed his lips, Jomsu instantly found himself thinking of schoolmistress Chun, Chairwoman of the Women's League. His instinct was on target.

Pang explained that the annoying behavior of the militia officer had been getting worse of late. He had tried to explain to the officer that he and Chun were like man and wife, but he refused to listen and kept saying comrades should share their pleasure since that, too, was the way of revolution. So, Pang said, what could he do?

Jomsu had never seen Pang in such a dejected and helpless condition. All because of that bastard he'd been faced with an intolerable affront.

"We ought to pull out that bastard's tongue and grind it up. Maybe he'd screw his own mother if she were a comrade in arms, eh?" Jomsu said, clutching at the stock of his rifle.

"Better lower your voice."

"He's a beast, worse than a beast. Gotta kill him, no time to waste."

"Please, calm down. I didn't tell you to enrage you this way. He's a man, after all. If we just get a woman for him, it'll all work out, won't it?"

Pang grasped Jomsu's arm as he spoke. Jomsu recalled his wife and gazed into Pang's eyes, those eyes that once had flashed so brightly but which now seemed dull.

"I see."

Even before they fled into the mountains, Jomsu had guessed the relationship between Pang and Chun. An ideal match, but not even as fugitives had they acted like a couple in love. Even so, everyone in the group had a hunch there was some such tie between them.

Now that he thought of it, for the past six months they had spent in the mountains, none of the men had been anywhere near a woman. Not that loneliness had never struck, but it was subdued by the demands of their anxious, hunted daily lives. When they raided a village it was an indulgence they couldn't afford, even if a woman stood right in front of their faces. Probably each man had dealt with the urge in his own way. Schoolmistress Chun had pulled off her charade for quite a while, but Jomsu now thought she might have broken away from the group long before had it not been for Chairman Pang.

The raid that night was different. Jomsu gave a special order: "Catch two women, no more. Don't lay a finger on any others."

Summer passed and autumn came. Mountain life grew worse and worse. The pursuit of the military police was visibly reinforced, penetrating further back into the wilds. Even the night, once their refuge, was becoming threatening. And the deeper they fled, the rarer were villages, and food became very scarce.

Then a cataclysm struck. At twilight one day, they were attacked. Close fighting went on for almost two hours before the gunfire ceased. On their side, the casualties were catastrophic. Out of seventeen in the group, seven died and three were wounded. Chairman Pang was shot in the thigh. Under cover of darkness, they hastened to flee. Jomsu carried Pang on his back, with schoolmistress Chun trotting alongside, clutching Pang's blood-soaked leg.

There was no medicine to treat the deep bullet wound. Pang moaned in agony, and Chun refused to leave his side even for a moment.

"Hyunwoo, dear, don't give up, please. It's getting a bit better."

Chun called Pang by his first name. It was the first time Jomsu had ever heard him addressed that way. Chun repeated the same thing over and over, her eyes streaming with tears.

Pang's wound wasn't improving at all. In fact, it was getting seriously worse. The herb mixture Jomsu gathered on the mountain was little help. Each day the mask of death thickened on Pang's face. As if a portent of his demise, the festering leg began to stink. The wound was gangrenous.

The sixth day came. Answering a summons, Jomsu followed Chun. Pang's complexion was terrible. For a moment, silence reigned among the three of them.

"Jomsu . . . " Chairman Pang whispered his name and held out his hand. Jomsu was startled by the way he called out to him, and, sensing the strange finality of the situation, took the pale hand offered by Pang.

"Jomsu, you should get away, tonight if you can."

"Wh-what?" Jomsu took a deep breath.

"Listen carefully . . . there's no hope for us anymore. The war can't be won. Our last chance was to go to the North by the mountains, but that scheme's been bungled. The whole front is closed off and we've missed our chance. We can't retreat forever. We've failed. Soon I'll die, but I worry about you. Since you first met me, you've had nothing but hard work and suffering. I don't want you to die in the mountains like a dog. The world is in turmoil yet, it won't be too hard to hide your identity. But the longer you stay up here, the harder it'll be . . ."

Jomsu felt the sky collapsing in on him. He had fervently believed that the day of victory would come sooner or later without fail. Without that faith, he couldn't have stood the harsh and barren life in the mountains.

"But, what about you two?"

"Don't worry about us," Chun said softly, her face thinly veiled with an enigmatic smile. As if to reassure him, she added, "You know what'll happen if this conversation ever leaks out, don't you?"

The consequences were all too obvious.

Jomsu emerged from the cave. Darkness descended around him, deepening the late autumn chill. He lay awake all that night. The night brought memories of his past deeds, a foreboding of the desolate future, and a despondency at having chased so many ghosts.

Dawn was breaking from afar. Then a shout.

"Someone . . . Comrade Chun hanged herself!"

Jomsu rushed there. Mistress Chun was dangling from a nearby oak tree.

"What about Pang . . . !"

Jomsu dashed into the cave. Pang lay dead as if sleeping. At once Jomsu knew. Chun had smothered Pang before hanging herself. At that instant something snapped within Jomsu and he made up his mind.

He held Chun's limp body while another man untied the rope around her neck. As he helped to lower the body down, his hands suddenly froze. Like lightning the thought flashed: Could she have been pregnant? The corpse's abdomen was strangely protruding behind the short skirt. Jomsu carefully felt again the lower part of the stomach. What his hand felt was identical with a feeling seven years before, that touch of bloatedness when his wife was pregnant with Chilsung. He had felt an indescribable elation back then that made his whole body tickle, but now an icy cold stiffened him.

What they've done is unpardonable . . .

Instead of cursing them, however, Jomsu ruthlessly bit his own lip. The desperation that drove them to end their lives was becoming his own agony. He was deeply moved, too, by their warmth the night before in revealing the truth.

Jomsu buried them side by side on a sunny slope of the mountain. What can I do now? I'm like a fledgling with its wings cut off. This image appeared before him again and again as patted down the loose earth on their graves.

"Their conduct was positively reactionary. I appoint you, Comrade Vice-Chairman, to be Chairman from today. You'll do a good job, won't you?"

The red militia officer wore a repulsive grimace on his face as he spoke.

"Thank you, sir. I'll bend over backwards to work hard, Comrade Officer."

Jomsu thus accepted the chairmanship with dignity. But two nights later, while out on a raid, he vanished into the darkness without a trace.

"It's odd, really. Your present condition is not good at all."

Even without his doctor's renewed concern, he knew only too well the gravity of his condition. But he was in no position to enter a hospital.

"Dr. Chun, give me one more night, then I'll make up my mind whether to enter the hospital. Just now I have some affairs too important to . . ."

His voice was anxious. The water was approaching flood stage, but the dam had no spillway to open.

"No matter how important your business may be, could it be more important than your health?"

The doctor meant "life" not "health," but he had used a tactful euphemism. Whether to stay alive or to deal with the crisis at hand, that was the dilemma he faced. Even if his health were to deteriorate further, only his own existence was threatened. The other peril could bring a catastrophe swallowing his three children and his wife, not to mention himself. Bound by this realization, he couldn't check into the hospital.

"The whole world's not worth one's health, they say. I'll contact you again tomorrow."

Without bothering to conceal his displeasure, the doctor gave up.

"Thank you very much, Dr. Chun."

For the first time he felt genuine gratitude to the doctor. He used to think all doctors were only after money, but the thought of doing without Dr. Chun displaced that prejudice and gave him a vague sense of security.

To him it seemed he'd encountered the true essence of loneliness. A state of being at once a part of everything and yet totally alone. How painful to have to pretend all is normal while enduring a private chaos even as the world outside goes on as usual. Never had he faced such loneliness.

Years before, while fleeing in the mountains through the directionless darkness, he had felt a similar despair. But back then he'd had the all-encompassing goal of survival, an animal instinct, and the yearning to recover his son, Chilsung. But now, sunk in the depths of despair with dangers converging to menace him, he had nothing to hang on to. His only hope was to meet Shin Bomho, his tormentor, in person. He was prepared to give up, not two hundred thousand, but half of all his property. To go into the hospital now was unthinkable, even if his condition worsened. Unless he could convince Shin Bomho to meet him, he had no choice but to sit and wait for the telephone rings that drove him mad. He had already abandoned the idea of searching out the bastard and killing him.

He lit a cigarette, puffed a few times, extinguished it, then lit another. He glanced about, always coming back to the clock hanging on the wall in front of him. It was almost five past ten. When no call came, his anxiety increased. He was short of breath, confused.

Ring. Rrring. Startled, he leapt to his feet.

"Hello, I . . ."

"How do you do, Mr. Bae Jomsu?"

He shuddered. The slow voice emitting syncopated syllables felt colder than ever.

"Look, young man, I'll give you half of all I own. Please help me. I'm serious, this is for real."

He poured out his rehearsed phrases in one breath.

"Heh, heh, heh . . ."

"Hello, hello?"

"Listen well, Mr. Bae Jomsu. After all, you, a beast, know only money. Half your property? An astronomical sum, I'm sure. But I'm not after money, so I'll decline."

"Well, what do you want, then?"

"I think I've made it clear."

His legs buckled at his knees.

"See here, it's been thirty years. Please think it over and let me live."

"Let you live? Some guts you have for someone who murdered thirty-eight people. I never said I'd kill you. You're free to go on living."

"No, my life is in your hands. Please, let me meet you."

"Well, that's enough for today . . . hold on, I forgot to mention one thing. Your oldest son lives in Kureum Apartments, doesn't he?"

"Wh-what are you planning to do?!"

The shock nearly did him in.

"Don't you know?"

"Not that, young man, please! I beg you . . ."

"It's your problem."

"Whose son are you anyway, so set on ruining my life?"

"If you're really interested, no reason not to tell you. But I doubt you would recall, having slaughtered thirty-eight in a bunch. Do you remember a man by the name of Shin Byongmo?"

"Shin Byongmo . . ."

His head was a chaos of screams, faces, and corpses.

"Well, well, like I said, seems you don't remember."

He was short of breath.

"Then . . . Shin Byongchul was . . ."

The face flashed before him—Byongchul who'd been mercilessly killed by Jomsu's sister Sunwol. Shin Byongmo was Shin Byongchul's younger brother.

"Th-then you, you're . . ."

He stammered, deathly pale, then lurched.

"Shin Byongmo was my father."

"Wha, what you say!"

Shrieking, Jomsu collapsed heavily onto the floor, thinking, "You must be my own son, my own" as the face of Shin Byongmo's young bride pulsed into his mind.

"Mr. Bae Jomsu, don't you think you've lived too long?"

These words buzzed from the receiver which by then had fallen to the floor. He sank into a coma without hearing them.

Human Door

1

"I prepared something for just this occasion. A photo of your father. He's quite young in the picture, but you'll recognize him right away."

Upon awakening, the same train of thought resumed. He must have dozed off there at his desk. Outside the window, he could see flower buds slowly unfolding under a layer of dew. Hyongmin could sense the vibrance of that invisible energy, but he was too numb to appreciate anything. He had been robbed of sleep by a perplexing and oppressive incident.

He sighed quietly and picked up a pack of cigarettes. He poked his finger inside in the usual way—empty. Savagely, he crumpled the pack, the cellophane crackling in his hand with a thin transparent wail. He flung the mangled package toward an ashtray heaped high with butts.

"No need to take my word for it. Check with your father."

Hyongmin relit a butt. All night long he'd wrestled with these imponderables, trying to grab the question by the tail. But the night had been fruitlessly consumed, and still he chewed on the same question.

Everyone has a secret weakness, they say. Hidden incidents of bedwetting, of fondling a young aunt's breasts while pretending to be asleep, of cheating on an exam, of masturbating five times in one day, of deserting a pregnant woman, and so on. In Father's case, however, his past was something entirely different.

"Your father's real name is Bae Jomsu. Your name shouldn't be Hwang Hyongmin, but Bae Hyongmin."

Faced with this jarring news, Hyongmin's reaction was to try to hide behind nervous laughter. Maybe it was an instinctual defense, triggered to shield one from undefiable shock, like a criminal's grin at the pronouncement of his death sentence, or a request for a final smoke in the shadows of the scaffold. The voice on the phone was no mere human voice, it was more like an oracle tolerating no contradiction. Hyongmin saw himself transformed into a goldfish in an aquarium which instantly froze. Even if the fish survived, what could it possibly do? The sleepless night he'd just passed had accomplished nothing. Was it actually possible that Father had done that? All he could do was gasp, over and over again, at these questions.

The call had come around ten-thirty.

Rrring. Rrring.

In a slightly exasperated mood, Hyongmin put down the book and went out to the living room. His wife was already in bed, complaining of the flu. The repeated rings grated on his nerves as he went to answer the phone.

"Hel-lo . . ."

"How do you do, esteemed professor Hwang Hyongmin?"

Instantly, Hyongmin grew tense, though he couldn't say why. It was a perfectly normal phrase for a caller to use, utterly banal, yet he felt an uncanny tension and coldness. It was the voice—unreal, syncopated in a flat monotone, uttering a syllable at a time. It was colorless and odorless, like the voice of a robot in some science-fiction movie.

"Who's this?"

Hyongmin grew agitated, tightly coiling the springs of his emotions.

"It concerns your father, Mr. Hwang Bokman. Let me speak to you about the matter."

Father? Dozens of little bulbs in Hyongmin's head began flickering in variegated colors.

"Listen. If it's business, you should call the company. I've nothing to do with that."

Hyongmin's reply was impatient, almost as if cursing. He was peeved by the speaker's abrupt shift from the honorific "esteemed professor" to the familiar "your father."

"Your mind runs too far, too fast. You're mistaken this time. It concerns the life and death of every member of your family. Hope this isn't taken for blackmail."

Hyongmin took a deep breath without being conscious of it. At the same time, he cut through the knots of foreboding clotting within him. To stand up to this stranger who, without a trace of excitement, had pronounced crisply and calmly a chain of rather long words, Hyongmin realized the need for absolute composure.

"Are you at least aware of the offense this constitutes under the Criminal Code?"

Like a boxer who has landed a right jab flush on the chin of his opponent, Hyongmin felt his spirits rise.

"Very sophisticated, worthy of a professor. The nature of the offense does not interest me. Just listen well, and consider where your father's crimes may fit. It should take you some time."

Hyongmin, after dishing out a single jab, felt he had been hit with a flurry of lefts and rights. Despite an urge to hang up, he grasped the phone tighter. He felt a terrible need to smoke, but his cigarettes were in the study.

"Your father at the age of thirty was an active communist."

"Communist?"

"Correct. Don't pretend you don't understand."

Hyongmin at once recalled his father's age as fifty-nine and calculated that it would have been twenty-nine years before. Then he felt all his strength drain away. At that time, Father had crossed the 38th parallel from his home in Hwanghae province in North Korea, coming south in defiance of the Northern regime, risking permanent exile from his birthplace.

"You listen to me! Cut the nonsense and hang up the phone right now."

Falling into his classroom manner, Hyongmin raised his voice.

"Isn't it premature to be so self-righteous? Your father's real name is not Hwang Bokman, but Bae Jomsu. His hometown is in Cholla province in the South, not Hwanghae in the North."

"Wh-who the hell are you?! Don't you know this is blackmail?!"

"Huh, huh, huh, why not shout louder? If your wife learns about these things, so much the better for me."

Hyongmin felt a sudden terror. That "huh, huh" could not be laughter. It was a curse, like a shaman's incantation. The voice seemed to leap out of the receiver, becoming snake scales encircling his throat.

"To conceal his treasonous communism, your father changed his name, his birthplace, even his face. All this was fabricated before you were born. Imagine if you can."

"Who are you, anyway? What grounds have you for such nonsense?"

Although he spoke fiercely, Hyongmin felt his heart strangely sinking. Maybe it was the stranger's remark that all of it happened before he was born. Those words jarred him with a mysterious hypnotic force. Already Hyongmin was entangled like a fish in a net of dreadful possibilities that it might be true, and his vehement tone was part of the struggle to get clear of the net. Intuitively, Hyongmin accepted the possibility because he'd seen acquaintances suffer from similar unmaskings.

"I'll identify myself in good time. You demand grounds, well, your father is still alive, isn't he? And besides me, if we count the people from your father's hometown, I think we'll have more than enough witnesses."

"Shut up. You've mistaken him for someone else."

"I've prepared something for just this occasion. A photo of your father. He's quite young in the picture, but if you correct for his present years you'll recognize him right away. I mailed it today, so you should receive it tomorrow. Don't destroy it, hoping to eliminate the evidence. I have the negative."

Hyongmin felt the net drawing tighter. He had no reply, and felt totally exhausted by this time.

"Your father is Bae Jomsu, so your real name is Bae Hyongmin, as I said."

"Shut up, you bastard!"

He couldn't deal with the terror that voice was carving into his forehead in the shape of the characters Bae, Hyong, Min, except by shrieking.

"Huh, huh, huh, I'm sure it must be a shock. But it's only the start. I'll stop here for today, Mr. Bae Hyongmin. Now, then . . ."

"Hello, hello?"

"Go ahead."

"What are you after?"

"After? Well . . . don't you think your father has lived too long?"

"What?!"

The voice was gone.

He hurriedly dropped the receiver, which suddenly felt slimy. His craving for a smoke was bad, but Hyongmin couldn't move. An indescribable terror was tightening its grip on him. The surroundings of his own house seemed unfamiliar. The sofa, tables, cabinets, wallpaper, pictures, clock, everything wore strange expressions. Suddenly, those familiar objects erupted into a chorus of laughter. Hyongmin peered about—from the bathroom, the kitchen, the room where his wife lay asleep, from his own study, the horror flooded upon him.

Why am I so afraid? Hyongmin barely caught this thought, struggling to compose himself. All at once he realized it was those words. Those words had rolled out of the phone and were still there, creeping about like parasites and spreading terror.

Hyongmin grabbed his head with both hands. He had no choice but to overcome this dense black fear. Never before had words been able to induce in him such a suffocating terror.

It could be true . . .

Hyongmin contemplated the worst with a clear mind, as if surrendering to the terror. But immediately he denied it, like a furry animal avoiding fire.

"Communist" was not a label that slumbered peacefully in dictionaries until needed. It was the horrid mark of traitorous criminals, of crimes transcending time and space. He knew nothing about the Communist invasion except what he had read in books, seen in exhibitions of photographs or heard from his elders. But he knew too well the heinous nature of the offense from seeing the scars it left upon his friends. And now, his own father was being denounced as a communist!

Father—the self-made man. An unschooled man who came empty-handed from the North and battled the world alone. With a resolve simple to the point of ignorance, he had led a life so frugal as to approach miserliness. His economic success of today was the fulfillment of his inner self. They say Abraham Lincoln shed tears at the mere mention of the word "Mother." Hyongmin choked up whenever he thought of Father's life. The only reason he had studied so very hard as a boy was to please Father. How delighted Father had been each time he brought home prizes or the best grades. In school, he was awfully perplexed when they had to name the person they respected most. Every time he wanted to write "Father," but the teachers wouldn't permit it. To admire one's own father was only too natural, they said, so he should choose someone else. Uncomprehending, he ended up writing names like "Tom Sawyer" or "Popeye."

Now this father of his suddenly, out of the blue, was being accused of having changed his name and birthplace to conceal having been a Communist traitor.

Who on earth could the caller be? Then, suddenly, Hyongmin's hatred for the stranger gave way to an intense concern for his father. He snatched the phone.

"No need to take my word for it. Check with your father."

But he couldn't dial. What could he do, bluntly ask his father if he'd received a call babbling about communism? What if his father had received such a call? What if the charge were true? In that case calling now wouldn't do any good, it would just torture him even more. If the accusations were true, Father would still try to conceal the truth from everyone at all costs. He would do all he could to solve the problem secretly, all by himself.

Hyongmin drew his hand back from the phone and sank into an abyss of despair. Not that he believed what the caller had said even for a second. But he was in no position to refute him once and for all. All he could do was to recognize the painful fact that he had fallen prey to the gaping-mouthed monster called ill fate.

"Don't you think your father has lived too long?"

Hyongmin shuddered. The voice, even then, was bland and colorless. Yet a definite threat of murder had been made. It had two interpretations: either his father should have died long ago, or he should soon die.

"Son of a bitch, I'll kill you first."

Hyongmin stood up ferociously, shaking. He had passed a sleepless night without solving any of an unending chain of questions.

Hyongmin heard his wife stirring. He hurriedly extinguished his cigarette, plucked a book at random from the shelf, opened it on the desk and set some blank paper beside it in front of him.

"Oh, dear, didn't you sleep at all?"

His wife's tone blended sympathy with a reproach. She had become his bride not long before, and there was a fragrance of fresh wildflowers about her.

An invisible wall had gone up in Hyongmin's mind to keep his wife out. Better for her to remain in the dark. After less than six months of married life, all she knew was that she, the daughter of a high government official, had married into a reputable family of solid financial power. Her intelligent husband was said to have bright future prospects. Hyongmin choked at the unwanted but necessary precaution of erecting a tomb of secrets.

"Urgent project to finish?"

"Mm, an impromptu seminar on short notice."

"Should have told me you'd be working all night. Look at you—utterly exhausted. If I'd prepared a little snack last night, you wouldn't be so tired."

"It's all right. You weren't feeling well."

"But you should have. If your father finds out I neglected you, he'll show me no mercy. Please, don't make me an evil wife, dear."

Her high nasal voice almost whining, Hyongmin's wife hugged him from behind, touching her cheek to his.

Had things been different, he would've gone on to tease her by saying, "So it's fear of your father-in-law that makes you care for me, eh?" That peculiar nasal voice, and her vaguely tantalizing scent, ordinarily evoked a strong masculine urge in him. But today it was just another sound.

"You look awfully overworked. Better get moving now and make your morning call to your father to pay your respects."

She must've sensed Hyongmin's indecisive mood.

"All right." Hyongmin rose ponderously from his chair.

Father—Hyongmin felt choked by emotion. His father was a man who tried to solve all crises by sheer will. Despite his being the eldest son, Father had permitted Hyongmin to set up a separate household after he married. He'd sacrificed his desire to have his eldest son live with him in accordance with Korean tradition. "A woman marries her husband, not her husband's family," he said.

"Intrusion from the in-laws can spoil a good marriage, and filial piety from a distance is more cherished and better appreciated than from nearby. I'm still able-bodied, and a doting daughter-in-law will soon age me beyond my years. I ask nothing more than that the two of you love each other, and see that you look after your student husband's health."

Such had been Father's words, on various occasions, countering complaints from his wife or Hyongmins's younger siblings. Finally it was decided that the newlyweds should live apart in a home of their own. The daughter-in-law's dutiful request that she serve her husband's parents was accepted, on the condition that she serve them only ten days instead of the one month she'd proposed.

Father was delighted and proud to be served by his daughter-in-law, who barely knew how to tie the sash of her own traditional dress. Despite his high blood pressure, he laughed and praised her salty soups and overly spicy salads. The more pleased Father became, the more critical Mother was of her daughter-in-law. But under the imperious sway of Father, Mother could wield no real power. Since they moved out, Hyongmin had been calling his father each morning to pay his respects. It was a practice initiated by his wife in affectionate gratitude for her father-in-law's progressive and humane attitude.

As he dialed, Hyongmin decided to make the usual inquiry after his father's health, and not only because his wife was standing beside him awaiting her turn.

"Father, it's Hyongmin. Did you sleep well?"

"Um, sure. You?"

Nothing unusual about Father's voice. It was resonant as always.

"Yes, your blood pressure all right?"

"Sure, sure, now put the little one on."

Following the regular procedure, Hyongmin gave the receiver to his wife. Even if Father, too, had received a threatening call, Hyongmin probably would not be able to detect it in his voice. He would try to sound more natural than ever. However grave the difficulties encountered by his company, Father always saw to it that the family never had the slightest hint of trouble.

Hyongmin drank two glasses of milk and ate nothing. He couldn't stomach the toast or fried eggs.

"You're in trouble again. Whenever you start writing you're like a pregnant woman."

"What do you mean? Are you trying to say you've been having morning sickness without letting me know?"

"Goodness, what a thing to say. I'll be in big trouble if I ever use the wrong metaphor."

His wife blushed and got up from the table.

Hyongmin was so absorbed in worrying about the mail that might arrive in his absence that he considered not going to his classes so he could receive it himself. But that would only steer his wife's attention to it, pouring oil on the fire. He finally reassured himself that she wasn't the type to open someone else's mail.

All day long he was distracted and couldn't teach properly. His mind was like a tangled spool. At one moment he could hear the voice on the phone, and the next he found himself doubting the family in which he had felt such pride. What if it were all true? Then, hurriedly he picked up the textbook and went off to his classroom.

In trying to suppress thoughts racing along ominous paths, Hyongmin succeeded in formulating a hypothesis about the stranger on the phone. He was not at all ignorant, and although the voice seemed devoid of feeling, he sensed an urgency in the speaker that led him to believe he must be on some kind of quest for revenge against Hyongmin's family.

Around four that afternoon Hyongmin returned home. Three pieces of mail were on his desk, and his instincts enabled him instantly to pick out the one from the caller. One was a plain letter, the second a large manila envelope containing a book of some sort, and the last was from him. It was an ordinary light brown envelope, folded twice to be almost square and so thin that hardly anything could be felt inside.

Hyongmin couldn't bring himself to pick up the envelope. An uncontrollable dread stormed within his breast like a furious cyclone. He feared that inside he'd find a picture of his father as a young man. Opening that envelope would be picking a number in a lottery of death. But it was a cul-de-sac. He stretched out his arm and grasped one corner of the envelope between his thumb and index finger. Despite his resolve to be strong, his hand trembled. His fingertips froze and the chill soon spread all over him. His whole body became tense as he struggled not to succumb to the cold—it was like a brutal force threatening one's very life. He tore the envelope with both hands. Then, in a continuous motion, he pulled out the contents.

"Don't be misled by the mole underneath the left eye."

This was written in a neat hand on a sheet of white paper. Hyongmin smelled an aroma of death, the same odor of peril exuded by warnings posted at forbidden places in big red letters under a skull and crossbones. He tore away the white paper. Inside was a photograph about the size of his palm. He drew a deep breath. At once he recognized the youthful face in the picture to be that of his own father.

"Dear, your coffee's ready."

His wife chimed in a melodious voice. Hyongmin quickly slipped the picture into a book.

"All right. I'm coming."

Hyongmin answered loudly, then rubbed his face with both hands. His face still seemed tense. Inside his brain, a ravaging series of tremors exploded. In the photo his father was stripped to the waist, waving a huge hammer in the air. There was no need to see more, he knew right away what his father's trade had been. Could he actually have been a blacksmith? He was from a proud and wealthy lineage. Still, undeniably, in this picture Father was a blacksmith. A blacksmith ... traitor ... metamorphosis ... a maelstrom of confusion shattered Hyongmin's composure.

"You look so tired. Try to take a nap, please."

"I will."

"What sort of seminar is it?"

"Same stuff as always, you know."

Hyongmin felt annoyed with his wife. It was the first time since their marriage he had felt that way. He knew it wasn't fair to her, but her existence had become a weight around his neck.

"I'll catch a wink of sleep."

Hyongmin rose from the table after downing his coffee. It had tasted like Chinese medicine.

"Sleep comfortably, in the big room."

"No, I'll do a little thinking in the study and take a nap there if I feel like it. I'll be in trouble if I lie down too comfortably."

"As you wish."

"If you're bored, go ahead and go out."

"May I, darling?"

His wife smiled like a bright flower, and Hyongmin nodded, embittered by his own duplicitous generosity.

Having sent his wife on a visit to her family, Hyongmin was alone and returned to his study. Suddenly he had an auditory hallucination of a hammer on metal, the regular beat of a blacksmith working, issuing from the book where he left the picture. The piercing metallic sound rolled in rhythmic waves, like the clapping of a well-drilled cheering section, roaming to remote ravines of his memory, to the innermost recesses of his soul, slowly penetrating further and further inside him.

As if he had once heard it frequently, as if he had once been utterly familiar with it, the sound was inside him. It was like the awakening of a long forgotten echo of woodcutters once heard on a moonlit winter night. When had he heard that sound? Hyongmin was furiously excavating the sediments of his memory, and meanwhile, the sound waves pierced deeper and deeper within him.

"Of course, that's it!"

Hyongmin moaned. It was back before he entered grammar school. He had gone with a friend to Father's factory, without Mother's knowledge. Men of Herculean strength were pounding with iron hammers in front of a towering crimson fire. And the stirring spectacle was complemented by the delightful clinks of all different sizes and shapes of hammers.

"Those sounds are like soap bubbles," Hyongmin had said, and his friend, pursing his lips, had remarked in turn, "Naw, to me they're like jaw-breaker candies."

Upon hearing his friend's words, Hyongmin had begun searching for his father. When they started out for the factory, Hyongmin had bragged to his friend how his father would buy them candy, and now his friend wanted the payoff. But Father was nowhere to be found. His impatient friend had interrupted the busy laborers, asking where Hyongmin's father was, until they realized that Hyongmin was their boss's boy. Father was away on some errand, but the two boys had returned home with handfuls of candy the workers had bought for them.

That same night, however, Hyongmin had to raise his pant legs to have his calves whipped by his enraged father. It was punishment for the crime of visiting the factory. Ever since then, Hyongmin never had dared to visit the factory, even in his dreams, and the incident had been completely forgotten.

Hyongmin faced a shock that shattered him into a thousand pieces. He took the photo out from the book again. It was not his present father, but himself, who most resembled the young man in the picture. Father, bare-chested, was about to strike down with a heavy iron mallet. The hammer had a long slender handle, curved like a bow. The muscles of his arms, lifting the hammer into the air, looked alive and rippling, and the shoulders and chest, massive as rocks, exuded an aura of boundless might. The face was slightly uplifted, glistening with sweat. The sparkling eyes were fixed in an intent gaze on the target of the hammer. The half-opened mouth was somewhat twisted, as if gathering reserves of power. The expression on his face bespoke a formidable strength.

Hyongmin absent-mindedly focused on the tiny mole visible on the cheek beneath the left eye, and the picture slipped from his grasp. Even without the warning scrawled in black on the wrapping of the photograph, the mole would never have prevented him from recognizing his father. The note called it a mole, but it must have been a tumor. Still, that thing, no longer there today and probably removed before Hyongmin's birth, was itself a clear sign, announcing his father's past.

"Father . . . "

Hyongmin clasped his hands, his elbows resting on his desk. Rubbing his forehead against his clenched fingers, he called out to his father in a choking voice. Nothing but pitch black enveloped him. In that darkness, he found himself fractured, broken, crushed, ground to dust and finally blown away by the wind.

2

Rrring . . .

Hyongmin answered on the first ring. He feared his wife, whom he had coaxed into retiring early, might awaken.

"Hello?" Hyongmin said hastily in a subdued voice, glancing mechanically at the wallclock. It was almost ten.

"Good evening, Professor Bae Hyongmin."

Just like the day before, the voice was devoid of feeling, chopping each word syllable by syllable. Hyongmin shuddered. The man had replaced "Hwang" with "Bae," and those words "Bae Hyongmin" stabbed his heart like sharpened knives.

"Received the picture?"

"Yes . . ."

"Was he unmistakably your father?"

"Yes."

"You're honest, worthy to be a professor."

Hyongmin had much to say, but was uncertain how to begin and felt the stranger was toying with him. He knew the man was cruelly gloating over this. As he knew Hyongmin's address and phone number, he also knew that Hyongmin was only a lecturer at the university. But he deliberately made a point of calling him "professor."

"Who are you, anyway?"

"Well, before finding out about me, isn't it more important to discover more details about your own father?"

"Let's meet. Let's meet and discuss the details."

"No hurry. I refused to see your father, so why should I meet with you?"

"You refused to meet my father . . . you mean . . ."

Suddenly nauseated and feeling dizzy, Hyongmin saw the two faces of his father. The face in the photo was superimposed on the face he knew so well.

"Is it so surprising? Did you actually think I'd deal with him through you without contacting him directly? That'd be a bit too stupid, wouldn't it?"

More jeering from the stranger.

"To my father . . . when did you . . ."

"Same day, yesterday, I called him in the afternoon. So several hours before calling you."

Father . . . yet he had been perfectly normal on the phone that morning. Hyongmin felt his heart bursting, and sobbed between chokes of sympathy. What a shock it must have been to him. All night long he must have agonized.

"Listen, sir, won't you leave my father alone? Please, don't kill him."

Hyongmin was almost crying.

"Calm down, please. I have neither the right nor the power to kill your father. So your request is beside the point."

The voice, still expressionless, mercilessly parried Hyongmin's plea. Such cruel modesty was a vicious resource to which only a powerful man could resort. Hyongmin felt the compound humiliation of one trampled on as he knelt to beseech forgiveness. His blood boiled now with an indignant rage.

"See here, right now you're committing a murderous act. How can you say you lack the power and the right . . ."

"Huh, huh, huh. You call this murder, uh? If a man is dying because of a couple of phone calls, don't you think there must be a very good reason for it? It can only be his own guilt, it's not my fault."

"Wh-what? What exactly are you accusing my father of? Don't you know there are lots of people leading respectable lives who once were communist collaborators?"

"Steady, Professor Bae Hyongmin, what you say may be true, but . . ."

The voice broke off there. Hyongmin felt dizzy at the abrupt silence. He repressed an urge, creeping up in his throat, to cry out, and instead hastily lit a cigarette.

". . . but, remember, not all communist collaborators acted in the same way, and don't forget that those now leading dignified lives have paid for their past by going through fair trials in the courts. But . . ."

Again silence. Hyongmin put out the cigarette with a twist.

"But . . . your father, who held the rank of Vice-Chairman of the Communist People's Council, slaughtered thirty-eight innocent people. Then he fled, changing his name, birthplace, even his face to escape the nets of justice, at last reaching his present position."

" . . . ."

Thirty-eight . . . thirty-eight people . . . thirty-eight innocent people. . . .

"That's a lie, a filthy lie. My father is not that sort of beast. Who the hell are you, anyway? Who are you . . . ?" Hyongmin asked, sweating like a dog.

"Calm yourself. This is only the start, if you're already this excited, you'll be in trouble. If you want to know who I am that badly, I'll tell you. I am . . ."

The voice stopped. Hyongmin imagined a perfectly straight thread, crimson like the color of blood, running through a vacuum—a symbol of rancorous rage.

"I'm . . . the son of one of the thirty-eight people your father killed."

The blood-colored thread instantly turned into a flame. Hyongmin was speechless at his own instinctively true aim. He felt engulfed by the venomous rancor oozing from the stranger's voice.

"Please, let me see you, we need to talk."

"It's unnecessary. You and I have absolutely no right to discuss that historical incident. There's no reason for us to meet, ever."

"But why call, then . . . ?" Hyongmin hastily replied, unable to accept the refusal.

"Because you, as Bae Jomsu's eldest son, have certain duties to discharge. You're responsible for knowing the truth about your father. That's the cross you must bear as a blood relation. Just as I for the past ten years have wandered the country in search of your father, now you have the obligation of going down to your father's hometown to verify the crimes he committed. My purpose in calling is now half-accomplished, and it will be fully attained when you depart for your father's hometown. That's all I've got to do with you."

"I see, I'll do as you've suggested. But later, after that, then what will become of us?"

"Us?"

"My family, I mean."

"Your father is the only guilty one in your family."

"Well . . . my father is . . ."

"That's not something the two of us should discuss."

"Sir, I realize it's rash and impudent of me to ask this of you, but won't you please try to forget what my father did, it was twenty-nine years ago, won't you please try to forgive him? Tell me how he can be forgiven."

"Sorry. It's not within my power. That's the prerogative of the spirits of the thirty-eight who were killed twenty-nine years ago. Besides, my mother lived her whole life with a rancorous heart and couldn't forgive your father even on her deathbed. The spirits of the dead are calling for your father."

"Sir, please . . ."

"Now, I'll direct you to your father's hometown. The place is . . ."

Toward dawn, Hyongmin slept for a few hours. Before going to bed, he had made up his mind to journey down to his father's birthplace.

"I need to gather some data for a comparison of features of different provinces. An overnight trip should be long enough. Lock up the apartment and go stay with your family."

His wife made no real protest. As far as his academic work went, she had been well indoctrinated by her father-in-law, and was very compliant.

"Writing your article is important, surely, but please be careful in an unfamiliar place."

His wife didn't forget to express concern.

Without a hint of emotional turmoil, Hyongmin calmly dialed his morning courtesy call. This call, which had been such an enjoyable way to start the day, had become an excruciating ordeal. Probably for his father, too. Actually, it must be more agonizing for Father. Concealing the mortal danger, he had to present a mask of placid well being. It became an act of torture instead of a greeting. Still, he had no choice but to dial.

"Father? Hyongmin here. Did you rest well last night?"

"Certainly, certainly. The two of you?"

Father's voice sounded dull, and it was not just Hyongmin's imagination.

"Yes, but are you feeling all right, father? Your voice sounds a bit . . ."

No sooner had he started saying that than Hyongmin felt regret. Disclosing that he'd sensed something amiss would only make Father more agitated and fearful.

"Nothing, I'm fine. Just a bit tired. Now, let me speak to her."

Father's haste was apparent.

"Sure, I will. For the next couple of days I have to take a little trip to do some research for a paper I'm working on."

"Trip? Where to?"

"Well, down to Chungchong province, not far. What do you think, father, about sending my wife to stay with her family while I'm away?"

Hyongmin had almost blurted out "down in Cholla province." Sweat beaded up on his forehead.

"If it's for your studies, you should go. And take care of yourself. Now put the little one on."

Father's harping on his "studies" struck Hyongmin as sad, and made him recall the blacksmith in the photograph.

Hyongmin overruled his wife's wish to see him off at the bus terminal and sent her by taxi directly from their apartment to her parents' place. Come back healthy, don't get sick. His wife was sobbing in the face of one night's separation. Darling, I'm sorry. I don't want to lie to you, but there's no other way. Facing his pale wife's tears, Hyongmin shared something of his father's burning pain.

Which bond would prove stronger, the affinity between man and wife or a son's devotion to his father? For a few brief seconds, Hyongmin turned this query over and over in his mind. At last he was overwhelmed by fatalistic despair. They were two utterly distinct kinds of love. With no common dimension, how could one decide between them? Still, he could not but consider the shock his wife and her family would feel if they ever found out about this matter. He was tormented by the thought that the tears now shed by his wife would take on a wholly different meaning.

Hyongmin compulsively lit a cigarette. He told himself that if those tears later bespoke a different distress, he'd be able to dismiss them without remorse. Six months of married life could never displace lifelong bonds of blood. Blood—the substance of immortality itself—remained undeniable and incontestable. Hyongmin suppressed the afterimages of his wife and hailed a taxi.

"One for Kwangju," Hyongmin said as he slipped the money across the ticket counter. The voice seemed unlike his normal voice and quite strange. The destination on the ticket he bought, the place drawing him on this unexpected pilgrimage, was one he had never had a reason to either like or dislike. It had always been just another of many cities in the nation. It was situated in exactly the opposite direction from Hwanghae province.

The express bus left on time. Hyongmin closed his eyes only to see his father's face appear before him. It was an angry visage, the face that had thrashed the hell out of him on the day he had gone to the factory. The furious glare that forbade him ever to go near that place—what was behind such fury?

His father wouldn't permit his own son to visit his workplace, still less would he have passed his trade on to his son. For he resented being a blacksmith, an accursed trade, all his life. A blacksmith was not a skilled worker like a mechanic and did not earn a good living. Like the brand seared on a slave's shoulder, the smith's hammer was a signifier of his low caste. If his father had known Hyongmin was on his way to his old hometown, he would've raised a rod against him with the same fury as he had years before. No, not a rod, perhaps. How could the visit to the factory as a child compare with this trip to his hometown as a grown man? The shock might kill him. Hyongmin reflected on how thorough and painstaking his father had been in both concealing his true origin and instilling family pride in his children.

"Father . . ." Hyongmin summoned his father, moaning in distress. Tears ran from his closed eyes.

"Young man, are you from Kwangju?"

The voice was accompanied by a nudge to his side, startling him into sitting up.

"I said, you from Kwangju?"

An old grandmother was speaking to him through a mouth full of hard-boiled egg. After a sightseeing trip in Seoul, she needed someone to talk with during the long ride back home.

"No, grandma, just on some business. Sorry, I'm not really up to chatting just now. I'm sorry if it means your trip will be boring."

It sounded heartless, but he had to politely discourage her at the outset.

"Yeah, you don't look so good. But don't worry 'bout me, rest, go ahead 'n rest."

The old woman clicked her tongue, tut, tut, and seemed to feel genuine compassion toward him. Hyongmin leaned back against the headrest and looked out the window. The bus already was accelerating through the outskirts of Seoul.

"Farewell, Seoul"

Hyongmin's vision was arrested by a sign with those words, but because of the speed of the bus it vanished instantly. That simple phrase struck him as something out of the ordinary. Farewell. And its opposite: Welcome. He felt lonely at the thought that before long he might never be greeted with a "welcome." He focused his vision to scan ahead into the distance. The highway stretched out white as far as he could see. The roadway was a greyish-black, but in his mind the color registered white. The horizonless white road seemed an expression of fate, pulling him at breakneck speed into the past.

Hyongmin in fact was journeying backward in time. It was an era altogether different from the evolutionary epochs that an archaeologist would find interesting. An archaeologist would be satisfied with the mere excitement of an intellectual thrill, wrapped in an expensive package labeled "research" or "theoretical accomplishment." But he was en route to an encounter with a monstrous fate that might very well annihilate all the presuppositions of his present fruitful existence. Perhaps it would end up being a reckless intrusion into history, leading to a realization of a predestined debacle. All at once his fate was tightly intertwined with a war which he knew about only from books, tales told by his elders, and pictures at exhibitions.

The Korean War—known as "6.25" because it erupted on June 25, 1950—had ended in 1953 and so lacked any concrete significance for Hyongmin, who was born in 1954. Objectively, the country was still divided in two by a Demilitarized Zone, with the two sides harboring enmity against each other and military service still mandatory. Subjectively, apart from Father being banished from his home up North, 6.25 to Hyongmin was little more than a historical episode before his time, like the Samil Independence Movement against the Japanese on March 1, 1919.

Hyongmin's great-grandfather, he had been told, was a noble courtier who had been greatly praised for his selfless benevolence. Following the Japanese annexation of Korea he'd been stripped of his rank and was forced to labor the rest of his life to restore the family's wealth. As he was discerning and disciplined in all his undertakings, the family so prospered that by his death his estate embraced nearly a thousand acres. Most of this vast patrimony had been lost by Grandfather, but no one blamed him for the reversal.

For Grandfather did not squander his inheritance on gambling or debauchery, rather he spread the family's money to the four corners of Manchuria in support of the cause of liberation. Grandfather was always away, sending news only through a furtive grapevine, and the family struggled just to make ends meet. That was why Father received no schooling despite the family lineage and was forced to become a manual laborer. Grandfather had passed away in Manchuria two years before the liberation from the Japanese occupation. The family had learned of it through hearsay, but they never received any formal notice nor was his body recovered for proper burial. The family had not even been able to mourn openly out of fear of the Japanese military police.

In the wake of liberation came the Communist world, and Father had been an obvious target. As time passed, life became still more intolerable than under the Japanese. Victims couldn't just sit still and persecuted people began joining together in an anti-communist underground. But that movement could not last for long and Father had barely been able to escape before being denounced. Nevertheless, retaliation fell upon his relatives. Father's grandmother, stepmother and half-brother were dragged away to be executed as Father risked death to cross the 38th Parallel in the bitter cold of January 1950. The following June the Korean War broke out.

Such was Hyongmin's family history. From the time he was a small boy until he reached adulthood, his father had recited this same story dozens of times. On such occasions Father's demeanor was most dignified and reverential. As for Hyongmin, though he knew the oft-repeated saga by heart, he never turned an inattentive ear to it. The repetitions were not tiresome like some overplayed popular record. With each telling, the story was etched a little deeper into his soul.

A family of noble descent, a heroic fighter for liberation, a lineage known to be anti-communist—that he was a son of such a heritage made him feel a boundless pride, and this feeling was the solid foundation of self-respect upon which Hyongmin had built his proud personality. Had it been in the second year of Middle School? In his Korean Composition class, he had been asked to write on the topic of "My Father." After a moment's reflection, Hyongmin resolved to write an account of his family history which was engraved inside his head as distinctly as the characters written on the blackboard in front of him. Once he started writing, the story unrolled itself as smoothly as a spool of yarn.

"In the whole world, there is nobody I respect more than my father. When I think of my father I feel deeply sorry, and he is to me the greatest of men. I am sorry my father wasn't able to study much. But he is a great man because he wasn't ashamed of that and instead worked very hard until he became the president of a company. I'm afraid of my father, but I love him most of anyone in the world and respect him most."

That was the closing of his composition.

An unexpected result followed. It won a prize as the best composition and was printed in the school magazine. Hyongmin had been extremely flustered, worrying to death lest his father happen to read it. And even though Father was always genuinely happy to see him bring home prizes, Hyongmin never told his father about that particular prize and hid it away. Not long after, however, it was revealed. Though busy with his company, Father made it a point to drop by the school or to invite Hyongmin's teacher out for lunch every month or so, and he learned the news from the teacher.

After reading his son's composition, Father stared down at the floor for a moment without speaking, and then, deeply moved, he hugged Hyongmin, who had been waiting anxiously, saying, "Splendid, Hyongmin, splendid. I'm blessed with a wonderful son."

Still, in the picture Father was a blacksmith. When you see a general with rows of stars on his shoulders, sometimes it seems like the man might have been born a general. Similarly, his father in the photo looked so perfect one had to wonder if he hadn't been a blacksmith from birth.

"Father . . ."

Hyongmin moaned, closing his eyes. He felt his father's anguish and vulnerability. A blacksmith and a scion of noble lineage . . . these were two extreme poles. The meaning of the fanciful tale his father had concocted penetrated deep into Hyongmin's heart, engendering pangs of sorrow.

"Don't you think your father has lived too long?"

He wasn't yet sure what the stranger on the phone really wanted. He would not resort to such a stupid move as murdering Hyongmin's father himself. But surely he would hurl a bomb of some kind. As he tried to regain his composure, Hyongmin felt he shouldn't try to intercept the bomb, nor should he be too obsessed with the potential damage. The whole affair was like a wheel already set rolling down a steep hill. The wheel would come to a stop only when gravity pulled it no more. Even if his enjoyable current state of life would all go up in smoke, Hyongmin couldn't lift a finger to prevent it. Maybe all of this was predestined to happen this way from time immemorial. It served no purpose for him to try to gauge the enormity of Father's crimes now. Besides, to do so would be an impious desecration of one's parent. He felt that, even should he learn that Father's offenses had been graver than expected, he would love him more, not less, than before.

3

It was nearly three in the afternoon when Hyongmin arrived by local bus at Hoejongri.

"Go well, uh?" the bus girl said with a grin. She had been chewing gum with alarming vigor. As she dangled from the doorway of the moving bus, her face bespoke her opinion that Hyongmin's urbane appearance was out of place in such a backwater. Though paved with asphalt, the country road was dusty. Hyongmin gazed vacantly at the bus as it receded into the distance, a plume of dust whipping up behind. "Go well." The normal "Go in peace" had become "Go well," and the girl's unfamiliar dialect still echoed in his ears. It reminded him he was hundreds of miles from home.

So this was where Father was born . . .

Hesitantly drawing a deep breath, Hyongmin took a moment to look about. Renovated farmhouses, low hills, rice fields full of ripening shoots, it seemed an ordinary enough hamlet. He could scarcely believe that not far away, before his birth, such an atrocious massacre had taken place here. Just as big cities maintain stability in their own ways, this place had kept the characteristic repose of a farm community.

After surveying the horizons, Hyongmin set off walking in what seemed a likely direction. Rice terraces, trees, hills, mountains, fields . . . suddenly his eyes were riveted on one spot. A very extraordinary shape for a mountain. Three summits looming side by side, holding one another's slopes off the central peak, almost like a trio of humps sprouting from a common torso. If a woman had three breasts, they might look something like that.

The three peaks were so densely forested that from a distance they appeared nearly black. In the intervening space stood several low hills, and beyond the peaks rose a rugged mountain range. The three peaks of the mountain bestowed a certain uniqueness on this otherwise nondescript village.

"Go to the police chief. Show him your university I.D., and he'll help you. It's entirely up to you now, to dig into your father's past."

Such thoughts flashed through Hyongmin's mind. What was the stranger's relation to the police chief? Had the chief been forewarned of his visit? For an instant he feared an ambush might've been laid for him. He thought it over. A conspiracy couldn't be ruled out . . . but it wouldn't be to plot some fresh crime. It was just an attempt to clear up an episode on the far side of yesterday. In any case, the man he had to deal with was a police officer, at least in name.

So if the stranger is in cahoots with the police, the chief might exaggerate some things. But Father's crimes were treason and murder—even if the police inflated the number of victims from thirty-eight to seventy-six, how much graver could the punishment be? Or if the number was diminished to nineteen, how much leniency could be expected? Hyongmin felt he'd be able to tell if there were any ties to the caller, once he met the police chief face to face.

By making a few inquiries Hyongmin had no difficulty locating the police station. He stood outside the building for a long time, filled with dread . . . never before had he felt so wretched.

"What brought you way down here to these parts, I wonder . . . ?"

The police chief, double-checking Hyongmin's identification, was extremely polite. He seemed a decent, humble man of about forty. Hyongmin at once dropped his suspicion of a conspiracy.

"Well, I've come here today because I'm doing some research for an article I'm writing. I need to gather and analyze some information about pro-communist forces during the Korean War, you know, the forces, other than the North Korean Army, that evolved somewhat independently, or shall I say, indigenously. I'm looking into the nature of such partisan forces, the damage they wreaked on the local villages together with the North Koreans, and the aftermath of it all. Such information isn't really available in any organized form. I thought each village and region must have its own peculiar characteristics, so I chose various places across the country for this research. This village happens to be one of the locations I chose, so here I am to ask for some help."

Without hesitation Hyongmin poured out the cover story he had concocted well in advance of his arrival.

"Ah, I see. This work of yours seems difficult, but important, no doubt. I'll do my best to assist you, naturally. But . . ."

The police chief rubbed his hands, an embarrassed expression on his face.

"You see, back then I was only about ten, just a boy, and this is not even my hometown, so I'm afraid I won't be of much help to you myself. But if you can wait a bit I'll introduce you to an old man who knows all about what happened in these parts back in those days. What do you say?"

The chief was so eager to please that Hyongmin was growing embarrassed, too. He was acutely conscious of the fact that, as the police chief, he should be an authority on past events within the region of his responsibility.

"Thank you very much. It was so many years ago it's only natural to go at it in that way."

Hyongmin embellished his gratitude a bit.

"They say the red partisans in this village were real savages. But time heals all, and as time flew by, most of the older generation passed away; only a few are left now. For the youngsters, it's all like a fairy tale. But these studies of yours are a good thing, worthy of a professor. We're still living in a virtual state of war, with anti-communism essential for survival. Studies like yours will help promote anti-communist consciousness."

Such were the chief's comments after he ordered his men to contact several people. Like a typical police chief, he bestowed upon Hyongmin's work a deep interpretation of his own.

"Oh, I don't know. I expect to come up with some worthwhile results, but what I know thus far is very little."

Hyongmin's response was evasive. He intended it as self-deprecation, but inside he sympathized with the humility of the chief.

"Sir, Mr. Shin Munjang is in, but the other two are out," one of the officers reported to the chief.

"All right, we'll begin with Mr. Shin Munjang. Let's go now, professor."

The police chief rose, apparently intending to escort Hyongmin himself.

"You must be busy, if you just call to advise him of my visit, I can go by myself."

"No, no. This is a small village, quiet like water in a cistern, not very much to be busy about. Besides, this man is old as the hills. I'd better introduce you myself."

The chief marched out of the station, leading the way.

"Things around here have changed a lot, but I'm told the whole area used to be practically owned by the Shin clan. Even with all the changes, you still can't underestimate the Shins. Wealth and whatnot, almost everything important is still in their hands. The man we're calling on, he's one of only a few older Shin men still alive."

The chief, walking briskly, continued his commentary. Acknowledging his remarks in a non-committal way, Hyongmin was organizing his thoughts. A feudal society, nobles and peasants, the stranger on the phone probably was a Shin, and Father's fabricated family history might well have been adapted from the chronicles of some line of the Shin clan.

"So, young man, you mean to say you're a university professor?" the old man asked, peering straight into Hyongmin's eyes after glancing down at the identification card clamped between two of his fingers. He was a man of about seventy, and gave an impression of being very fastidious.

"Yes, but I'm not a tenured professor yet, only a full-time lecturer, a beginner, in other words," Hyongmin answered, agitated by an obscure feeling. For the first time, he was acutely aware that his real family name was not "Hwang" but "Bae."

"I see, but what's the rank got to do with it? Police, corporations, they have ranks, too, but rank goes up as time goes by, everyone gets older, isn't that the truth?"

"Certainly, of course, sir."

Beneath the old man's gaze, the police chief seemed to turn to jelly.

"Um, commendable, commendable, indeed."

The old man once more looked Hyongmin over, his expression a blend of admiration and skepticism. Hyongmin immediately understood the old man's ambivalence. As a member of a noble family, he valued scholars highly, and undoubtedly would regard a university professor as worthy of respect, but Hyongmin looked too young to deserve such a title and deference.

"So . . . the chief is asking me to tell what happened here during the war, is that it?" The old man spoke abruptly, rotating his head toward the chief so quickly as to stir up a breeze.

"Yes . . . I know nothing about it myself. I tried to contact some other people, too, but none were available, so, being in a hurry, we came to see you."

The chief was cautious, offering excuses.

"That detestable tale . . . I can't, I cannot do it." The old man was firm, shaking his head vigorously. His wrinkled face all at once grew hard like a mask of plaster. His frozen countenance made it seem he was reliving all his ugly memories of that time.

"But sir, this man has come all the way here from hundreds of miles away . . ."

The astonished chief moved and sat closer to the old man.

"I know. I know that. But . . ."

Staring into space, the old man sighed heavily. Hyongmin realized from the old man's face that mental scars never heal with the passage of time.

"As for me, I am a grave sinner against this family. I'm a grave sinner with no right to talk about those times. So, go find someone else. I cannot speak."

The old man's voice was full of restless remorse bordering on delirium. Without knowing the source of the old man's guilty conscience, Hyongmin judged it would be impossible to persuade him to talk and with his eyes signaled as much to the chief.

"Grandfather, it seems my unexpected visit has needlessly reawakened painful memories. I'm so sorry, I don't know how to apologize," Hyongmin said, bowing deeply.

"No, no. You've come far, I'm the one to apologize. But it's the rancor in my heart that's to blame, young man, can you understand?"

The old man's brief words were an apology of sorts. Hyongmin thought he could fathom the deep wounds troubling the old man's heart.

"I understand. I can understand your suffering, I think."

"It was a foul, detestable time. Detestable indeed."

As Hyongmin emerged from the house into the yard with the chief, the old man's voice followed.

"Hey, Chief Kim, remember Junggol who runs Kyongsong restaurant?"

The chief turned around and answered hurriedly. "Sure, I know him."

"Go and see him."

"We'll do that, sir."

Hyongmin offered a cigarette to the chief once they were away from the house.

"You're taking too much trouble on my account."

"Not at all, isn't this the kind of service police are supposed to provide in a democracy?"

Hyongmin gave a curt laugh and so did the chief. But it was just a gesture, for his heart was clouded by a cold fog after meeting the old man.

"How touchy that old fellow was. Such a big to-do over ancient history."

Fuming cigarette smoke through the chimneys of his mouth and nostrils, the chief voiced his discontent.

"He may have his reasons. Maybe he went through some awful times he'd rather not remember."

As he spoke, Hyongmin had his father in mind.

"It's five already, looks like you won't be able to make it back to Kwangju tonight."

"Well, I was planning to stay the night here. Is there an inn?"

"Don't worry. There're a couple, not very good ones, though. First, let's go see the restaurant owner, Mr. Shin Junggol. We can find you somewhere to sleep later."

The chief was willingly arranging things for Hyongmin. It seemed a natural outpouring of his kind nature, but Hyongmin wasn't up to further formal gestures of gratitude.

"A little awkward for a man from a proud yangban family to be running a restaurant, eh?"

No sooner had he said it than Hyongmin regretted this remark. How could he have been so thoughtless? It had not been premeditated, but how would the chief take it? Hyongmin was surprised to find himself already feeling antagonistic toward the Shins.

"Yangban? It's a long while, isn't it, since the aristocrats became scarecrows. High status, noble descent—only in old legends can you live on such distinctions. Today money, not yangban blood, and an I.D. card, not a pedigree, are all we need. When there's money to be made, the descendants of yangbans don't even mind being butchers, not to mention restaurant owners, don't you agree?"

His remarks were like bullets straight into the bull's eye. Hyongmin was speechless. He had no way of telling whether the chief's own ancestors were yangbans or slaves. It wasn't clear whether he'd been expressing satisfaction or regret at the decline and fall of the old aristocratic order, few traces of which survived.

The restaurant proprietor, Shin Junggol, was a sturdily built man of around sixty.

"So, your family name is Hwang. Good thing it's not Pang or Bae," Shin Junggol uttered abruptly, peering intently at Hyongmin's name card. At that instant, Hyongmin felt a shock like a spear puncturing his heart.

"I beg your pardon, sir?" the chief asked with a blank face.

"Reckon you wouldn't get it even if you'd been to paradise and back, so why don't you just be on your way and go about your business."

Shin Junggol waved his arms, as if shooing away a flock of birds from a rice field.

"Even if I was of a mind to, I couldn't stay right now. But will you help the professor here, or not?"

"See here, man, what's there to help about? It's a tale of how we Shins were done in by lowly peasants. To vent my spite I don't mind telling it hundreds of times."

Shin's face flushed red. Hyongmin again realized, as he had with the old man, that time doesn't heal scars of the soul. The inclinations of the two men were opposite, yet the feelings of both seemed to flow from a common source.

"All right, all right. Then I'll leave you in peace."

"You know, my story'll be like reciting the whole Samgukji. Are you ready for that?" Shin Junggol asked Hyongmin, referring to the famous Chinese saga known as the "Chronicle of Three Kingdoms."

"Don't worry about that. He's already decided to stay over here tonight," the chief quickly responded, and only then did Hyongmin realize what Shin had meant.

"No problem, then. Eat your dinner here, and by the time my tale's done, dawn'll be breaking, so you won't even need an inn. I won't charge you more for using my place overnight. What d'you say?"

The question was directed at the chief. Hyongmin grinned silently, picturing the cash register in Shin's mind.

"Couldn't be better. Kyongsong has the best food, so we would've had to come here to eat in any case."

Owing partly to his profession, the chief handled the situation smoothly.

"Right. Go on, then."

"Wait, uh, why not come back after work and join us for dinner?" Hyongmin grabbed the chief as he headed out.

"Yeah, why not? You've helped the professor, too," Shin Junggol chimed in.

"Will that be all right with you? It'll pain me to no end to see this old man's business flourishing 'cause of me, eh?"

The chief smiled broadly, lapsing into the local dialect for the first time. Hyongmin immediately caught the chief's familiar use of "old man" instead of the honorific address he had used with their first host. The change did not seem to stem only from the difference in the ages of the two Shins.

"Now, now, just listen to that crooked mind of his. You hurry now and head on back here later."

Shin Junggol rushed the chief on his way.

Dinnertime was at hand. Shin Junggol said he had to serve his customers before starting his story, then vanished. Left alone in a corner of the room, Hyongmin lit up a cigarette.

"So, your family name's Hwang. Good thing it's not Pang or Bae."

Bae meant his father. But Pang, who could that be? His name had preceded Father's. Did that mean Pang was more fanatical than Father? If he was more fanatical than Father, how many could he have killed?

Hyongmin lit up another cigarette, then gazed out through the window. He decided not to ruminate any further until after hearing the story.

Darkness was unfolding itself over the still country roads. The lights shining from the windows of small shops nearby had a simplicity befitting this muted hamlet. What would this placid little village have looked like thirty years before? As now, the struggle for survival must have been the main thing.

To survive, what does that mean? Is life not always and everywhere vain and empty in the face of death? But life is in the process, not the outcome. The process is innocent of the outcome, but the outcome can illuminate the process. Perhaps that explains the competitive struggle that's come about.

"Professor Hwang, sorry to keep you waiting so long."

Hyongmin hadn't noticed the chief's return.

"Oh, no. Have a seat, please."

"Looks like old Shin's gone off somewhere."

The chief looked about the restaurant discontentedly.

"Yes, but he said he'd be back soon."

"Some hospitality this is. I'm awfully sorry."

"No, quite all right. Please do sit down."

The chief hesitantly took a seat, still wearing a look of displeasure.

"Do you have recollections of the war?" Hyongmin asked to distract the chief, without any real curiosity.

"Not as many as the old folks, but I remember quite a bit. Mostly dreadful things. Shelling splitting my ears, corpses, hunger, cold, sonic booms, all ghastly."

The chief shuddered as if those memories were back before his eyes.

"It's embarrassing to say, but from the time the war broke out till it was over, and even for a few years after, I used to wet the bed. It was an illness, yes, definitely an ailment I caught from seeing corpses of our neighbors all piled up in heaps. But nobody saw it as a sickness. I was punished. They treated me like an idiot. The tenser I got and the harder I tried not to do it, the more I peed the bed. I was so ashamed I felt like dying, but I couldn't help it. Bedwetter and policeman, odd combination, isn't it?"

The chief laughed good-naturedly, but Hyongmin couldn't laugh. It was too realistic, a pitifully true instance of what war can do to a young boy.

"At first, they sent me out with a winnowing basket on my head to beg for salt, but when I kept it up despite the constant humiliation, they decided I needed some medicine or else my weenie never would grow to work properly. The so-called medicine, now, was nothing else but cat urine, the only instant cure, they said. But nobody had any bright idea how to collect it. Cats, you know, piss a tiny bit here and there as they please. Finally, someone had a brainstorm, and they confined a cat in a tin drum, with the top covered to make it dark inside. Then, every so often, they suddenly beat the drum like hell. This was supposed to startle the cat into pissing.

"The plan had a plausible ring, really. So, a tin drum was found, a cat trapped inside, and I sat by it with a wooden stick in my hand. I waited a while, beat the drum, waited a while more, beat it again, all the time praying desperately: 'Dear cat, please piss up a storm.' All day long I repeated this hideous ritual. At long last the cover was taken away. The cat leapt out with uncanny strength as soon as the lid was off. My mother, who was opening the cover, screamed and fell back flat on her back. I ignored her and peered impatiently inside the drum. Only a few bits of fur here and there, and not a drop. The only result was a scar on Mother's hand where the cat scratched her. Whether cats ever piss has been an open question in my mind ever since."

Again the chief laughed pleasantly. It was astonishing beyond anyone's wildest imagination that such a statuesque, imposing man on whose chest the police insignia was most becoming could in boyhood have beaten a tin drum containing an imprisoned cat in a futile effort to gather a bed-wetting remedy.

These subconscious scars had emerged from his memory on their own. Realizing this, Hyongmin told himself that everyone who lived through those terrible times must have scars of some sort deep inside. And so he gained a new perspective on the "6.25" war.

"Know what my mother said when my first son was born? 'I thought it'd be a blessing to have a granddaughter, but you had a boy . . .' She stopped there, realizing her slip, and then she held me and wept for a long while. She must have never expected that I'd become a real man someday. I never felt my mother's love more deeply than then. After seeing me have three sons in a row, she passed away in peace."

"You're a lucky man indeed. You've done your duty to your ancestors."

"Oh, I don't know. Maybe so, but the real trouble's in raising them. It's nearly thirty years since the war was over, but I still get depressed whenever I hear a jet fly by. I get nervous and anxious, like a bomb's going to drop or a machine gun may come strafing at any moment. Anyway, it's a horrible feeling. Maybe it's my being a country bumpkin, but I'm too ashamed to mention it to others. It's not the kind of thing for a man in uniform to bring up."

"No, it's quite possible," Hyongmin said in an unnecessarily loud voice, trying simultaneously to capture an image flitting through his memory.

It was about a year before in September, and the whole campus was showing early signs of autumn. After a lecture, he'd run into an elderly professor in the hall. The two of them were about to step out into the quadrangle when suddenly a sonic boom from a supersonic jet exploded, shaking the sky overhead. The old professor froze in his tracks, holding his head in his hands. He seemed about to faint.

"Professor, are you all right?"

Hyongmin hastily moved to prop him up.

"Yes, I'm fine, just, just . . ."

The old professor spoke in a moan, frowning awfully. The sound of the jet meanwhile faded into the distance.

"That noise doesn't remind you of anything?" the old professor asked, slowly taking a step.

"Probably a dry run for the flyovers on Armed Forces Day?"

Having said this, Hyongmin felt the old professor's gaze rest on his face. Turning around, he saw the old professor staring at him. His look was neither cold, nor calm, nor cynical; it was too complex to decipher.

"Well, sir, is something wrong?" Hyongmin had asked confusedly. The professor walked on ahead, repeating "Nothing, nothing at all." What had he done wrong? Looking at the old professor's bent back, he was at a total loss to understand what was going on.

Now, a year later, Hyongmin at last understood what a non-sequitur his reply had been. He had belatedly grasped the meaning of the old professor's complex expression. Just like this police chief hundreds of miles away, he was terrified by a jet's sonic boom, but for Hyongmin, that noise was no more than a physical phenomenon caused by the jet's supersonic speed.

"You were expecting a feast of some kind, showing up here so early, uh?" Shin Junggol said in an absurdly loud voice as he approached their table.

"Old man, how can you treat your guest this way? I'm really disappointed." The chief assumed a tone of mock anger, and the old man responded brazenly, "I knew you'd be entertaining our guest, so I went off on an urgent errand."

"The professor's bound to be tired, so please get on with your story."

"Right. Let's head over to that room there. What d'you want for dinner?"

"First, let's have beer and some roast beef," Hyongmin answered right away.

"Roast beef and beer?" The chief and the old man spoke almost in chorus, "Not bad, not bad at all."

"No need to make a feast of it, we'll have a simple meal," the chief said.

"Uh-uh, just watch and eat your fair share," the old man growled.

"It's only right for me to treat you. It's all covered by the research grant, so don't think twice about it," said Hyongmin, winking at the chief.

"Okay, but let's have *soju* instead of beer. Roast beef and *soju* is a meal fit for a king, don't you agree, old man?"

The chief spoke in a firm tone, unheard until then.

"Right, right, a wise man you are, and Confucius himself might've said the same."

Old Shin Junggol was quick to smooth out the situation. Hyongmin grinned as he entered the room. The chief's selfless concern was pleasing, and the undisguised greed of old Shin was not unbecoming either.

As the beef was roasting, liquor was poured all around. For lunch Hyongmin had only grabbed a glass of milk while transferring buses, but he didn't have much of an appetite now. He was more attracted to the *soju* than to the meat. The clear *soju*, with its characteristic cool glow, was served as always in small glasses. Every time Hyongmin drank *soju*, it reminded him of a surly woman. He was impelled to drink it by a mysterious impulse, and that urge was as forceful as ever on this night.

"How did you come to look me up?" the old man asked, turning over the beef.

"First, we paid a call on honorable Shin Jangmun."

"What? So, what happened with him?" shouted the old man abruptly. Hyongmin and the chief were too amazed to open their mouths.

"Wait, what's wrong?"

"Go on with what you were about to say, and be quick about it!"

The old man was red-faced with excitement.

"Nothing much came of it. We were advised to come and see you, so we did."

"Him, what did he say when he sent you over here?" asked the old man, looking the chief straight in the eye.

"He said he was a grave sinner against the Shin family and had no right to speak about the past."

"Uhm, even a flea tries to save his face, so he spoke the truth!"

The old man vigorously wiped off his mouth, though he hadn't yet touched any food.

"You mean there's some secret about it?" the chief asked in disbelief.

"See here, Chief Kim, you better pay attention if you're gonna be a proper chief around here. That man was a Red himself in those days!"

"Wh-what?!" the chief blurted out, almost choking, and Hyongmin was as startled as if he'd been socked in the face.

"Now, then, drink down your glass and we'll move along with the tale."

The two men lifted their glasses, following the old man's lead, and like oafs, emptied them in one gulp. Hyongmin felt the sharp, venomous *soju* flow into his empty belly, and a deep confusion began to envelop him.

"Now, hear me well. During the Jap occupation, that man went through school all the way to university, one of the few of us Shins to get so much modern education! But while he was away at school, he wasn't studying like he should've. The underground movement and—what'd they call it—student movement. He was busy, busy all the time with movements and such, worrying his parents to death. In the end, he never finished school at all, got chased around by MPs, and fled all the way to Manchuria. Up there, he wanted to work for the liberation underground. So far, except for worrying his parents to death, his deeds were admirable—all for the cause of recovering our lost homeland, you know.

"But after Liberation, he came back, and, being an educated man, he took to playing around in the bigger streams up in Seoul. Every so often ugly rumors floated down to us though the grapevine, rumors he'd been playing commie in Seoul. The elders in the family, whenever those winds blew our way, damn sure kept the rumors quiet. Well, I'll be damned if that sort of stuff wasn't true. When war broke out, he showed his true colors out in the open, and if he wasn't quite a pillar of the Communist Party in the South, he was at least big enough to be a rafter.

"But the real shock came later. A Communist himself, he didn't know nothing about his family getting massacred at the hands of other Reds. Lazing about up there in Seoul, not knowing a damn thing when, you know, his own father, uncles, cousins, second cousins, all got murdered at the hands of his own goons. Now, listen, see, there's more. After the war, we of the Shin clan spent good money and signed our names to get that man released from prison. That's why he's still walking around alive, so if he's not a grave sinner, who is, eh? That man's life's just opposite of mine, so it was natural for him to send you fellas to see me."

Hyongmin thought of the fastidious old man. Never had he imagined that such a truth lay behind the old man's calling himself a sinner and his refusal to speak of those times. How heavy a secret can a man bear? Hyongmin felt giddy.

"Well, you really can't tell about some men. Who would've thought such a thing?"

The chief smacked his lips bitterly.

"Why then, do you suppose, man has long been called the most dreadful of creatures? Of all the beasts, man is the one capable of the most horrible crimes, and then he conceals his crimes behind a smile so natural-like."

Hyongmin watched the old man with renewed interest as he said this. His words were hardly ordinary, and the old man, in his own way, seemed to command an insight that laid bare human nature.

"Now, time for me to get on with the tale of the persecution of my clan, no?"

As if to collect his attention, the old man drained his glass in one gulp. Then, he stuffed his mouth with meat. Watching the old man, Hyongmin felt a constant grip of tension.

"Well, what was it, a week or so after the war started? Before the North Korean Army reached us, the peasants rose up. God almighty, how senseless it was! Until the day before they didn't dare open their mouths against us, the lowly creatures, then one morning they woke up to play the lords. The police were taken away to the town hall, leaving the police stations empty. Before those fiery-eyed peasants with their sharp spears, we Shins were scarecrows, nothing more. Confound it, an outrage it was!"

The old man wore a bitter look as he again emptied his glass at a single gulp.

"And that's not the only confounded part. It turned out those base creatures had long been planning to rise up together. But we were blind, wandering in the dark and clueless about the whole business. They weren't so vicious at first, but then the North Korean Army came. Almost overnight they all became butchers. They say the tigers up in the Chiri mountains are ferocious, but they're nothing compared to a man gone wild. We'd been living together for ages, knowing each other through and through, like mirrors for each other, and that makes for the most savage enemies. Red armbands on, spears in hand, they dragged people off like dogs. What man worth his salt would have done different? The world had turned upside down in the most horrendous way."

The old man drank half of another glass and took out a cigarette. As he lit it, his expression gradually changed to resemble that of a shaman capturing a spirit.

"The most confounding thing of all was discovering who their leader was. It was none other than Pang, a grade school teacher. He'd always been quiet and submissive like some shy girl. That's how scary a man can be. Who could have imagined the nice, angelic Pang harboring bloody red ideas deep down inside? The deputy to this Pang was a common creature, a blacksmith by the name of Bae Jomsu, and the whole mess was cooked up between those two bastards."

Hyongmin stopped breathing and clasped his hands under the table. Those three syllables of his father's name had come bursting out at last. He was worried that the tension building inside him might surface on his face.

"That bastard Pang who turned Bae Jomsu into a Red was no good, true, but the bastard Bae himself was a far worse monster. God, his evil's beyond telling. If, and I tremble to say it, but if their world had dragged on another couple of months, they'd have exterminated every man and boy in the Shin clan. We'd have been gone for good. In other villages wood spears were used; it was only in our three villages that iron spears were waved in our faces, all thanks to that bastard Bae Jomsu. Just think of it, for months before, that son of a bitch was forging iron spears right behind our backs, sharpening them to murder us. Even today, it makes me shudder. We were living peaceful lives, accepting humble greetings from those bastards, oblivious to what was really on their minds."

The old man drained another glass. Hyongmin followed suit. The chief refilled the emptied glasses.

"When Pang and Bae became Chairman and Vice-Chairman, they started carrying on like rabid dogs, no lie. Overnight, all three villages became their playground. The decent folk of the Shin clan were all taken away at their hands. If a single one of us ran off, they swore they would kill everyone already taken away. The ones not taken yet, like me, wanted to run, but their threats stopped us in our tracks. We spent every night sweating in fear, and come daybreak, there they came again to take away more men. I can talk about it now, but back then I felt like shitting in my pants and dying. I couldn't run, and I didn't know if I'd be the next to be dragged away. And guess what, that very night they came to get me!"

Hyongmin and the chief were so startled they sat up very straight. The old man had suddenly raised his voice to a shriek and pounded on the table with his fist. Then he cleared his throat a few times before emptying his glass again.

"Will you be all right, drinking so much?" asked the chief, cocking his head to one side.

"Why, do you think I'm getting too drunk to tell the tale? Don't worry. This is medicine, not liquor, medicine, you hear? My nose, my chest, you know, stink with the smell of blood, and this medicine cleans away the stink. You made me tell this story, and now you don't like me drinking, huh?"

"Not at all, please drink as much as you like, sir. Chief Kim was only concerned about your health. Help yourself, by all means."

Hyongmin spoke hurriedly, giving a couple of nudges to the chief beside him.

"Really. I wasn't complaining about the liquor, no, I was only thinking about your health."

The chief played innocent.

"If that's so, thank you kindly. But I can't keep on with this tale of lunacy unless I'm in the right mood, so don't make it any harder for me, all right?"

The old man looked at his two listeners in turn, as if for confirmation. The two men nodded.

"Where was I?"

"Well, they were coming to get you," the chief quickly picked up the thread of the tale for him.

"See, you being such a nuisance, I forgot where I was."

The old man frowned and stuffed some beef into his mouth. Hyongmin lit a cigarette, reflecting that the narrator had been well-chosen. Like a tape recorder, the old man had warmed to his task and went on and on without any prompting. If he'd been the type who only answered questions, the whole thing could have turned out to be painful. Now, all Hyongmin had to do was listen, and when the old man finished his story, ask him any questions that might be left.

"So, three of those bastards came after me, Bae Jomsu, some guy called Lee, and another, name of Pansul. The spear tip glistened even in the dim lamplight. They ordered me to follow them, sticking the spear here, right here (the old man was poking his index finger into his throat). It drove me up the wall. If I didn't follow, I could see that spear jabbed in one side of my throat and out the other. But to be dragged away like a corpse, well, who the hell were they anyway?

"God, life itself was the real enemy then. I needed to say something, anything, but my tongue turned to stone. So, I got dragged out into the yard like a dog. It was pitch black outside. Soon as I saw how dark it was, the thought of escaping flashed through my head. Problem was that bastard Bae Jomsu. I'm all spent now, but back then I was no slouch. I would have been tempted to tangle with them, even three men with spears, if Bae Jomsu hadn't been there. Blacksmiths have always been known to be strong, and this bastard Bae, big bones and all, was strong enough to kill a tiger with his bare hands. And on top of that, he was waving a spear. I couldn't lift a finger as they dragged me out through the fields. Instead of tying my hands, they took my belt away, so I walked, holding up my pants with both hands, legs shaking, stumbling, all the while thinking how cattle must feel when the butcher leads them to the slaughterhouse. Then, the Mountain Spirit gave a hand, a helping hand to me!"

Once more the old man was shrieking, pounding the table. This time neither Hyongmin nor the chief were startled. Both had been intently following every word of the tale. The old man lifted his glass to moisten his lips.

"I'm off to take a leak, be right back!"

The old man jumped to his feet and left. Until he returned, Hyongmin and the chief were both absorbed in deep thought. Even as a middle school student, Hyongmin couldn't open even the little finger when his father made a fist. Later, as a high school student, when they arm-wrestled, his whole hand was no match for his father's two fingers. Until his university days, that mighty fist had been looming over him. But among his peers, Hyongmin had always been known as strong and tough.

"So, where was I?"

The old man belched loudly. This time it seemed he knew perfectly well where he had left off and was asking mainly to arouse the attention of his listeners.

"Aye, the Mountain Spirit stretched his helping hand down to you."

Like a quick pupil, the chief was quick to mimic the old man's manner of speech. In a leisurely manner, the old man finished his half-filled glass. Then he stuffed some beef, cold by now, into his mouth.

"Well, professor, was it worth listening to?"

"Certainly, better than Samgukji."

Though improvised in a moment of bewilderment, Hyongmin's answer could not have been better, he told himself.

"Ha, ha, ha . . . good, very good. After all, what's Samgukji except a tale of killing and being killed, and lots of fighting. Well, let's get back to our tale."

The old man seemed in a fine mood. He noisily swallowed one more swig of *soju*, and the chief grinned at Hyongmin, a meaningful twitch at the corner of his mouth.

"Why do I say the Mountain Spirit's helping hand came down to me? Well, the fiery-eyed tiger, that bastard Bae Jomsu, just headed off. As we headed round a turn in the road, Jomsu says, 'I'll head back to see what's happening, so you two take him on.' God, my ears opened wide, and I tell myself, now I'm saved. The bastard went on his way, and after I thought we'd gone far enough along, I stopped and said, 'Hey, Lee, how about letting me take a piss!' 'Shut up and go on, quick now,' barked Pansul, who was still wet behind the ears.

"If only I'd had a belt on my pants, I wouldn't have had to beg to take a piss like that. Spears and all, that old spineless Lee and mushy-headed Pansul, shit, I could handle both of them, no sweat. But how the hell could I fight with one hand holding my pants up? If I just tried to slip my pants off, in a wink a spear'd be stuck in my belly! Asking to take a piss was just to buy time, you see. 'Hey, Lee, even a sinner's got to piss, let me go, please,' I kept on begging in a dying voice.

"Then, Lee said 'Hey, Pansul, let him take a leak. Fact is, I gotta piss myself.' God, when I heard that, my blood began to boil, and strength suddenly sprouted in my trembling legs. (The old man raised both arms high and shook them.) 'Hurry, go on and piss, hurry,' yelled Pansul. I took a few steps down the road, then let my trousers drop. They fell to my knees, without a sound, and before you know it my feet were clear of them. Those two bastards were busy pissing, whispering something to each another. God, what better opening could I ask for? 'Life or death,' just like they say. I rushed over and knocked right into them point blank—there was no time to think—pushing, punching, biting, in the dark none of us could see.

"In the midst of fighting, first on top, then beneath, I feel something in my hand, guess what? A spear! A spear! I snatched it and jabbed all around. A little later, silence. Both bastards dead, you know. When I realized what I'd done, all I knew was I couldn't go back home, so off I ran with nowhere to go. As I ran I noticed I was heading up into the mountains. Only after passing through the next valley did I feel like I was out of danger.

"After taking a deep breath, I looked at myself holding the spear in one hand. My chest and thigh hurt something awful. Without thinking, I rubbed my chest and leg. God, I nearly screamed with pain. I felt them again gingerly and there was something real sticky. Blood. Soon the sun came up, and I could see the long cuts, and my whole body was caked with dried blood after running so far. God knows the agony those wounds gave me, hah, that story can wait, let me show you the scars."

The old man unbuttoned his jacket and shamelessly lifted his shirt. Sure enough, across the right side of his chest was a ghastly stretch of scars. The old man didn't stop there, either. He sprang up, undid his belt, and dropped his trousers. On his left thigh was a scar much worse than those on his chest, with hideous protuberances that looked as though they might burst at any moment.

"From that day till those vicious bastards finally ran off, three long months under the scorching sun, I was more dead than alive. God almighty, I can't tell you the suffering I been through in those days! Even now, just thinking about it's enough to make me shudder and grind my teeth. Think of it, bleeding something awful from my wounds, cuts and scratches from running through the woods, and the world was those bastards' playground, with nowhere for me to hide. What situation could be more desperate than that? Even so, I had faith the Mountain Spirit would save me.

"To crawl back down into the village would've been like throwing myself to the lions, so I had to keep climbing even if I dropped dead. I aimed to find a hut far up on *Sambongsan*, where an old man used to live, digging herbs and carving wood. For years he'd been bringing rare herbs down to us Shins, and we called that hermit a holy mountain spirit. If only I could find him, he'd cure my wounds and save my life, I thought. After a long day and night of climbing I reached the hermit's place, but I was near dead by then. Just as I hoped, the old man took care of me like I was his own son. But his kindness was in vain, and my wounds kept getting worse. The old man's herbs were for boiling and drinking, not to make plasters, and they did me no good.

"Then he brought me some iodine and other medicine from the village. I kept shivering with a high fever, like a man stricken with malaria, but slowly my wounds started to heal. I never knew a man's life was that tough, like jute rope. In another month and a half, my wounds were all healed up, and meantime the village was in chaos. The two bastards, Pang and Bae, along with North Korean soldiers, had been killing the men of my clan like dogs.

"By that time, my wife was flat on her back in bed, beaten half to death by those scum. The old hermit couldn't bear to tell me about that, so I only found out later. Now, God hear me, a curse on those bastards and strike them dead! The way they slaughtered our family, so many Shins! They did their killing right on *Sambongsan*, a place our family has held sacred for generations. They made us dig into the veins of the mountain, and buried the corpses in those very holes! You know which of those bastards thought that up? The blacksmith, Bae Jomsu, that son of a bitch, you know!"

The old man was clenching his fists, quivering, and the flush in his face was not just from the *soju*. Sheer hatred, unabated by the lapse of time, was exuding a boiling heat.

"Have another drink, please, and calm down," said the chief, offering him another glass.

"Right, right, got to drink to calm down. Well, you two fellows not thirsty?"

"Sure, we'll have one more with you."

The chief lifted his glass and Hyongmin at once followed his lead. Hyongmin thought to himself that the three peaks which had attracted his attention that afternoon could only be *Sambongsan*. Quickly he deduced the interrelations among its geomantic significance, the Shin clan and the lowborn blacksmith.

"When they say life's but a dream, they must mean a life free of rancor. Plenty of time has passed since those days, but the outrage and thirst for revenge are still green and fresh like it was only yesterday. I can't understand it myself."

The old man lowered his glass with a pained look. Such heated talk was far from normal for him, and his advanced age had begun to show. Rancor. What is the source of such hateful rage? It's more than just a scar left in one's soul. Much more must be involved. Obscure feelings overtook Hyongmin as he reflected upon the nature of rancor.

"Excuse me a minute," the chief said, rising halfway to his feet. His eyes were beckoning and Hyongmin stood up as well. Hyongmin glanced at his watch. Quarter till ten.

"You must be exhausted; why don't you head on home now?"

"Nah, who knows when I'll have another chance to hear this tale? By the way, professor, with the story being all about himself, will it help you any?"

"Sure, it's all new to me. After he's finished, I may ask some questions if I need more details."

Hyongmin ordered some more beef and liquor. As soon as they sat down again, the old man cleared his throat once or twice, getting ready to go on.

"Where was I? Well, that devilish idea, I learned, was Jomsu's, that son of a bitch, I could hardly believe it, you know. The old hermit was beside himself, saying I couldn't go anywhere in my condition, but I couldn't just sprawl up there doing nothing. So, I decided to go down to see for myself. The veins of *Sambongsan* all dug up, our clan members standing there, backs to the holes, and then slaughtered with spears. Bae Jomsu and his men acted like they were butchering cattle. The very Shins who'd been feeding and clothing them, those bastards returned kindness with revenge. Through the trees, I saw their evil deeds with my own two eyes, and I swore to Heaven, swore to my ancestors, that I'd surely get even with them, come what may."

The old man's voice suddenly took on a hoarse, ragged edge. Glistening tears welled up in his eyes, and he seemed to be choking with emotion.

"I couldn't bear to visit *Sambongsan* after that. Nightmares tormented me every night. My anger was boundless and I almost went stark raving mad. With each passing day I got bonier, feeling like I'd starve before our world returned. How many of those days of madness passed I don't know, but one day the old man come up from the village with news that the red bastards had all run away overnight. In a flash I ran down the mountain and rushed into the village. The wife of that bastard Bae Jomsu already had been stoned to death under the dangsan tree. Samjung and Minju, two reds who couldn't escape, were killed at the school playground. That was not the end of it, though, no. There was still plenty for me to do, and my thirst for revenge couldn't be quenched that easily."

Old Shin licked dried spittle from the corners of his lips and then wiped his mouth with the palm of his hand. So, my father's first wife was lynched, stoned to death. Hyongmin took a deep drag of smoke, trying to picture a woman whose face he had never known, and even imagining her futile screams.

"So, how many of the Shins were killed?"

Hyongmin looked up. The chief had posed the question he himself hadn't dared to voice.

"Well, you won't believe it, but thirty-eight departed for the other world. Those damn bastards, no, no, those two sons of bitches, Pang and Bae, cut down that many. Pang was evil, no doubt, but Bae was worse. That the bastard's son's been fed and still lives here today, that's only because of the Shin clan's kindness."

Hyongmin almost leaped up at this sudden revelation. So, he had a half-brother alive! He took a deep breath before speaking.

"Sir, you mean to say the man called Bae Jomsu has a son still living here?"

"That's what I said. A half-wit he is, must be thirty-four or thirty-five by now."

"A half-wit, you said?"

"Not exactly insane. I mean, he went through too much and had a breakdown. A tough life he's had, what with his father's crimes all burdening the son. It was a miracle he didn't get stomped to death when his mother was stoned under the dangsan tree. The sight of his mother being killed must've terrified him half to death. For days afterward he had fits and all. Somehow he lived through it, but ever since he's been like a half-wit. And to feed that imbecile, clothe him, and let him stay on in our village all these years, what do you call that except the kindness of the Shin family?"

Hyongmin repressed a moan, feeling at the same time a thin, grey anger. His father was the target. Was he aware of this or not? In the course of his nearly perfect metamorphosis, had he never once returned here? Even a fugitive should have come back to see what happened to the wife and son he abandoned. Shouldn't that bond have been stronger than the fear of retribution? Could Father have smothered even that instinct for the sake of his own safety? Or had he returned only to find his wife dead and his son an idiot, and then left for good? Hyongmin told himself not to jump to conclusions too hastily, but he couldn't help feeling another new agony.

"So, that idiot is Bae Jomsu's boy."

The chief nodded to himself in recognition.

"Besides him, there must be lots of poor souls who lost their parents," said Hyongmin.

"No doubt. They range from boys who lost their fathers when they were three or four to some not even born when their fathers died. The boys who never knew their fathers' faces, they're the ones I pity. Well, professor, satisfied?"

"Ah, yes, very satisfied, you've done me a great favor indeed."

"It's already almost midnight."

The chief got up.

"You must be awfully tired."

The old man quickly emptied his glass, saying in a yawning voice as he rose.

"Well, sir . . ."

Hyongmin hesitated for a moment.

"You want to say something more?"

The old man prompted Hyongmin, his chin wagging.

"Well, the thing is, I was wondering if tomorrow morning you could show me a few of the old places you spoke of?"

"Sure, sure, for the research, I'll be glad to show you around."

The old man consented with pleasure.

4

"You have a duty to know the truth about your father."

The stranger on the phone never said too much. It was entirely an illusion that Hyongmin somehow felt he had heard a great deal from the caller. Father's real name, his hometown, the crimes committed, the number of victims, the dispatch of the picture—these were all the man on the phone had spoken about, apart from short replies to Hyongmin's confused questions. In the turmoil ensuing after the first drastic shock, he had been straining to dissect, reconstruct and extrapolate from the little he had been told, and then had mistaken the results for things actually heard on the phone.

It gradually dawned on Hyongmin that the caller might be a coldly rational man. He knew far more than Hyongmin would be able to discover in this village, but he had related no more than a few facts. Hyongmin wondered whether, in the stranger's position, he could have been so cold-blooded.

How young would he have been when he lost his father? Was he one of those who, unable to recall his father's face, grew up bowing at a sacrificial altar to a ghostly father? How had he come into possession of Father's picture? Still, Hyongmin, as before, consciously avoided thinking about the future course of this disastrous situation.

Why did Father have to kill so many? Unfortunately, it seemed he could not distinguish the resentment of downtrodden peasants from revolutionary communism. Had it been so unbearable to be pressed into becoming a blacksmith?

What about his half-brother? Was it possible Father never found out he had survived, a helpless idiot? Under the circumstances it seemed natural to infer that Father had deserted his family in perilous times to save his own skin, and then never went back to look for them. Inhuman. If that wasn't what happened, what if he actually had returned, but quickly left again after confirming his wife's death and seeing his son reduced to a blithering idiot? Again, not the conduct of a decent man. No matter how hard he tried,

Hyongmin could conjure up no plausible excuses for the abandonment of his half-brother.

Near dawn, Hyongmin finally fell asleep for a few hours. Even then he was tormented by a succession of nightmares and could not really rest. The fatigue that had been accumulating over the past several days weighed down on Hyongmin, and he felt as if his body was bloated with filth. He took his time in the bathroom washing his face, but still it was barely seven o'clock. He could not bear to stay in his room any longer, so he left the inn. Slowly, he walked down the main road. Only a few people were outside. There was a deep quiet and freshness in the air, worlds apart from what one encounters on the greyish cement streets of the city, where each morning starts out restless but tired.

Kyongsong restaurant, like all the other shops, was not awake yet. Hyongmin walked on past it and further down the road. His mind, oddly enough, was blank. Not that his head was clear. Rather, it was empty, almost like a perfect vacuum.

Startled by a sudden, screaming horn, Hyongmin jumped to the shoulder of the road. A bus marked "Kwangju Express" whizzed by and disappeared into the distance, slicing through the autumn. All at once Hyongmin thought it might have been a misstep to have indulged his impulse the night before by suggesting they pay visits to local landmarks. The undreamt-of discovery that he had a half-brother was such a shock, and the idea occurred to him because he felt obliged to see him. But the sight of the bus gave him a strong urge to flee from this place. A bitter grin came to his lips—emotional pendulum swings like this made him loathe his own weakness.

After absent-mindedly watching the bus fade from view, Hyongmin focused his eyes on the horizon above the road's vanishing point. The mountain with three peaks loomed there. The shapes of the peaks could not have changed overnight, yet to Hyongmin's eyes they looked totally different today. A mountain with severed veins—he squinted, straining to make out bare spots on the slope where the graves had been dug. He figured no trees or grass would grow there, and the reddish-brown soil would be exposed, like the scars on the old owner of Kyongsong restaurant.

Those holes dug into the mountain were vessels in which two opposite streams of rancor had been mixed by a merciless fate. At that place the rancor of the peasants, descendants of slaves, had collided with the rancor of the yangban landlords. By forcing them to dig thirty-eight holes, by killing thirty-eight men, had his father completely extinguished his own rancor? Hyongmin recalled Shin Jangmun, the first old man he'd visited the previous day.

For a while Hyongmin was in a confused state. The lives of the two men—Father and Shin Jangmun—on the surface seemed similar in some ways but at bottom they were totally different. That both had joined up with the communists seemed to make them alike, but, viewed more closely, even that had been clearly different in the two cases. Father had joined uncritically, a raw recruit, but old Shin must have done so based on an exercise of his own critical judgment. What followed brought them two disparate lives. Father fled, but the old man was arrested. Father had undergone a metamorphosis, while Shin Jangmun endured the judgment of law. If one could live without objective recognition of his guilt, the other was doomed to live in the snare of his relatives of the Shin clan. But, then, Father had led a fugitive's life, haunted by unrelenting fear and jeopardy; and the old man had not been subjected to that kind of misery.

Hyongmin turned about, unable to bear gazing at the mountain any longer. The three peaks seemed to howl like immense beasts, and streaming down from the dense woods he thought he could hear anguished shrieks of pain.

He looked at his watch. Nearly eight. Hyongmin slowly trudged back the way he had come.

The stranger must have phoned again last night. To Father, too. How would Father try to deal with it? Hyongmin shook his head. He did not want to get mired in thoughts he had managed to suppress up to then. The problem was more urgent than ever, and since arriving here he had confirmed it was beyond solution. All that remained was to figure out what the future would bring, and that seemed to depend entirely on the whims of the stranger.

Kyongsong restaurant was open, and the owner, old Shin Jungol, was energetically sweeping the already clean path out front. His bamboo broom raised a breeze that bore off nothing more than a few fallen leaves.

"You're up and about real early, Professor. I've been waiting for you, anyway."

The old man was in high spirits, showing not a trace of fatigue from the night before. Hyongmin said hello and then followed him inside the restaurant.

"All I have for breakfast is rice gruel, what'll I do?"

"That's just fine, let's eat together. It's my treat."

"Well, you shouldn't. You spent more than enough last night."

The old man, though pretending to decline the offer, seemed pleased and required no great persuasion to change his mind. Apparently, his satisfaction came less from the sale of another bowl of gruel than from authentic satisfaction at the respect accorded him as an elder.

Hyongmin ate barely a few spoonfuls. He tried to eat more to avoid inviting the old man's concern, but his stomach rebelled.

"What do you want to see?" The old man asked through a mouth full of rice.

"Well, the smithy where the man called Bae Jomsu used to work, and his son, that'd be about all."

Hyongmin stopped short, lest he subconsciously betray himself by a sinking voice.

"Want to go see *Sambongsan*?"

The old man's tone indicated an affirmative response was presumed.

"Sure, if there's time."

Hyongmin replied as expected, but already he had decided not to go there. The decision had been made as he gazed up at the mountain earlier that morning. Thirty-eight spirits of the dead, he felt, still roamed up there. Surely, their graves even now must show blood-red soil and not grass or trees.

"You're looking at a long trip home, so let's hurry."

The old man rose as soon as he finished eating.

"By any chance, sir, do you know the background of Pang or Bae?" Hyongmin asked, trying to adjust his gait to the old man's jumpy manner of walking.

"Sure, I know. Pang, the teacher, he was an outsider, not from these parts, so I don't know as much about him as Bae. Anyway, Pang got schooling during the Japanese occupation, one of those base creatures who got lucky and got educated. But he couldn't hide his origins, and so became a Red. If not for that little bastard, our village wouldn't have been teeming with so many red devils, either.

"The bastard Bae turned red all because of Pang, who was always filling Bae's ears with talk about workers, peasants, and the like, sugary stories about nobles and landlords, and so on. If that's not scratching boils, if that's not pouring oil on the fire, what is? For generations, the Baes tilled our clan's land as serfs. Can't say I know how he got to be a blacksmith. Anyhow, peasants, blacksmiths, same kind of low lives. That bastard Jomsu was famous for his bad temper, nothing like his father. Only good thing about him was his work. With the skills of a blacksmith he could've fed his wife and boy with no problem. He could've lived well enough in a world where a smith has plenty to keep him busy, and a good one can live comfortably enough. But no, he had to take the lives of others and shorten his own. In the end he did in his own kin, like a goddamn cannibal."

Hyongmin trudged along silently for a while.

"There, that's the smithy."

The old man was pointing at a spot where the square, rough-earthen chimney of a forge shone in the early morning sun. The structure's roof was covered with corroded green tin sheets, and the walls were plastered cement. No sign of the old days was evident.

"That's not the original place, is it?"

"Of course not. After that bastard Bae and his gang run off, the villagers grabbed his wife and burned down the smithy. But a forge, like a slaughterhouse, is supposed to prosper if the same site's kept, so newcomers came in and built this on the same spot."

Hyongmin wheeled about to head back.

"What's this, you don't want to see it close up?"

"No, it's all right."

Hyongmin walked briskly, leaving the old man trailing behind.

"Got a smoke on you?"

Hyongmin halted and waited for the old man to catch up. He handed him a cigarette and lit a match.

"Where does Bae's son live?"

"Him? Well, he's got no home, so he just stays wherever he lays himself down."

"Then it won't be easy to locate him."

"No problem at all, come sunrise, he's out walking the streets, easy to spot him."

"How far gone is he? Does he remember anything?"

"Nah, not a thing. He doesn't know what money is, all he knows is eating and shitting . . . an idiot, he is."

"Must've been badly mistreated, eh?"

"Not really, he may not have much upstairs, but his heart's in the right place and he does what he's told. If he'd been born with his father's temper, he'd have been dead long ago, but a good heart he has, to be living this life, you know."

For an instant Hyongmin thought it might be best not to see him after all. He didn't think he could bear witnessing with his own eyes such a miserable being.

"By the way, one thing's always been a mystery. That idiot somehow always knows when summer's coming. Every year in the summer, right about when his mother got stoned to death, he always falls sick. He boils with fever and starts blabbering like he's having fits. People say his mother's spirit possesses him and makes him feed her, what do you think about that?"

Hyongmin felt a heart-rending pain. All these years the man must have constantly suffered from that mortifying trauma. Even if they'd driven him from the village, back he would've come. Even if they'd stoned him to death, too, he would have returned again and again. It was the idiot's sole memory, with roots sunk deep down in his mind. Maybe it was his only light, the only reason for his existence. A sigh rose from the dark recesses of Hyongmin's troubled soul.

"Let's take that path, it leads to the dangsan tree."

Hyongmin tramped wearily behind the old man. The fatigue he felt was almost overwhelming.

The tree standing in the center of a big empty space was huge. Its immense branches had a bark of metallic texture, and the dome of thick leaves soaring overhead marked the ages it had endured. The vast form of that tree, swathed in the profoundly silent shadows of first light, was wondrous to behold. The emotion Hyongmin felt was not unlike that evoked by *Sambongsan*.

"How old is this tree?"

"Well, I'd guess more than three hundred years."

"A living witness to the village's entire history."

"Sure, sure, seen the good and the bad, all of it. But, can't tell us nothing."

"Was Bae's wife the only one killed here?"

"Nah, everybody we caught, and those caught by the army or the police, left for the other world from right here."

"Why here of all places?"

"This dangsan tree, along with *Sambongsan*, are like roots that nourish the life of our clan. Long ago our ancestor dreamed he should settle on the land fed by the veins running under *Sambongsan*, and he planted this very tree as a monument."

When Hyongmin looked at it, sure enough, the tree directly faced the central peak of the mountain. A peasant, his father, had killed two birds with one stone by burying the murdered Shins in the heart of *Sambongsan*, but the Shins had taken revenge by dragging the insolent peasants to meet their deaths in the shadow of the dangsan tree.

"Let's head back now."

Hyongmin turned around, even more exhausted than before.

"Should've dragged those two bastards Pang and Bae down here and lashed them to the tree, too. Even now, to think we didn't catch those two irks me to death, it's like having my own feet axed."

The old man shook his fist in the air. Hyongmin walked quietly, looking at the cosmos blooming alongside the road.

They arrived back at the street lined with shops.

"That idiot must be around here somewhere."

Peering about in all directions, the old man was searching for Hyongmin's mindless half-brother. Hyongmin felt his heart thump.

"Dear, are you sure nobody's left alive?"

Until Hyongmin entered high school, his mother used to ask his father this question all the time. Each time Father replied the same way: "I told you so already." Mother was anxious to know, in case the North and South reunited some day, whether any living relatives would step forward. It would never have occurred to her how mercilessly cruel such interrogations were. She kept on out of an icy desire to confirm that Father's first wife and their children in fact were all dead, unable to threaten the security of her own position.

"There's the idiot, right over there."

The old man picked up his lumbering pace. Hyongmin halted abruptly and looked over in that direction. A man was standing awkwardly in front of a shop. At that distance Hyongmin could not make out his face. All he could see was that he was rather tall. As if pulled by gravity, Hyongmin mechanically followed the old man.

"Chilsung, did you eat yet?" the old man asked loudly as he stepped up close to him. The lanky and ill-postured man gathered himself up and looked around. Hyongmin stopped breathing. Just as with the photograph of Father, at a glance he was certain this man was his own half-brother.

"Ahh, morning, Uncle."

The man greeted old Shin in a slur suggesting a lack of full control over his tongue.

"Belly full?" the old man kept shouting. Perhaps the man was hard of hearing, too.

"Yaaa, Uncle."

The man opened his mouth in a broad grin, looking at the sky above. He was tall with a perfectly proportioned figure. But his face was dull, and his eyes seemed dim as though befogged. Unmistakably, the cloudy eyes and face were those of an idiot. As he observed the man, Hyongmin felt a crystal of pity expanding and expanding until his soul seemed ready to burst.

What crime had he ever committed . . . ?

Hyongmin thought of himself, a full-time university lecturer at the age of twenty-seven. He had a solid status, envied by everyone around him. On the way to this position, he never once had experienced the pangs of hunger nor encountered a single incident meriting sympathy.

"Hey, why you staring that way? This here's a great professor, so greet him properly, and be quick about it."

Pointing at Hyongmin, the old man yelled in a raucous voice, and the idiot staggered off, fear on his face.

Hyongmin turned and briskly walked away. He was oppressed by a guilty conscience of unfathomable depth.

"Now, then, ready to go have a look at *Sambongsan*?" the old man asked, hurrying after Hyongmin.

"I'd like to, but my time is short. I have a few other villages to visit. I saw the mountain from a distance this morning."

"Did you, now? Well, it can't be helped if you've got no time."

The old man sounded disappointed.

"Sir, you've done me a great service. Thank you very much. I'll drop by and see Chief Kim on my way back."

Hyongmin bade farewell to old Shin Jungol, then briefly stopped in at the police station to say goodbye to the chief.

All the way to Kwangju, Hyongmin kept thinking of Chilsung, his half-brother. There was no progression to his thoughts, his consciousness was just fixated on the idiot. In the presence of someone who'd spent more than thirty years in utter oblivion, Hyongmin found even his guilt a mere conceit. He was ashamed to indulge in such sentimentalism and vaguely resolved to do something for Chilsung.

Sitting on the express bus bound for Seoul, Hyongmin felt a lethargy rushing over him. Before arriving yesterday, he'd been tense, consumed by anxiety. Now, however, his mind was like a foggy plain and his vulnerability seemed total.

The bus accelerated as it pulled onto the highway. Hyongmin had an indistinct notion that upon his return to Seoul the pattern of his life would undergo a great change, never to be the same again. As he gradually slid into sleep, he reflected that from that day on he would be able to speak with the stranger on the phone without the terror he had formerly felt.

When Hyongmin opened his eyes, the bus was still cruising along at high speed. Though he was awake, he didn't recognize the sights passing by outside. Vacantly he peered out the window.

Seoul 6 Miles—a mileage marker flew by. Hyongmin realized he had been submerged in a deep, dreamless sleep for four solid hours. He smoked a cigarette, inhaling deeply. As he smoked, his knotted mind gradually became untangled. Such was the fleeting comfort provided by a cigarette. He relished a moment of serenity, reflecting that the good things in his life he'd taken for granted for so long might all fall apart at once.

He stepped out of the taxi in front of his apartment, hoping his wife would be back from her family's place. Exhausted, Hyongmin left the elevator and stopped short as he was about to ring the doorbell. A memo had been stuck on the door. He read it:

"Father hospitalized. XX Hospital, Room 705. Heekyong."

Hyongmin tore the note from the door, then raced down the stairs like a man possessed.

Human Stairs

1

Mother barely made it to midnight before drawing her last breath. That she had survived that long shrouded Changyu's heart in a mist of grief. It may have been a moist echo of the countless sighs that had punctuated her days on earth, or steam from the frigid water with which Mother had quenched her burning anger.

Changyu knew. Mother had refused to surrender to death because she had to see her son one last time. If he had come a day earlier, she would have passed away the previous night. And if he had not arrived until a day later, somehow she would have held on until the next night. Certainly, Mother had no mysterious command over approaching death, like someone granting an audience only to a favorite visitor. But this was no precipitous demise ensuing from a sudden trauma; her chronic ailment permitted advance or postponement of her exit by a day or two. For his mother this much was not impossible, and Changyu had no doubt her will was strong enough to control her fate to that extent. For her entire life, she had relied on that reservoir of iron will.

Changyu was not alone in his emotional interpretation of Mother's death. Watching his mother on her deathbed, his aunt, Mother's sister, said in a sobbing voice, "She was only waiting for you to come." Only waiting for you to come . . . . The unexpressed sequel was clear from her tone . . . having seen you she at last closed her eyes.

Now, his mother had prepared a testament, a terrible testament, something that Changyu never could have dreamt. Even without that murderous urge buried deep in her heart, she never would have allowed herself to depart for the other world without seeing her son. At twenty-three, Mother had been made a pregnant widow. All alone she had brought up a fatherless child for twenty years.

Pulling out a photo from beneath the mat on which she lay, Mother said, "Look carefully at this picture." Her voice was almost like her voice before she fell sick. Changyu knew she was gathering all her remaining strength just to pronounce those few words. He took the picture from her quaking hand. As Changyu looked at the photo, she suddenly spoke once more.

"That bastard's your enemy, the one who murdered your father."

Her howling voice shook the room.

Changyu convulsively bit his lower lip, fixing his gaze up at the ceiling. Her bony, bloodless face already resembled a death mask. He couldn't believe it had been the source of such a loud and resonant voice, nor could he comprehend the uncanny sparks in those eyes sunk back in a face already chilled by the creeping certitude of death.

"You must take revenge on your father's enemy, without fail. The bastard's still alive, that's certain."

Her voice was much calmer than before, pronouncing each word distinctly. Her injunction was so unexpected that Changyu was at a total loss to respond. Mother shut her eyes, and around them ripples of tension were detectable.

"And . . . and . . ."

She was trying to lift her arm, then it dropped back heavily onto the mat, like an inanimate object falling.

"Mother!" Changyu embraced his mother, and his aunt, who had stayed nearby all this time like a silent shadow, rushed to her sister in tears.

"Chaaangyu . . . the bastard, the bastard's name is Bae Jomsu."

Mother's voice dissipated like vapor as it issued from her mouth.

"Mother, come back!"

Changyu grasped her shoulders, plunging into dark despair.

". . . there's more to say . . ."

Changyu felt his mother's voice growing distant, less a voice now than agonized moaning.

A faint pulse was still discernible in her emaciated body, and her shallow breathing managed to push but a trace of air out of her nostrils. Her only movement was shivering from chills.

"She's been this way many a time before," said his aunt, looking a little relieved as she stretched herself. She seemed to think Mother would regain consciousness and wanted to spare Changyu from too much worry. As he did his best to reconstitute his fractured and strewn thoughts, he noticed tiny beads of sweat on his mother's forehead. He started to reach for his handkerchief, but instead impulsively put his hand to her temple and carefully felt her head. Dread overwhelmed him, for her forehead was as cold as ice, and what his palm felt was the skin of death itself. He hurriedly checked her pulse. It was like a faint breeze in the distance. Upon his arrival two hours before, when he'd felt Mother's forehead, there'd been enough warmth to allay his anxiety.

Changyu picked up the photograph from the floor. It was about the size of his palm, and at a glance one could see it was very old. He intensely stared at the man in the picture. But it lit no fuse of hatred in him. That this was father's murderer against whom he had a duty to take revenge was utterly unreal to him. Before he realized his lapse of dutifulness, the picture engaged his interest in an unexpected way. It was at least several decades old, but despite its age there was something very modern about it. Old photos like that seemed destined to end up as faded sepia images on the black pages of an album, the people all looking as if they were wooden objects in a still-life. As though by concerted efforts, the subjects were always in rigid poses or wore absurdly stern masks. But the man in this picture contradicted the characteristics of the time and refused to be an inanimate object.

The man was alive and moving. He was a blacksmith, no shirt, hoisting a huge hammer in the air, about to strike down with it. The heavy hammerhead made the thin handle flex like a bow, and the muscles in his arms were vibrant and moving. A broad chest with the dense mass of a boulder, a face shining with sweat, bright eyes fixed on the target, firm lips slightly twisted as if to focus all his strength, from these details emerged a vivid impression of dynamic power. The liveliness of this figure was all the more striking against the faded background of the print.

Who took this photograph?

All of a sudden Changyu was extremely curious who the photographer could have been. Somehow the man who had managed to snap such a picture seemed far worthier than the blacksmith who had struck that pose.

A blacksmith's hammering was mechanical, repeated over and over, but to capture the activity at precisely the perfect moment called for an artist's intuition—Changyu wanted to find out who it had been. But his mother had plunged into an abyss of unconsciousness. He wondered, too, how the photo had come into her possession. Had she tracked it down somewhere just to show her son the face of his foe? Where could she have gotten it? From the blacksmith's own house? Changyu lost his train of thought.

In those days, could a blacksmith even afford to have a photograph taken? Photographers were few and far between, and besides, the vocation of blacksmith was nothing to be proud of. The image of a bare-chested man with a raised hammer in hand was less a cause for pride than for shame. It would be like a butcher seeking to preserve for eternity an image of himself slaughtering a cow.

Such were Changyu's ruminations as he stood the deathwatch beside his oblivious mother. Then, her coma merged into death without even a fleeting reprieve of lucidity. Like water saturating a sheet of ricepaper, death slowly invaded Mother's unfeeling form.

Mother . . .

Powerless to do anything, Changyu watched his mother's life slip away. She looked far too spent and decrepit for a woman who had lived only forty-four years on this earth. True, to their own offspring all parents seem old, even ancient. Still, from her ravaged corpse Changyu realized she had endured torments far out of proportion with her years. Physically, she may have suffered the knots of only forty-four years, but her soul had borne burdens of one twice that age, of eighty-eight long years or even longer.

That, perhaps, was why Changyu felt her departure at an early age was no great injustice. Fate had not been heartless in spiriting her away. Rather, this death may have been pre-ordained long before, and he himself had rehearsed it in his mind every now and then. From the time he was a small boy, Mother, despite her delicate constitution, had done all the chores on the farm all by herself. Occasionally, when she seemed unable to bear it any longer, she suffered from attacks of a burning in her heart. Once this burning commenced, the agony never abated until she was half dead.

Each time Mother had an attack like that, she placed on her chest a large slab of heated quartz, and lay there grinding her teeth, writhing all over. Sometimes when the pain grew intolerable she made Changyu stand on her chest. He could remember no moments more terrifying in his whole life. To do as she ordered was impossible, for to him his mother seemed as fragile as a dry leaf blown helplessly by a capricious winter gale. He was terrified that her skinny ribs would crack the instant he stepped on her.

Still, he couldn't disobey the tearful orders from his mother, with her eyes blanched white and her mouth coated with dried saliva. Trembling, he would fearfully step up on her chest, trying to put as little weight as possible there lest her bones break into pieces. Perched there, he couldn't hear or think, even his breathing seemed to cease. When at last he stepped off her, he would be soaked with sweat. As he wiped the sweat from his brow, his heart pounded with fear that Mother's malady would be the end of her. He tried not to dwell on the horrid thought that she could die at any moment, but the ominous fear recurred whenever that burning heart plagued her. As time went by, each fiery attack grew graver. Changyu didn't recall exactly when, but at some point he started pressing Mother's chest with his arms instead of standing on her.

From grade school through middle school, Changyu's ambition was to become a doctor some day so he could cure once and for all that evil burning heart that tortured his mother and threatened to steal her away from him for good. One day, while shelling green beans beside his aunt, Changyu had revealed, with an awkward pride, this plan of his. Upon hearing his dream, his aunt caressed his hand, repeating a heartfelt "Thank you, dear Changyu."

Then, heaving a long sigh, she said what a terrible shame it was that the sickness was not the sort a doctor could cure.

Changyu asked his aunt what she meant by that. She said he wouldn't be able to understand, but it was a sickness all tangled up with rancor and resentment, something invisible, not like boils on an arm or leg. So, she said, it wasn't the kind of sickness a doctor could cure. The strange words she used were incomprehensible to him. Who could cure her, then? Only she herself. It was still more incomprehensible. Auntie, what was it you just said, about rancor? Let me see, how can I explain it? Rancor is . . . rancor means . . . rancor is just rancor. When you're grown up, you'll understand even if you can't define it in words. When he reached high school, Changyu vaguely started to grasp some of the shapes of rancor. The notion of becoming a physician by then had slowly slipped from his mind.

"No, no . . . there's more to say . . . ."

What else had Mother meant to tell him? Was there another untold tale? On the brink of death, even her will had crumbled before she could finish her last words.

Witnessing his mother's death, Changyu finally saw clearly the essence of that rancor that had been responsible for her attacks and that had slowly gnawed away at her life. Keeping the picture of her husband's killer, for two decades Mother had gone on with an unquenchable thirst for revenge boiling inside her. The urge for retribution was the virus behind her burning heart, much in the same way a lighted candle consumes itself. She had been tormented by a searing rage that little by little consumed her own living heart. Her sister's words of long ago, that the sickness was all tangled up with resentment and rancor, came back to Changyu as though his aunt was now talking at his side.

For many years, all Changyu had known was that his father died in the Korean War. War was a game in which human lives were snuffed out, and in its course many a life was snatched away, so he'd regarded Father's death as a common misfortune of wartime. Not that he hadn't suffered from being a posthumous son, but the tragedy of never having known his father seemed to have been felt more deeply by his mother and the others around him. As he had come to realize, it was less painful never to have known one's father at all. Other children around him, slightly older, had vague memories of their dead fathers that tormented them and left painful scars. A few still entertained wishful hopes that their lost fathers may have survived, while others were obsessed by useless conjectures of "what if Father had lived?" Changyu at least had been spared such things.

Until he finished grade school, Changyu believed his father died a hero on the battlefield. While in middle school it was revealed to him that his father had died not in battle but at the hands of red partisans in his hometown. When he reached high school he realized how uncertain the relation between Father and the war actually was. These insights he acquired with no help from Mother, and they were not expressions of any rancor. He had heard the facts from someone, he couldn't say exactly from whom. Often he felt he had seen it all in a dream, but all the same he was sure it was not lies but the truth.

As Changyu went through these changes, Mother continued to suffer from constant attacks of burning heart, but not once had she said a word about Father's death. Of course, he often pestered her for details of how his father had died, but each time she only heaved a sigh and repeated, "That damned war, that damned war." Sick of that unchanging reply, he eventually gave up asking.

In the grey and silent aftermath of his mother's death, Changyu could remain alone no longer. Summoned by his aunt, the relatives rushed over despite the hour. Surrounded by a gaggle of family members, Changyu had to hide his own grief as the private shroud of death veiling the household was parted by the bustle of a growing crowd.

The funeral date and burial site were to be decided by Changyu in accord with recommendations by the clan elders. It wasn't just his lack of experience with such affairs; he felt all such funeral devotions were meaningless to the deceased.

"Should've lived ten years more, not even forty-five and left us for the other world."

"Just what I've been saying. It's a pity if you think only of her years, but with the rancor in her heart, she did well to hang tough as long as she did."

"Right. Without her strength of will, she couldn't have raised a fatherless child after such terrible ordeals."

"Sure enough. Nobody else could've endured such misery and then live on straight as an arrow. A wretched fate she had."

No one felt Mother's forty-four years to have been a short life, those years of exhaustion and trial that made up her ill-starred life.

"Fate's a strange thing. Such a noble woman living like a flower in the shadows."

"But for the war, she'd have had a long and happy life."

"That detestable war and those awful bastards—their atrocities are not done yet."

"Enough about that. No use talking, it's all over and done with, it'll only set our hearts ablaze again."

His relatives wore expressions of indignation, hatred, pain. One feature they all seemed to share was that each was remembering incidents of over twenty years before and none was ready to forgive the perpetrators for their crimes. Changyu felt like asking questions but didn't open his mouth. He wanted to hear more about Bae Jomsu, but somehow he also dreaded knowing too many details. He thought of his aunt. Surely she could tell him whatever the others could. He would rather ask her when they were alone. That way he could unravel what he did not understand about Mother's last request.

Changyu felt a dark unknown secret lurking in Mother's testament. It was hard to understand. Why on her deathbed would she command her son to avenge the death of her husband twenty-two years before in a war that saw countless people die? By emphasizing that the enemy was still alive, she had clearly implied what he should do to settle the score. And, by handing him the photograph, she was in effect charging him with the duty of revenge. Had it ever occurred to her what would become of her son if he succeeded in tracking down and killing that man? Mother was not that ignorant or thoughtless a person. Amidst the bustle of funeral preparations, Changyu kept wondering what else his mother had meant to say.

The burial was on the third day after her death. The coffin was black, a color fit to betoken the emptiness of death. After it had been lowered Changyu picked up a shovel, quaking with a loneliness amplified by the blackness of the coffin. Images of his mother's life of solitary pain engulfed him.

"Go on and say your final farewell," someone said in a muted, solemn voice.

His head swimming with impressions of his mother's presence, the scent of her body, Changyu lifted some soil and tilted the shovel. . . .

The lumps of earth and tiny rocks pelting onto the coffin echoed in his heart. Instantly, he held his breath and shut his eyes. Sorrow showered through the indescribable loneliness. It was a solitary sadness much more intense than that he had felt as she drew her last breath, or as her small body was laid in the coffin, or as the nails were hammered into its cover.

"You're gonna collapse any second. Hurry, hold on to me here," said one of the men, supporting Changyu. Two of them held his arms as he sat down on the grass. Tears streamed down his cheeks, running down his chin and along his neck. As he tried to compose himself, Changyu felt an acute sense of guilt, for he had not yet made up his mind to carry out her testament. Instead, he was skeptical about it. This world was no longer like that of the Yi Dynasty. His thoughts were punctuated with such doubts. The dirge began to play.

Now you depart,
When will you return?
Uncertain is our life
Uh-uh-hung, uh-huh-tal-kong.

The melodic notes reverberated far and wide as they all tread on the grave to pack down the earth. With mystical power, the dirge seemed to command the mountains, to make the trees tremble, and to still every blade of grass.

Across the rivers
Beyond the mountains
No return on that road
No return
Uh-uh-hung, uh-huh-tal-kong.

Immersed in the endless cycles of the funeral song, Changyu thought of Hakgoldaek. Like his mother, she had been renowned as a virtuous widow. Their two lives had many similarities. Of similar age, both had lost husbands in war and brought up their children alone without even considering remarriage, waiting to be reunited with their lost husbands. The difference was that Hakgoldaek's husband had gone off to war and never come back.

It was pathetic to watch Hakgoldaek pour her soul into longing for her husband's return. No matter how tired she was she stayed up until midnight every night, never failing to light a lamp in the main room before retiring for the night. Each night she made ready the bed for her missing husband. At dawn she went to the brook to get pure spring water to keep on the terrace for the day. At dinner time she always served a portion of rice for her absent husband. She never forgot his birthday, and on all holidays she religiously laid his best clothes out for him. She kept all this up for twenty long years.

With each New Year, Hakgoldaek paid a visit to a fortune teller. The divinations always indicated that her husband was still alive. The constancy of her annual consultations with the fortune teller was incredible, but more so was the fortune teller's gall in interpreting the divination that same way year after year.

Hakgoldaek was still alive and in good health, but his own mother had closed her eyes for the last time. A question arose and answered itself immediately in Changyu's mind. The fortune teller. Hakgoldaek lived a life of ceaseless anticipation while Mother's had been a life of unrelieved indignation. The two lives were insurmountably different. The first hung on a hope, the second was bound down by despair. For Hakgoldaek each tomorrow was bright and promising, but Mother stayed immured in a dark yesterday. What if the fortune teller had for once told Hakgoldaek that the portents meant her husband was dead? Hakgoldaek might have dropped dead on the spot.

Mother performed none of the rituals of waiting that Hakgoldaek observed. Mother never laughed out loud, nor did she audibly weep. Only cold melancholy was constantly there behind her expressionless face. She seldom spoke. If she opened her mouth more than once or twice, it was a talkative day. And all the while, like one prone to fits, she had attacks of burning in her heart. Changyu knew she couldn't last very long like that, but he was still surprised when the end finally came quickly.

Rancor had tortured Mother and in the end carried her off to the other world. What in the world was this rancor? Did it have a shape or a volume? Was it a product of vengeful resentment? No, the urge for revenge alone was not the cause. Hakgoldaek also was said to carry a thirst for revenge coiled like a serpent in her heart. Is rancor unique to women deprived of their husbands? No, that wasn't it, either. Changyu had heard of Chomchondaek, an old grandmother who wept for ten long years out of boundless rancor after sending her three sons off to war and never hearing a word from them again.

Rancor may be like a tumor in one's soul, a tumor spawned by a confusion of feelings, of being wronged, of unjust suffering, of sorrowful yearnings, of cruelly disappointed hopes, and of regrets for what might have been. Maybe it bears the bright color of blood dripping onto a white field of snow.

"Changyu, let's go now."

Changyu sat motionless, peering blankly at the mountains far off in the distance. One mountain carried another on its back, and that one in turn bore another on its shoulders and so on until the mountain range merged with the sky. Embracing the crimson blood of rancor, was Mother's spirit even now weeping on its lonely journey, flying over mountain after mountain and up into the sky? There, at the gate of heaven, would she rejoin her husband and tell him of her last request to avenge his death?

"It's getting dark, let's go down, I say."

Still Changyu couldn't get up. He lacked the courage to look directly at the round, raised mound of the grave.

"So, now you're a university student. Time's not so heartless after all. Father must be smiling and nodding in the other world. Smiling, he'll surely be smiling."

But Mother shed tears as she spoke. The tears flowed uncontrollably, and she bit her lips to stop them from twitching. It was the first time Mother let the word "Father" pass her lips, and the first time she had openly wept. In the face of this woman, Changyu could say nothing. But he felt he understood what was in her heart, which bore a spectrum of dark colors remote from the radiance of a rainbow, a heart with an untold number of layers, more than any earthly rainbow.

When his mother departed for the other world, nine months, no, eight months, not counting summer vacation, had passed since he had left home. Could she have been relieved at seeing her son grown? Or had her energy all been drained, with nothing left to sustain her? Changyu had to struggle to pay for his education, but he'd not formed any definite goal for the future.

Strangely enough, what they called life, livelihood, existence, all seemed to him no more than rain and wind. Something had always been missing from his universe. Even so, in the uncontaminated part of his heart he never gave up hope for his mother. He fondly wished she would hold on until he could care for her properly. But this normal yet desperate desire of his was to no avail, and like a passing breeze she had left him behind forever.

In Mother's place only a void remained. The gaping emptiness expanded when he returned to the house, now a cavern, dark and silent. Changyu felt trapped in the solitude and finality of his abandonment.

"You must be tired, get some sleep now," said his aunt.

"Auntie, when you finish what you're doing, please come inside, won't you?"

"What d'you want? You should just get some rest."

She waved her hand like she already knew what he would say next.

"Can't sleep right this minute. Hurry up and then come in, please."

"All right, I'll be in shortly."

She entered with a sweet rice drink on a tray.

"Try this, then you'll feel better."

Changyu pretended to drink but only wet his lips. Then he pulled the picture out.

"I've got to head back up to Seoul for school. Anyway, I ought to know about this and there's no reason to put it off. Now or later, pus never turns into good flesh. This guy, Bae Jomsu, you knew him, too, didn't you, Auntie?"

"Yes, indeed."

Already she had grown tense and cold.

"Please tell me more about him."

"Why do you want me to tell that god-awful story, there's no point. He murdered your father, and he ruined your mother's life, too, you know that much. So you've got to avenge your parents, that's all."

"Auntie, please, be sensible and try to understand. In the old days, a son would be praised if, after a lifelong hunt for his father's enemy, he succeeded in taking revenge. But today the world's not like that. If you do the same thing nowadays, they don't call you a dutiful son, but a fool, a lunatic, or just another murderer."

"So, you're telling me you can't do it, is that it?"

His aunt raised her voice, her rising anger becoming venomous.

"That's not what I meant. First, I'd like to know what he did, then I can decide what I should do about it. It all happened over twenty years ago, and besides, it was wartime. I'm not saying this is what happened, but if he committed the crime because Father had wronged him somehow, then I might not be able to . . ."

His aunt was shaking and shrieked, "Shut up! Just because there's a hole in your face, do you think you can say whatever pops into your head?!"

Instantly, Changyu regretted it. It was impossible to expect reasonableness from his aunt. Mother had been the same way.

"Calm down, please, Auntie. I said the wrong thing."

"Nah, nah. Can't take two steps at once. Husband and wife share different feelings from parents and children, so I shouldn't be surprised at that coming from you."

Her words were jumping to a wholly different tack.

"Auntie, I said I didn't mean it."

Vexed, Changyu, too, raised his voice a bit.

"No matter what you think, it's your thinking and I can do nothing to change it, but don't forget one thing, never. Remember how your mother was trying to tell you something but couldn't?"

His aunt stared directly at Changyu with resentful eyes. He didn't turn away from that stare.

"That bastard, see, that bastard didn't just kill your father. He violated your mother, too."

"What?!"

"You were inside your mother's belly. That was what she couldn't bear to tell you before she died. Every year on your father's day to receive the ancestor sacrifice, you and your mother always washed your hair with salt-water, remember that? Do you know what that was for? To wash away the sin against your father."

Mother's rancor, her seared heart, her tears, her dying request. In Changyu's imagination the blacksmith in the photograph was looming larger and larger, rushing right at him. He became deadly tense.

2

She always felt ill at ease in the presence of her husband, Shin Byongmo. She felt even more fettered and awkward in dealing with him than with her father-in-law. They lived by themselves, so she seldom saw her father-in-law. On the occasions when she did, it was easy enough to play the dutiful daughter-in-law by observing the expected decorum. But a husband lived under the same roof, and the curious interactions of husband and wife called for more than the ritual courtesies that suffice with a father-in-law.

Even sitting in the same room, she always felt a certain distance from her husband. A cold wind blew through that intervening space. It was a wind generated by her husband and to her it was inescapable, she could not redirect its flow. Even when they slept together, the chill of that wind never abated completely. She could not understand how that coldness even wedged itself between their naked bodies as their flesh commingled. Desperately she sought to rid herself of such thoughts, at least during those interludes, but in vain. He did nothing to dispel that wind, even in the most intimate moments.

"Can't understand what you're living for, sister. It's like living with the Buddhist saint of Daedok village. Hold on, though. At least the Daedok saint had a magic power to make you bear a son, but that husband of yours doesn't even have that. Well, ain't it the truth?"

Her husband's older brother's wife used to whisper such things, looking her in the eye.

"Oh, how can you?"

And then either she would blush beet red or else make some sort of fuss to change the subject. Meanwhile, she suffered from an inexplicable sadness and loneliness all this time. Never once was she energized by what her sister-in-law, between giggles and gossip, termed "womanly pleasure in living." She could not bring herself to blame her husband for making her as frigid as a slab of stone. What was regrettable was that after losing their daughter, Kyungja, there had been no sign of another pregnancy. If only she could have a baby she felt she'd be able to breathe freely at last. She wondered if the lack of any sign of another child wasn't due to the chilly wind invading their bed.

Her husband's personality was exactly the opposite of his older brother's. Her brother-in-law was carefree, loved his liquor, always wore a smile on his face. But her husband avoided socializing, when he drank he preferred to drink alone, and he was always absorbed in some profound concern like a man in grave trouble.

"From the beginning your husband was always different from his brother, but he didn't used to be like he is these days. He was drafted into the army out of school, and ever since he came back he's been a different man."

Her sister-in-law's observation was accurate. Barely a month after their wedding, her student husband had been conscripted by the Japanese and sent off to war, but back then he'd not been at all like he was now.

He used to laugh quietly, and certainly never surrounded himself with this wall of cold wind. His young bride often blushed at his heated passion, unlike now.

It was a rushed marriage. There was no escape from conscription, and her father-in-law wanted his son married before he was drafted. Naturally, the two of them opposed the idea, but the parents on both sides resorted to high-handed measures and hastened them into matrimony.

She had not been at all pleased. True, he was a college student, with a solid family background and good looks, but a conspicuously fatal flaw overshadowed all of those attractive qualities. It was the fact that he had been dragooned into being a student-soldier and was headed off to war. Still, she had no choice but to mount the marriage palanquin without uttering a word of protest.

"You're paying for your beauty, sister. Your face is like silk, without one blemish. The mountain goddess is depriving you of womanly pleasure because she's jealous."

So said her sister-in-law cruelly, a deceitful grin on her face. That "mountain goddess" was none other than herself. Because she was oversensitive about her own appearance, her sister-in-law gloated over her insecure marriage. Listening to these veiled curses from her sister-in-law, she felt an unbearable indignation that raised goosebumps all over her. Still she displayed no trace of emotion. If she ever let slip an ugly remark, it might end with more pain for her. Besides, she didn't want to sully her husband's name by fueling gossip among the womenfolk.

Despite its vagaries, her husband's love was something she believed in. She knew that she herself was not the source of the frigid air that enveloped him. She couldn't be certain, but she guessed he had undergone some trauma. Upon his return home he seemed more burdened with worldly cares than other men. Somewhere in the unplumbed depths of her husband's heart, she thought there must still be a place where she was wanted.

"Take good care of yourself. Parents aside, I'll not fail to come back alive because of you."

Those words he had whispered in her ear as he held her on the night before his departure. With his elegant deep voice pouring over her, she felt the sudden stirrings of pure passion, and then as quickly was overwhelmed with embarrassment, trembling that her careless desires had been revealed. In fact, before a month was out she had overcome all the fears and misgivings with which the wedding had been infected. Her husband by then had taken undivided possession of her heart, and she was ready to live with the reality of her husband's conscription.

Two months after his departure, the symptoms of pregnancy were manifest. Thanks to the understanding of her husband's parents, she was allowed to stay with her own family. In February of the following year, she gave birth to a girl. Then, with the liberation in August, her husband's family suffered hardships. Her father-in-law was hounded for having been a Japanese collaborator, and during the chaos the infant Kyungja contracted the measles. The baby struggled with all her strength, but in the end she succumbed to the disease. Her own grief at the death of her daughter was swept away in the chaotic confusion of the family's travails.

Her husband, having left his family with only anxiety over uncertain portents, gave no indication of returning. No one dared be glib, yet a certain atmosphere descended over the house. Throughout this period, her mother-in-law had been seeking the counsel of famed fortune-tellers.

Near the end of the year, on a day when heavy snow had fallen, out of the blue her husband walked into the house like a ghost. His hardened, expressionless face looked hollow. The whole family was deeply moved and at first welcomed him with open arms, but then grew troubled after noting that face of his, devoid of feeling.

Sitting at the dinner table after hurried preparations for a meal, he sluggishly lifted his spoon as though he had no appetite at all. Showered with questions, all he said was that he would talk about things by and by, otherwise he limited himself to an occasional "yes" and "well." His refusal to converse became a cause of embarrassment to those asking questions. As if worn out by the fruitless inquiries, his mother started instead to tell about the important events the family had been through while he was away.

First was the trauma of his father being denounced as pro-Japanese.

But what was wrong with her husband? He merely raised his bowed head slightly and glanced quickly at his father, then lowered his eyes again at once. He almost imperceptibly nodded and that was all.

Next he learned of the birth and death of Kyungja. Displaying somewhat more feeling this time, her husband raised his head. For a moment his eyes seemed to glisten with light. Yet, that was about all. Oblivious to these reactions, his mother kept dragging out story after story, but he seemed to pay no attention at all.

Then he stood up and calmly said, "I must rest for a while. I'll hear the rest of the news some other time," and his voice was like a cold breeze.

From that day onward, her husband never emerged from behind that wall of coldness. He remained so for the next four years.

"My dear, you've suffered greatly. I know it hurts, but try not to think about our baby's departure from this world so young. Our little one wasn't the only one lost in this god-awful time."

Her husband said that after they had retired to their room, but he had not even looked at her. She felt anew the same alienation and fear she had experienced on their wedding night. When she went out to wash and returned, she would find him curled up fast asleep in the corner of the room.

Apart from waking long enough to swallow a few spoonfuls of soup, he slept for the next three days. Watching his emaciated figure as he departed into the abyss of slumber, she felt deeply sad. What awful battles and what dreadful suffering had sapped his strength so completely? Her own suppositions haunted her. Even after a long stretch of sleep, he would not leave the room. He tried to avoid even his own family.

About all she ever said to her husband were things like, "Your water's ready," or, "Please do eat something now." He did absolutely nothing, just sat there in the room gazing into thin air. After several days of inert sitting, his attitude changed all at once, like someone roused from a nap by a douse of cold water. He sat up at his desk and began studying. His father was the one most delighted by this change, and kept incanting the same refrain, "Now, he's all right, he's fine, now." Judging from this reaction, his father must have been awfully worried about his son.

She dimly understood the nature of her father-in-law's feelings, based on what she had overheard passing between his mother and his elder brother's wife from time to time. A distillation of these opinions was that her husband, though astonishingly brilliant, was an eccentric, hypersensitive and extremely stubborn man.

"Do tell, the boy goes off to Japan, then sends us a letter saying he's studying to be an artist. In middle school, he brought home prizes for painting and all, but nobody ever dreamed he'd go to a university to try to take up painting seriously. My lord, I can't say what an awful commotion that stirred up around here."

Her mother-in-law had described the time from memory as if it happened yesterday. At first she was only bewildered. Her husband—a painter? She could not grasp it as an actuality. A painter husband and herself, it seemed even more remote to her.

He sat at his desk day in and day out. He spoke to her but rarely. She knew nothing of the hardships he had endured, of battlefields, of how wars were waged, or of how terrible war could be. Apart from their sleeping in the same room, there were no intimacies between them, nor was there any secret sharing that the two of them kept to themselves. Her everyday life was superfluous and the tension and indecision she felt were getting to be more intolerable than the anxiousness she had endured when he was gone.

Seizing opportunities when he went out for walks, she would look attentively at the books he'd been poring over and the writing he'd done, but it was all beyond her comprehension. Never before had she felt such despair over her paltry grammar-school education and the resulting ignorance. If only she had at least finished middle school . . . She often lapsed into loneliness, plagued with uncontrollable dread.

Entombed in his study, her husband passed almost a whole year. She couldn't believe there was that much to study and only felt downcast at the relentless tenacity which drove him to spend every day seated at his desk for a solid year.

With the coming of the new year, her husband became a teacher at the local agricultural high school. She was told he would teach history. Her timidity deepened. From various sources she knew only too well that he was a man of great ability, yet she never had dreamed that overnight he would turn out to be a schoolteacher. Wife of a teacher—she felt a suffocating fear and a thickening of the barriers between her husband and herself.

At first he refused to accept the teaching appointment, not because he disliked teaching, but because he felt he lacked sufficient knowledge to instruct the students. His father, who had exerted efforts to arrange the offer for his son, was restless, and the school authorities became even more eager to have him. His reluctance seemed to stem not from humility alone, but also from a sincere belief of his. He would have preferred to have finished up his interrupted university studies; however, there was a shortage of college faculty after the Japanese left, and it was far from easy to resume one's higher education in that time of turmoil.

"My Byongmo, that's fine, you're making me so proud. A fine place in life being a teacher. You know teachers, like parents and officials, have always been at the top, and nobody dares to step on a teacher's shadow. Fine, indeed. And just imagine, if you'd been stubborn at the start, you might've ended up a painter. What a shame that would've been, becoming a painter."

His mother was so gleeful she could have danced a jig. And so it was like a new sun had risen in the family, flooding the household with brightness.

But the happy days did not last for long. With North and South pitted against one another and ideologies clashing, instability came to the nation, and the pervasive air of unrest spilled into the schools. The subject her husband was teaching, history, was not wholly irrelevant to the currents in the world outside. He was respected as a knowledgeable educator, but as time went on he was swept up in the troubles of the time.

As the number of students favoring the North grew, they began vocally criticizing her husband's teaching. He tried to persuade the students to concentrate on their studies, and explained why they should not blindly accept the Northern propaganda, but this only resulted in further discontent among radical pupils.

These accounts of what happened had reached her through her sister-in-law. Her husband never talked about events at school, and she dared not ask questions. To be learning about her own husband's affairs through his brother's wife, practically a stranger, increased her misery and discontent.

"Shin Byongmo is the son of a Japanese collaborator." "Shin Byongmo is an enemy of the people." "Shin Byongmo is incurably counter-revolutionary, so out with him!"

Such epithets were being spread around the campus by students sympathetic to the communist North, she was told, and sometimes they shouted such things at his back. She passed each day in trepidation, dreading that something awful might happen to her husband.

One day a bloody riot erupted among the students, a collision between one faction leaning toward the Northern ideology and another adhering to the South. There were injuries on both sides, and the police intervened to quell the outburst of violence. The commotion turned the whole village inside out.

She paced back and forth in the house, not even daring to go out to see. She couldn't shake the ominous premonition that her husband had been waylaid by some grave disaster.

"Sister, how devoted you are! So loyal and faithful! Constantly worrying, so concerned about a husband who's so thoughtless of you is something to behold, truly a loyal wife."

The sarcastic sneer behind her sister-in-law's words was plain enough, but she was too flustered to argue, and anyway was in no mood to blame the speaker. A new affection for her husband had sprouted in her heart, and she felt no shame or embarrassment at revealing that love.

He came home very late that night, safe and unharmed, without a scratch. For the first time in her memory, at the moment she saw him she felt an impulse to cry out loud and embrace him.

"Oh, please be careful!" she barely managed to say as she brought his dinner in on a tray.

"Why, what've you heard?" he asked, looking up at her.

"Rumors."

"I'm being careful, so don't worry too much. And don't believe everything you hear. Rumors tend to blow things out of proportion."

"I know."

Listening to the beating of her own heart, she imagined a blooming flower bed bathed in brilliant sunlight, a place somewhere in his soul where instinctively she knew he cared for her. All at once she felt that her long life in her husband's shadow had been the right life for her to lead.

The unrest in the outside world worsened as time passed. The communist students, she heard, were more and more prone to violence, and even the faculties were splitting into overtly hostile factions. She tried to figure out what the fighting was all about. Based on the occasional news that reached her, to make out the situation was harder than sorting rice from barley. Still, she vaguely grasped the main outlines of it. If ignorance is bliss, knowledge perhaps is a disease. And a little knowledge may be even more perilous. Day and night she was plagued by anxiety. The dread that her husband at any time could be exposed to great danger was a suffocating yoke stifling her soul. She vaguely calculated that the humble and the impoverished made up a majority in this world, and based on that fact alone she concluded her husband was in imminent peril.

It happened that these worries uncannily hit the target.

It was around the opening of the spring term at school. Her husband, drenched in blood, was carried home by the neighbors. He had been badly beaten in a dark alley by two men. While he recuperated in bed for several days, he refused to answer any questions from the elders. Indignant rage beamed from his face as he lay staring at the ceiling. The household silently concluded that students must have been behind it. And they had a feeling Byongmo knew who they were.

When he finally rose from bed, he was a different man in everyone's eyes. It was hard to pinpoint exactly where the change lay, but now he had a certain hard and fearless quality about him. His glance was like ice, and his hardened lips looked like they might never part again. This metamorphosis of her husband brought a new anxiety over the family.

"Stay away from the school for a while," his father advised.

As her husband silently stared at the floor, the muscles in his cheek protruded from where his jaws met. He must have been gritting his teeth with all his might.

His brother said to him, "Better listen to Father. The government's rooting those bastards out from their holes. You should stay clear for a bit till the big flames are put out."

He continued to grind his teeth.

"Well, what do you say?"

His father was pressing him.

"Can't starve yourself to death because maggots turned up in your food," he blurted out impatiently, standing up.

Nobody could stop him from returning to school. People said he had become a fierce character at school. His role abruptly changed to that of disciplinarian, and he took up fencing again after a long lapse. She was surprised when she later learned from her sister-in-law that her husband's swordsmanship was quite impressive. Evidently he had resolved to meet force with force, but this change gave rise to a foreboding in her that he was about to leap into a fire holding a bundle of cotton.

Then things began to look brighter. The government commenced a nationwide crackdown to ferret out active communists. She heard the police station was overflowing with those arrested. The quicker ones were seeking refuge in the mountains, it was said. Students also seemed to be fleeing in groups. In the midst of this turmoil, her husband was busy each day going back and forth to the police station. He spared no efforts to get as many of his students released as he could, and his efforts had a considerable influence. The parents of some of those students visited their house to express their thanks, grateful for her husband's assistance. But what pleased her most of all was that he was no longer in danger, and the venomous chill about his face had diminished somewhat.

At this time, the communist forces had been pushed out into the mountains or else driven underground and relegated to clandestine activity. The world seemed to regain normality. But her husband still wore a heavy expression as though burdened with concerns, and his attitude toward her remained remote and cool. After several hesitant attempts, one night she gathered enough courage to open her mouth.

"The Reds are all gone now, so why still so troubled?"

He gazed into her eyes with a look so intense she had to turn her head away.

"What's wrong, does it choke you to look at me?"

" . . . "

She was sure her response would be too loud, but actually her voice was inaudible.

"I can't say how I know," said he, "but the communists aren't gone. None are in the open because they've retreated underground now. And being invisible makes them more dangerous than before, when they were out in the daylight."

Like mountain after mountain with no end. What was to be done? How long do you intend to go on like this? She had a million questions but they all had to stay inside her heart.

Free from serious turbulence, the school was almost back to normal. Occasionally a fugitive student would come back all emaciated from the mountains, and about the same time one or two others would abruptly vanish into thin air. From time to time, people one never would have suspected were unmasked as communist spies and arrested. With each such case people were astonished, repeating, "The least likely are the most dangerous sometimes."

By then another year had come and gone. With the advent of the new year, she secretly grew restless. Already seven years since they married, and four years since her husband's return, but still there was no sign. She had lost face before her husband's parents, and could maintain no dignity in the eyes of the people around her. But he, the person who ought to be most concerned, seemed utterly indifferent about his lack of progeny.

The disquiet she felt was growing more unbearable. What if there'll never be any child at all? She suffered in solitude from a pain she couldn't even share with her own husband. The only thing to be grateful for was that his parents had not been overbearing about the subject. Apart from him being the second and not the eldest son, probably they had sensed there was something missing from their son's marriage.

When April came she did not overlook the fact that her monthly flower did not appear, yet she dared not hastily attribute it to pregnancy. At one point she had missed her period for three months and even suffered from morning sickness. She had been absolutely sure she was pregnant. Everyone in the family knew about it. Then, inexplicably, in the following month she resumed menstruating and was mortally disgraced as a silly woman.

"Sister, you're just dying to have a baby, eh? No point in wishing, your body's got to get pregnant along with your mind."

Faced with her sister-in-law's jeering, she felt like killing herself.

The following month, again, no flower. Without saying a word to anyone, she secretly and desperately prayed day and night. Please let it be a baby, their own little one. June came and a few days after she assured herself that her period had been missed again, she heard war had broken out.

Once more the world fell into chaos and turmoil. Her husband looked much more distressed than actual conditions around them warranted. It was the most anxious and confused she had ever seen him. He rarely ate or slept. After a sleepless night, he would hurriedly depart for school at the crack of dawn.

In the evenings the whole family assembled in the house of her husband's elder brother and talked until late. Nobody seemed to know how the civil war would unfold. Out of fright and anxiety, all of them were hoping that somehow the war would quickly die down. Several days passed in this manner.

She woke up, startled. Outside the door she distinctly heard people moving about, and she saw that her husband was already sitting up. He held her hand. Again she was startled, his hand was freezing cold and trembling awfully.

At that moment she heard the sound of heavy steps across the floor of the house's main room. Her skin crawled. Then loud mumbling in low voices was heard. She almost screamed in terror. Someone suddenly began shaking the door wildly. She grasped her husband's hand once more and found it quaking even worse than before. She felt the breath of imminent death, and was obsessed by a desperate notion that she had to reveal to her husband that she was pregnant.

"Shin Byongmo, come on out, right now! No use resisting!"

With these words, something was thrust into the room, tearing through the rice paper in the door. She ceased breathing. In the translucent darkness could be seen a long metal spear. Faced with this murderous spear, she almost died from fright.

"Shin Byongmo, out here, now!"

Her husband got up. She grabbed him by the arm. He shook free of her hands. Again she clutched at him. This time he shook even harder. Then he unlatched the lock. The door slammed open, and three shadows thrust spears toward her husband's chest.

"Shin Byongmo, recognize me, no?" one of the shadows asked.

". . . ."

"It's me, Bae Jomsu, Bae Jomsu."

". . . ."

"I'm disappointed you don't seem to know Bae Jomsu. Well, then, do you know the blacksmith, huh?"

"My god . . ."

"Why the hell you acting so surprised? The world's got different masters now!"

The blacksmith . . . a picture flashed by in her head.

"Hurry, now, off with his belt, and drag him along!"

Upon this command from the blacksmith, the other two shadows rushed in and dragged her husband out.

She rose quickly, then froze in her tracks. A spear tip was stuck right underneath her nose.

"You stay right where you be. If you try to run or scream, we'll butcher you and your husband both with these spears."

". . . ."

She collapsed back down where she was lying. The door slammed back shut in front of her face. She buried her face in the covers, too petrified to cry, and shivered piteously. Dear . . . oh, dear . . . dear . . . she couldn't think straight, all she could see in her head was the dejected back of her husband.

The door suddenly opened once more. She looked up with a start. A black shadow filled the portal. Instinctively she cringed, wrapping both arms tightly around herself. The peril was primordial.

"Don't make a peep if you want to stay alive," ordered the shadow, taking a step inside the room. As she moved back away she thought . . . pregnant, husband, death . . . there was no escape.

Bang! The door was shut.

There was nowhere to retreat, her back was to the wall.

"Lie down, now!" spat the shadow as he removed his jacket. She pressed herself against the wall, thinking she'd rather die first.

"I said, down, quickly!"

These words poured from the shadow's mouth as he tossed his pants away and rushed toward her. She bit her lip and pushed at the lunging shadow. But he grabbed her hands and soon her body was cast like a puppet onto the covers.

"Listen when I tell you nicely. Struggle uselessly, and your precious life won't last long," said the shadow slowly, as he kneeled on top of her thighs.

"There's no law that only that bastard Shin can enjoy this pretty face. A blacksmith like me's a man, too, y'know, I've been known to get excited, too."

The blacksmith tore off her top and her underpants. She quaked, her body buckling in two. He pressed himself down on her as she was. She twisted her legs, pushing him away.

"What's all this fuss, what's this fuss!?"

The blacksmith lost his temper, forcing her hands above her head, pinning both her arms to the floor with one hand. Then he mercilessly planted his knees between her writhing legs. With painful moans she fell limp. There was no fighting his strength.

"Uhm, uhm . . ."

She moaned, feeling agonizing pain as if her lower half was being torn in two. Pregnant, pregnant, pregnant . . . she thought it'd be better to die. Beastly smell, beastly breathing, beastly ferocity, beastly filth . . . on waves of pain, she heard the screams of a new life already polluted. Better off dead.

Eyes wide open, she silently shed tears.

"Different masters rule the world now, so don't be imagining you've been wronged," said the blacksmith, gushing heavy breaths. Then he started to put his clothes back on. She barely managed to turn around and burst out weeping.

"Bear me a son, then maybe I'll take you as my concubine."

The blacksmith chuckled as he rushed out.

She wept and wept, calling out the name of her husband who had been taken away.

3

All at once the world had turned inside out, beyond imagining. You could not believe your very eyes. Like the compound disorientation when masked players first appear and then reappear without their masks, the shift in the world was bewildering. She had no time to grieve over her husband's abduction or her own rape. The reality that had burst upon her in the hours before dawn permitted no such sentimentality.

On that night, her brother-in-law's house had been turned upside down, too. Her father-in-law and her husband's elder brother also had been dragged off. For some unknown reason they had taken her sister-in-law, too. Her mother-in-law was almost out of her mind, so she felt her first duty was to care for the feverish old woman who kept on chattering mindlessly.

"Nah, hah, you goddamn bastards. Dear, dear, Byongchul, Byongchul, nah, I said. Nooo! Oh, Byongmo, my Byongmo, what happened to Byongmo. Dear, dear . . ."

As she pressed a cool cloth to her mother-in-law's forehead, she kept thinking about what her husband had said about it being more dangerous when the Reds were underground than when they acted in the open. Truly, he was a man of deep insight who had foreseen the future.

The blacksmith—who could've guessed he would turn out to be a communist—a man who barely eked out a living working scrap iron at his rundown forge out on the market road on the outskirts of the village.

All of a sudden something flashed through her mind like lightning. That speartip he had aimed at her husband's heart, it shone before her mind's eye. She shuddered. The blacksmith must have made that spear. Not one or two but . . . She was gripped by an unholy fear. That man who wore an obsequious grin and ostensibly was making hoes, shovels, scythes, had secretly been turning out those diabolical spears when no one was looking. Anyone who could do that easily was capable of hauling any number of people off to who knows where.

She was outraged. What had the government been doing all that time, and what of the police? But the indignation soon turned into despair. She grew pale and blue when she set out to try to learn where the men of the family had been taken. Upon being told that those arrested were held at the police station, she couldn't figure out what on earth was happening. Later she discovered that most of the constabulary had fled to the provincial capital the afternoon before, and the communist partisans had taken over the police station. The few who resisted were killed with spears.

Before learning of this state of affairs, she had no idea things had gone so far. Only later did she learn that the police station had already been taken over on the night the intruders raided her home. The blacksmith's boast that the masters of the world had changed echoed in her ears with new meaning.

The only hope she could cling to was that the police forces who had retreated to the provincial capital would return and drive the communists out. This hope was soon shattered, for several days later there appeared in the village not the police but North Korean soldiers.

Meanwhile, the blacksmith had broken into her room the last four nights in a row. Each time she trembled and looked death in the eyes, but with the coming of dawn she had to go on caring for her bedridden mother-in-law. Summer, the season of heat, humidity and mosquitoes, was hatching other conspiracies. Summer itself seemed to be allied with the North Koreans, and there was no power that could stand before them.

It was the day after the North Korean soldiers arrived when screams were first heard from people being executed on the central slope of *Sambongsan*, for generations a place believed by the Shin clan to preserve their good fortune. She heard they had dragged the Shin men up the mountain, forced them to dig holes, killed them with spears, and then buried them in the holes. It was a double revenge: the taproot of the Shin family, running deeply and broadly through the three villages, overnight was severed from its bedrock. It was a mortal blow nobody could parry.

Despite her own boundless terror, she did her best to console her mother-in-law, who, taken ill at the shock of her husband's seizure, slowly had been recovering until she heard about the murders on *Sambongsan*, which made her lapse again into a cold sweat, shivering all over. Then, on the third day, the news of her father-in-law's death blew into the house.

"No! No!" Her mother-in-law screamed, leaping up, and then she just collapsed in a heap onto the floor.

"Mother!"

She held the old woman in her arms, but she was already dead. Her eyes remained open and white.

Numbed to fear, she spent the night in the company of three cousins, watching the corpse. Theirs was not the only house in mourning.

It was a little past noon the next day when she heard that her husband, too, had been executed. She sat, grabbing a post with both hands, showing no reaction except the tears flowing down over her cheeks.

Gradually, the darkness before her eyes began to lift and slowly she recovered her composure. Reflecting on overlapping images of her husband, she kept repeating to herself one thing, that she must not die yet. For reasons unclear to her, that thought obsessed her soul.

She arranged the burial of her mother-in-law without observing any ceremonial formalities. The corpses of neither her husband nor his father were recovered, and even her mother-in-law barely escaped burial in a straw-mat shroud.

They were not content with killing all the men they had taken away. They returned to ransack every single household, now inhabited only by women and children in mourning or trembling in deepest fear. Not just their valu-ables and food, but even the furniture was confiscated and carted away. Those energetic, lively men in red armbands only yesterday had been neighbors with familiar faces. Whether they liked it or not, they all had been living off of the Shin clan.

It was early morning when they ransacked her father-in-law's house, where she was staying. She was in the middle of preparing breakfast and met them without any serious fear. It was an attitude of resignation that followed upon her caring for the family dead.

"In the name of the People, we are confiscating all your property," said a man with a slim build and keen eyes, accompanied by four other men. Emerg-ing from the kitchen, she was relieved to see that the blacksmith was not in the group. By this time, she had heard that the blacksmith, Bae Jomsu, was the Vice-Chairman of the People's Commissariat, and that the vile creature was the one in charge of all the killing.

"Open the door of the barn, now!" yelled one of the men. Just then, Tongmyong, her oldest nephew, jumped out from the main room and shouted, "Teacher!" A fifth-grader in grammar school, Tongmyong ran unreservedly into the arms of the keen-eyed man. To be more precise, the man stood mo-tionless and the boy spread out his arms wide and threw them around his waist.

"Why, isn't this Tongmyong?"

The man looked embarrassed at the embrace about his waist.

"Teacher, this is our house."

"Really."

She was deeply confused for a moment. Why in the world would a teacher become a communist? Outwardly, he educates the young ones, but inwardly . . . Such duplicity was far more troubling to her than that of the blacksmith.

"What now, Comrade Chairman?"

To this inquiry from one of his men, the teacher replied, "Proceed, at once!"

The teacher was the Chairman, and his calm, cold command befit a Chairman.

"Teacher, can't you please save my mama and papa? What's happened to my mama and papa?"

Tongmyong was imploring the Comrade Chairman. As of then, her husband's brother and his wife were still alive.

"It's all right, you just stay home and study."

The Comrade Chairman tried to shoo the boy away, and made a grimace, motivated by embarrassment or hostility, it wasn't clear which.

"Teacher, I'll study for sure, but please promise you'll save my mama and papa, please."

Tongmyong was still clinging onto the Chairman, begging desperately.

"Look, let go of me. I said all right, didn't I?"

The Chairman shoved the boy roughly away. As he turned his back to her, she felt outraged.

"Finish up and return without delay!"

With that order, he left his men behind and rushed from the house without looking back. She had no way of discerning whether he was leaving in accordance with a prior plan or because of the awkward circumstances. Tongmyong watched his teacher leave, and kept sobbing quietly.

They scraped up the last of the grain and took it away, leaving them nothing to eat. Now they had only lettuce from the back garden with soybean paste for dinner, and once in while rotten persimmons they found and washed in warm water to make a semblance of a meal. It seemed that hot and tedious, hopeless and terrible summer would never end.

The only thing plentiful was sunlight. The hot sun burned down day in and day out.

Ever since the day when she made up her mind not to give up and die, she'd been doing something secretly. Early each morning she washed herself with salt water. Otherwise she couldn't bear the feeling of impurity and filth. The mere thought of that beastly man touching her made her itch intolerably. She felt guilty because of the effect on the innocent, unsullied life within her, not to mention the impiety towards her husband who already was beyond the pale of this awful world. She was gnawed by worry that the blacksmith might boast to others about raping her. If there were rumors, the unborn child surely would be claimed to be that bastard's. Despite the discrepancy of several months, the facts would never stand up against the power of rumor, especially when many took for granted that her husband had been unable to conceive a child with her.

The executions at *Sambongsan* seemed less frequent now, but they still had no word about her brother-in-law and his wife. She tried every possible way at her disposal to find out about their fate, but had no success. True, there was never any formal notification whether relatives had been killed or spared, but they had adopted the odd practice of leaking the victims' identities on the very day they died. Even with the unrelieved dread, she had not completely abandoned hope that the couple somehow might still be alive.

Tongmyong's teacher naturally had not shown his face there again since the incident. The little boy went out into the hot sun each day to gather whatever word about his parents he could and always returned home dead tired.

One day she was grinding barley to make gruel. As she mechanically crushed the grain in a wooden mortar, she thought the waning moon setting over the western mountains looked as cold and white as a widow in mourning clothes. The sky never changed its color, the stars kept twinkling, the trees and reeds stayed just the same, and only humans felt a restless urge to change. She heaved a deep sigh, wondering how long this life of hers would go on. The sigh had become habitual, a part of her.

July passed and it was now early August. While summer lasted it was possible at least to make soup from a few squash and some greens, but she fell into a bleak despair when she wondered what winter would bring. The whole harvest had been handed over to the People's Commissariat. If present conditions continued, they would not escape the fate of rabbits cast out into a frozen wasteland in the dead of winter.

Sick and tired of it all, she drew another long sigh as she reached for the pestle. At that moment she heard somebody approaching.

"Sister, you're up awfully early today."

It was one of her cousins by marriage, walking up at a brisk pace. Intuitively, she knew something had happened and her heart sank with an almost audible thud.

"Sister, heard about your brother-in-law?"

Her cousin whispered, swiftly looking about.

"Hear something? Well, what happened?"

She grabbed her cousin by the hand, greatly agitated.

"Calm down, sister."

"All right, just hurry up and tell me. What happened?"

"Well, he passed away last night."

"Wh-what?"

She felt her heart crumble and fall like rocks in a landslide.

"His wife, too, both gone."

Dizzy, she braced herself on a screen and sat down. It was as if the last thread of hope had disappeared once and for all. No one else was left to die, no one left to wait for.

"Sister, know who wanted to kill them? It was Sunwol, Sunwol."

"Sunwol?"

The name was unfamiliar to her.

"You know the blacksmith, don't you? The Vice-Chairman."

"That bastard's wife?"

"No, not wife, his sister."

"What in the world, that bastard's sister . . . ?"

"God only knows why."

Just then there was a flash in her head.

"Then, she's the bitch who's been holding the two of them all this time?"

"That's right."

She bit her trembling lips and shut her eyes. At last she knew why they had never been able to discover where they had been taken. Her cousin went on, "The bitch killed them in such a dreadful way, who knows what god-forsaken revenge she was after."

"What did you say?" she asked drowsily, slowly reopening her eyes.

"See, that bitch's been keeping the two of them in some hole up on *Sambongsan*, and every day, she takes a couple of hacks at their flesh, little at a time, and still feeds them once a day, so they've been dying real slow, slow . . . ."

"Stop! Enough! Go, now, go!"

She closed her eyes tightly and shivered.

Their flesh carved away with a knife day after day, and still fed, how could they have survived a whole month? What had they done to her? Feeling herself the agony of being butchered like that, she wept and wept. But a still more horrifying thing happened the afternoon of that same day.

She had given strict orders to Tongmyong and his two sisters not to leave the house lest they find out about their parents. Though they were poor pretexts, the boy was told he had studying to do, and the girls were told to stay in because it was too hot that day. Tongmyong snapped back at once that he wasn't going to study communist teaching. Her eyes screwed up to show him she was serious as she reprimanded him. But the boy managed to sneak out anyway and found out how his parents had died, which by then was common knowledge in the village. Like a man would have, he resolved to exact revenge and went to the office of the Women's League. When he encountered Sunwol, he started brandishing a kitchen knife, but he was immediately arrested and shot to death by a North Korean soldier.

She was summoned to the People's Commissariat.

"That bitch sent the boy to do it. That bitch should die, too!"

"Comrade Bae Sunwol! Quiet down!" shouted the Chairman. His face was contorted and his eyes shone fiercely.

"Answer me. Did you send Tongmyong to do it? Yes or no?"

Down on her knees, she looked straight up into the Chairman's eyes. She knew that this moment would decide whether she lived or died. She was obsessed by the thought that she should not die yet.

"No," she said in a clear voice. "If ever I had a notion to use that little knife, I would have done it myself."

Sunwol shrieked again, "What the hell did you say?!"

"Comrade Sunwol, I told you to be quiet!"

The Chairman pounded the desk.

"Are you insane or what? Shut up your goddamn mouth and be still!" spat the Vice-Chairman, the blacksmith, in a harsh voice. She had deliberately avoided looking at him.

"Then, how do you explain the knife Tongmyong had?"

"That's not our knife."

"You mean he stole it somewhere?"

"Looks that way."

There was a temporary silence in the office. She hung her head. She kept thinking she should not die yet.

"All right. You can go now!"

It was the Chairman's voice.

"Comrade Chairman, what kind of sentence is this? That bitch ordered me killed, how in the world can you be on the side of that bitch?"

Sunwol vented her rage.

"Comrade Bae Sunwol! Pay attention and listen carefully. Reckless killing is not our mission. Don't ever forget that your irresponsible actions may damage the revolution or even ruin our cause. From now on take heed when you act. If you ever repeat what you did, there'll be no forgiveness. Don't you know how counter-revolutionary such atrocities are?"

Freed from their clutches, she was completely exhausted. Facing the fact that her life was no more secure than a fly's, she no longer felt sadness or despair. In a brief span of time, she had lost too many relations to allow sane responses to prevail. Life may be vain, but it is tenacious as well. During these horrid episodes she had not experienced any morning sickness, rarely had enough to eat, was tortured by heart-shattering shocks, yet her abdomen kept growing larger and larger.

With the deepening of autumn the skies were yawning wide, the clouds dispersed and the midday sunlight beamed down in gradually slanting rays. Utterly indifferent to the travails of humanity, the seasons slowly rolled by. She worried about how she would care for her two nieces, the only other survivors, through the winter.

Then, one day, she awoke to find the universe entirely changed again. Just as they had appeared, they disappeared under the cover of darkness. The villages and towns in the area were all turned upside down. Those communists who had not managed to escape were seized and the families of the fugitives were all rounded up. The atmosphere was frenzied and out of control.

Upon hearing that the blacksmith's wife was being stoned to death under the dangsan tree, she rushed out of her house. When she reached the place, the woman was already dead.

"Shouldn't have done it, why the wife, what's she ever done? Everyone's gone mad!"

She went back home, mumbling to herself. She held her stomach with both hands. With every shocking event, pains stabbed through her abdomen.

The next day, among the reports she heard was one that Sunwol, along with some male partisans, had been dragged from village to village until they died. Hearing of Sunwol's end, she felt the opposite of what she felt about the death of the blacksmith's wife.

The enraged retribution went on for days. The heated violence slowly cooled down only after the arrival of the South Korean Army and the reestablishment of the police force.

Now she had to endure renewed sorrows. With her body getting heavier, several times she walked up *Sambongsan*. Each time a grave was exhumed, the sound of women weeping spread on the autumn breeze through the valleys, echoing in the distance. The exhumed bodies were already decomposing and were hard to identify. The women trembled, cursing the cruelty that would not even let them retrieve the bodies of their lost men. She had no success in finding the remains of her husband, his father, his brother or her sister-in-law, who had not been the only woman killed.

The number who lost their lives at the hands of the Reds had been thirty-eight in all, most of them members of the Shin clan. The clan council decided to bring down the right number of corpses, selected at random, for a mass funeral. Since they all belonged to the same clan, it did not much matter which family took charge of the ceremonies, and they supposed the dead would have understood, under the circumstances. There was no other way.

Following the funeral, she was sick in bed for several days. Troubled by a high fever, she felt an indescribably strong bond to the life growing inside her. Perhaps it was what had made her cling so desperately to life. True, there were two nieces besides the unborn baby. But toward them she felt only a duty to bring them up, there was no link of common blood. The child inside her was the only trace left of her husband, or was it he himself, reincarnated?

As the winter grew more bitter, she left her two nieces in the care of relatives nearby and went to stay with her own family. It was time to prepare for the birth of her child. On the way, walking through a wind-swept field, she thought of Bae Jomsu. That beast of a man at least had not blabbered about it before departing. She could not stop thinking of the filth she tried to cleanse away each day with saltwater.

About ten days after rejoining her own family she delivered a child, a son. As soon as she heard her mother's shouts mixed with tears, all the suppressed sorrow of her victimization overwhelmed her and she cried out her dead husband's name.

"Heaven'll watch over you for the rest of your life."

Those words from her mother implanted a mysterious strength in her heart. As she sank into a long, deep sleep, she kept telling herself that from then on she had to live with all the strength she could muster.

By the time she awoke, the baby had been washed and was sound asleep. Just as she expected, he was truly the reincarnated image of her husband. His forehead, nose and chin all took after his father. Peering down at the baby, she nearly wept. What pains to preserve that life! What a sorrowful conception it had been! What a pitiable entrance into the world!

Her heart was torn by the thought that her son was destined to grow up never having known his father. As for her, she had gained a new strength by bearing this child, but how could she fill the void when the child felt the void of fatherlessness? She believed she understood what was meant by "fate." It was entirely beyond human will, controlled by heaven alone.

She had to spend the winter with her family. After a month she expressed an intention to leave, but her mother was adamant that she stay. In the Shin household no elders had survived and there was not enough food, not to mention the severe cold, so her mother said. The two nieces were a concern, but in the end neither she nor any of the other relatives could replace their parents, so it would be better just to send them food for the winter, such was her family's opinion. Actually, she was still exhausted mentally and physically, so she decided to follow their advice. She returned in March when the sunlight began softly to shine. Her family wanted her to help dispose of the Shin estate and then move back near them, but she strongly opposed that idea.

She had no right to deal with the property of her husband's family as she pleased. Anyway, she would never leave the land where her husband was buried.

In far off places the war still raged on. She took her nieces back and slowly began rearranging the two practically empty houses. The burden of bringing up three children was now hers to bear.

One day as she cleared her husband's desk she came upon an album of photographs. Quickly, she thumbed through it. The photo was somewhere in the middle and the instant she saw it a shiver ran down her spine. It was a picture of the blacksmith, bare from the waist up. She recalled his bestial odor, and the memory of those horrid nights rushed back upon her as vividly as if she was reliving it all over again. Carefully, she took the picture off the page, afflicted by sudden nausea as she held it between her fingertips.

Before he left for the war, her husband once had shown her his photos. They were mostly of himself in cap and gown at his college graduation. From rows and rows of such pictures, the blacksmith had jumped out. Her husband was going to pass it by without any explanation.

"This is . . ."

She murmured as if asking herself something. She started to ask, but marking the vulgarity of the half-naked figure, was about to swallow her curiosity.

"This? A sad story of my past," her husband said, laughing briefly as if to himself. His words were incomprehensible.

"To make a long story short, it was a hobby I took up to console myself for the frustration of my dreams. Anyway, this received first prize at an exhibition. That's all you need to know."

Saying nothing further, he had moved on to the next page. Out of curiosity, she asked her sister-in-law if he had ever worked as a photographer. Her reaction was an exaggerated gesture.

"What a stupid thing to say! Calling an artist a commercial photographer, what a ridiculous thing to say!"

She was perplexed as her sister-in-law kept on giggling, apparently greatly amused. Her response, with its affected air of profundity, revealed something she had never dreamt about her husband. He had been compelled to abandon his ambition of becoming a painter because of his father's strong opposition. His father had even made a scene by traveling to Japan to see his son, who in the end changed his major to history. But, unable to renounce completely his dream of being an artist, he got a camera for himself. It was not cheap, but to distract his son from painting, his father had little choice. With that camera, her husband had never taken even one picture of family members.

Photography was an art, he declared, so he was not about to waste film on just anyone. During vacations when he came back home with his camera, the family still had to fetch a photographer from town if they wanted pictures taken at family events. Nobody could bend her husband's stubbornness. And, incredibly enough, the pictures he did take were no more than a farmer carrying a shitbucket, or an old man with a long pipe in his teeth, drooling as he slept in the shadow of a tree, or roosters fighting in the marketplace with feathers all ruffled, or a small boy leading an ox along a country road at dusk, and so on. The blacksmith picture was one of those. Judging from the fact that such a piece of trash won the top prize at some contest, her sister-in-law scoffed, the photographer and the judge both must have had poor eyesight.

She wrapped the picture of the blacksmith in a piece of white paper. Then she opened a drawer in the dresser and placed it in the bottom.

She forced herself to adapt to farm work. With four mouths to feed, she had nothing to rely on except the land. The other property had all been lost, but the land itself came back to her. Even their cruelty could not destroy it. She had to borrow others' hands for the rice cultivation, but she tried to teach herself all she could about farming. Even when she hired labor to help out, she thought it would be easier to understand their pains if she herself knew more, and then she wouldn't be as likely to be cheated, either.

Much of the field work she did with her own hands, both to save the cost of hiring help and to keep from having too much time alone. To be lonely with nothing to do was the most dreadful thing for her. At such times, without exception, horrible memories came to haunt her. Often, on nights when she lay down to sleep without having worked hard during the day, she was tormented by nightmares.

She sought salvation by immersing herself in work. She battled the scalding sun and wrestled with the soil. She poured her soul into the crops as if they were her own offspring and devoted herself to the fields with a sense of destiny. Her fair face developed flaws from the heat and wind, and her hands and feet grew coarse and ugly with the scars and callouses of constant toil.

Her tenacious working astonished the people around her. They had imagined she would soon tire of the labor, and some even said she was not working at all but merely venting her rancor. She worked on without respite until the harvest was in. On winter nights, she never climbed down off the loom until very late. Watching the strands of hemp woven together on the woof and warp of the loom, at last producing a sheet of cloth, she learned the way of human life. She firmly believed her backbreaking work would bear fruit one day in the achievements of her young son, Changyu.

Her sister, while paying her a visit one day, said in a voice on the edge of tears,

"Oh, dear sister, look at yourself. Only twenty-four years old, and already you're an old hag."

"What a thing to say. If I don't become a hag, maybe I'll rise to be a high government official?"

"That's not what I meant, I mean you should live a more comfortable life. This is no way for a woman to live."

"Wake up. Since when am I a woman? Now I'm the head of a family with three little ones."

"Still, things needn't be so painful. I mean, leave the hard work to the servants."

"I don't want a comfortable life anymore. Do you know who died in the war? Those who lived comfortable lives and let their servants do all the work. Those working bastards turned around and poked us with spears like they'd been slaves and never even been paid. Heaven strike them dead, why'd they suddenly make every well-off soul a mortal enemy?!"

"Sister, settle down. I must've said something wrong, calm down."

His sister shook her with both hands. She was so enraged her face was white as a sheet and her breathing was galloping out of control. Whenever the topic came up, her heart began pounding and she started panting for air. She tried to control herself but just couldn't and was beside herself.

Her son Changyu grew without any illness and reached his first birthday. She took out the grain she'd been stockpiling since the previous autumn and made a big platter of ricecakes to share with all the neighbors. She knew only too well how scarce rice was in those times, but she felt she had no other choice. It was the only thing she could do for her son, and she was obsessed with the notion that following that tradition was the only sure way to give him a promising future.

Spring came and the field work began all over again. About then she felt an odd change in her body. Even while absorbed in her work, all at once she would recall an incident from the past, which set rolling a whole chain of memories and made her heart pound. At such times, she grew short of breath, feeling suffocated as though her heart might explode. After these attacks, her body would be soaked in a cold sweat and all her strength drained away. She kept telling herself the affliction was only in her mind and tried hard to repress the morbid memories. But it was no use, and again and again her intention was betrayed as those haunting memories kept coming back.

On the second anniversary of her husband's death, she rinsed her son's hair in saltwater and had him bow at the sacrificial altar. Of course, she had done the same thing the year before, too, sitting before the ceremonial table with her son in her arms. She washed her own hair with saltwater, too, intending to cleanse the filth and sins of the past before meeting the spirit of her husband.

"Now, Changyu, let's bow to your father."

Holding the child, who could barely walk, she helped him bow twice, as tears began to flood. Changyu had learned to say "Mama" but "Papa" was totally foreign to him.

"Dear, your son already can bow. Please accept his bow. How do you like him? He looks just like you, doesn't he? Don't worry, I'll bring him up a proud man, even if it does me in."

She carried on interminable one-sided conversations with her husband. While he lived she had felt a great distance between them, but now that he had crossed over to the other side she felt no distance at all, possibly because no responses were to be expected from him.

Autumn came and another year was about to slip away. There was talk of her sister marrying one of her neighbors. It was no mere coincidence, for her father had her situation in mind when he started the matchmaking arrangements. After about a month of deliberations on both sides, the betrothal was fixed.

"You two help each other in this life. There's an old saying that when you grind rice in a mortar, the work's easier if somebody nods along with you."

So Father had said when he dropped by on the way to his would-be in-laws' house. She hid her hardened hands in the hemp kerchief she used to tie her hair back, and tears welled up in her eyes. Her sister's wedding went forward late that autumn, and at that time she moved close by.

Sitting at the loom, she often groaned and grasped her stomach as her affliction of shortness of breath worsened as time went by.

"Sister, when did you start having those attacks?" her sister asked when she dropped by one day and was surprised to see her in pain.

"It's nothing . . ."

She was so out of breath she could barely speak.

"It's no minor complaint. It's the very sickness, the burning heart, suffered by those who've been wronged too often, they fall stricken like that. Of all illnesses, it's the worst, like fits. Nobody can see it, no medicine can cure it, the only way to overcome it is in your own mind. Forget it all, everything, so you can start a new life with a new mind. That's the only cure."

Her sister was right. But this "mind," how can it be controlled when you can't even locate it? The unfathomable mind, doesn't it have a life of its own?

The war ended the following summer. She was numb at the news. To one whose burning heart worsened with each passing day, the news brought no joy or pleasure. A few days later, she prepared a sacrificial offering for the third anniversary of her husband's death and washed her own and her son's hair in saltwater.

One day her nieces had a sports festival at school. She went to the market for the first time in a long while to get some things for them. She could feel that the war was really over from the general air in the marketplace. The vendors looked full of life and people wore vibrant expressions.

She was about to head home after finishing her shopping when her sister said, "Sister, do you know who that beggar is over there?"

She turned to see who her sister was pointing at. It was a boy in rags chewing what looked like a cuttlefish tentacle. Even at first glance he seemed dull-witted.

"Do you recognize him?" her sister again asked.

Shaking her head she felt instinctively that the boy must have something to do with her, else her sister wouldn't have bothered to pose such questions. Soon that feeling took on an ominous quality, and her heart started pounding fiercely.

"Don't be so surprised, it's the blacksmith's son."

"What!" She staggered, bringing her hands to her forehead.

"Sister, calm down now."

Trying to focus her thinking, she looked again at the boy.

"No wonder you're shocked. But if the blacksmith himself ever shows up alive, the shock'll kill you before you can take revenge. Anyhow, he doesn't know a thing, an idiot, they say. He saw his mother get stoned to death under the dangsan tree. Somehow he was spared, but after seeing his mother killed that way, he had some kind of fit and has been an idiot ever since."

"How old was he then?"

"Maybe five or so."

Five years old . . . she gulped.

"By the way, how'd you come to know so much about it?"

"Everybody's heard the story, except you, buried in your work on the farm and in the house. You don't even know what's been happening under your nose. You really should get out once in a while, you know."

Her heart grew heavy. What had the little thing ever done to deserve this? She shook her head again and again to dispel the image of the blacksmith's wife tied to the dangsan tree, blood all over her. Could the blacksmith possibly . . . She had been about to speak but stopped herself short. The thought flashed through her head that Bae Jomsu might know his son was still alive. Even after their flight into the mountains, there had been some signs that some of them had returned to the village a few times.

On her rare forays into the marketplace, she went out of her way to avoid the blacksmith's son. For, despite the compassion she felt for the boy, a lump of fire still burned in her heart.

With the summer heat the searing affliction to her heart grew considerably worse. Then, as cool winds came, it gradually subsided. It was like a terrible boil arising in the summer which disappears with the approach of cooler weather.

A few months had passed since the sixth anniversary of her husband's death when her sister brought the most unexpected and incredible news, casting it before her with a loud thump.

"Sister, take care not to be shocked. Please, promise me you won't be too surprised."

Her sister tried to calm her in advance, having little faith in her terribly weakened heart.

"All right, just tell me, what is it?"

Though she said this, her heart was already beginning to race. From her sister's grave expression and the precautions, she sensed it had to be something very unusual.

"I'm telling you this only because I think you ought to know . . ."

"You'll kill me with all these warnings," said she, growing impatient.

"All right. I'm telling you now. The thing is, the blacksmith is alive."

After her sister said it all in one gulp, she shrieked,

"Whaaat?!"

Just then she felt faint and dizzy as her breathing was cut short.

"Sister, get a hold on yourself. I told you again and again not to be too surprised."

Her sister supported her with one hand under her shoulder, and with the other rubbed her back, half crying.

"Where is the bastard? Tell me at once, where?"

She was gasping for air.

"Well, I don't know where he is now, but not long ago he was seen in some tavern over in Toksongri, they say. The owner of the place is an outsider, so he didn't know who the bastard was, and besides he wore glasses and a western suit. Even with those, our neighbor would've recognized him right off except the bean-size mole under his left eye was gone, so he wondered if it could really be him. Still, on his way home, the more he thought about it the surer he was that it had to be Bae Jomsu, the blacksmith. Our neighbor realized his mistake and hurried on back to the tavern to try and catch him."

"And then?!"

She was pale and trembling.

"Well, when he got back, the bastard had already disappeared."

"Where to?"

"Well, he'd been asking the owner a thousand questions, but the man just kept saying he didn't know where he'd gone after he walked out the door. So he ran out and searched all over, but by then it was dark and he lost him."

"The fool, who was the oaf who caught sight of him anyway?"

Her gaping eyes were bloodshot and her voice shrill.

"It passed so many mouths . . . I don't know exactly who saw him . . ."

Her sister could not even finish her mumbling.

"No! Must be some mistake! That bastard died long ago! Died long ago!"

She howled, trembling.

Her sister gazed at her with fear and wonder. It wasn't clear whether her elder sister really wished the blacksmith was dead or wanted him to be alive so she could kill him with her own hands. The younger sister hesitated to go on, but decided to tell it all.

"That the bastard lives is a fact," her sister said firmly, as if nailing it down.

"What're you talking about?" she asked lethargically, as if the excitement had spent her energy.

"Apart from the bastard making endless inquiries about what happened after the war, the next morning his son, the idiot beggar in the marketplace, was wearing a brand new pair of shoes. Nobody around here bought shoes for the idiot, so who could've done it but that bastard Bae?"

"What devilish nonsense is that? If it surely was him, how on earth could he only buy a pair of shoes for his son and not take him?"

She shook her head, her lips contorted in a skeptical sneer.

As if to awaken her, her sister raised her voice, saying, "Sister, that's just why it had to be that bastard Bae! Listen, now. Looking for his own whelp, he found an idiot, not remembering what happened to his mother, not even recognizing his own father. Bae figured it'd be hopeless to bring him up like a normal person, so he just gave him a pair of shoes and took off."

"But how . . . ?"

"That 'but how' fools you too easily, don't you know? You see, with a cruel heart like his, he could've done the same thing a dozen times over."

All at once she felt a tension pressing her whole being. Bae Jomsu was a man, not a woman. And among men, he was merciless, cold-blooded. She couldn't blindly trust the man who claimed to have seen Bae, but she couldn't ignore his words entirely, either. There must have been some cause for him to take the stranger for the blacksmith Bae Jomsu. And it could not be overlooked that the idiot, who was lucky if he begged three meals a day, overnight turned up in new shoes. Who else was likely to buy shoes for him?

The times were so hard most children went to school barefoot in summer, and even adults had their shoes resoled again and again before buying a new pair.

She hoped the blacksmith was still alive so she could take revenge on him. But so far it had been merely a vague longing stemming from a lifetime of resentment and rancor. Now that it seemed likely he actually was alive somewhere, she felt off-balance, confused. Oddly, fear and hatred oppressed her with equal force. And like living parasites, they penetrated into every recess of her body, sometimes leaping right before her eyes in the form of an abominable monster.

Unlike before, after that she frequently encountered the blacksmith in her dreams. Gradually, she became convinced that he must indeed be alive somewhere out there. And the affliction searing her heart became graver with each passing day.

4

Ten years passed before Changyu tracked down the blacksmith. To be more precise, nine years and three months after his mother died, Bae Jomsu in the flesh miraculously materialized one day right in front of Changyu's eyes. On that day he had been heading into the gate at the entrance of Sun Corporation, carrying the new catalogue of books he was selling on the installment plan.

"Hey, Mr. Shin, come on over here, right away!"

The guard recognized him at once and beckoned him over.

"How are you, Chief? Something going on?"

Changyu quickly strode toward the head guard, wearing the subservient expression and empty smile that had become second nature to him.

"Curfew time. Go over there and stay inside for a while," said the guard pompously, adjusting his gold-trimmed cap. It was a haughtiness reserved for occasions when he had some special assignment.

"Visit from some big shot?"

To puff up the guard's self-importance, he made this inquiry without any real curiosity.

"Yes, a big shot all right. Hurry on over there."

He put an unnecessary emphasis on his words, without even glancing at Changyu, who swiftly walked into the security guards' office, thinking he'd have to dole out some cigarette money today, too. To address this guard as "Chief" had been his own idea. The shallowness of the human mind was something to behold, and his obsequious use of that inflated title was surprisingly effective. Such tactics of salesmanship were particularly useful with people of humble occupations. As drivers became "chauffeurs" the term "driver" seemed disreputable; once bus girls started being called "conductresses" the old "bus girl" took on a scornful tinge; and when charwomen became "house maids" the old label quickly became taboo.

The calling of guard, or "gatekeeper" in the vernacular, was not a vocation of which one could be overly proud. They were not the only ones who found it demeaning, but they did seem to hate to be addressed as "Mr. Gatekeeper" or simply "Mister" as much as a maid hated to be called a "charwoman." So, Changyu quickly transformed "head guard" into "Chief," calling to mind a white-collar "section chief." The results had been even better than anticipated.

The richest fishing grounds for selling books on the installment plan, all things considered, were the big corporations where staff was paid well and bonuses were frequent. Naturally, those waters were the hardest to enter. Without exception, at the main gate you ran up against outrageously uniformed so-called guards who shooed you away. Getting access turned entirely on one's aptitude in making allies of the guards. Make your face familiar, offer them cigarettes, bewail misfortunes together with them, buy them Chinese noodles, share a few glasses of liquor, and then, when they can relate to you on the human level, present them with a free set of books for their children and pass some cash under the table on the pretext of buying cigarettes. Then the precious fishing ground will be yours. Meantime, the head guard is revered as a section chief, and with proper indulgence for the other guards, eventually they all will entertain an illusion that the guards' office has become a management bureau of some kind.

Until such a friendly alliance can be formed, patience is needed to endure the unavoidable transitional period, which sometimes takes months. Then, even after the right relations have been established, one must not forget to keep slipping them some pocket money. The key to the strategy is to have them unconsciously waiting for you. Once they're habituated, their help knows no bounds. Not only will there arise an unspoken understanding that no other book salesmen will be admitted, but they may promote sales by encouraging purchases by female clerks with whom they are friendly. Consolidate your foundations in this way with a few big corporations and office buildings, and making money becomes as easy as floating on dry land.

Sun Corporation was one of the companies Changyu had cultivated by such methods. Nobody had taught him the ropes, of course. Through four years of struggles to earn a living as a book salesman he had developed these tactics on his own.

"It's up!" said one of the guards, slamming the phone receiver down, and the others hurriedly picked up their caps and rushed outside.

Changyu idly watched the three guards making absurdly frenetic gestures as they stood at the main entrance to the building on the marble floor, which was polished so perfectly that even licking it wouldn't turn up a speck of dust. The glistening marble and the busy gestures of the guards . . . suddenly Changyu glimpsed weary shadows. How many months of their pay would it take to buy the marble floor? What sort of men could make those guards so keyed up and eager to please? Absorbed in such ruminations, Changyu felt the same awe and remoteness he always felt when visiting grand edifices.

According to the head guard's orders, two men opened the main doors all the way outward and then snapped to attention at each door. The head guard stood at attention in front of the elevator. They all acted like soldiers. Soon the elevator doors parted. As two men walked out, the guard made a military salute and shouted out something briefly. The two men completely ignored him, crossed the front lobby and then stopped in its center. They talked for a moment about something, then laughed aloud.

"My God . . . !"

As he watched the two men, Changyu sprang up in spite of himself.

"That, that is Bae, Bae . . . ."

His eyes gaped and his whole body grew rigid.

Older, glasses, no mole under the left eye, but there could be no doubt. It was the blacksmith, Bae Jomsu, nobody else but the bastard in the photograph.

The two men shook hands, then one walked out through the door and the other turned back. Changyu watched all their motions, but he could see nothing but the aged face of Bae Jomsu.

"What is it, not feeling well?" asked the head guard as he removed his cap.

"No, sir, just . . ."

Changyu did his best to hide his emotions.

"Don't 'no, sir' me. Your face is the color of chalk. Sure you didn't have an attack of indigestion or something?"

"No. Dizzy for a moment, that's all. Now, have a cigarette."

Changyu was evasive and quickly took out a pack of cigarettes.

"Take it easy, now, money's not everything. Health comes first, you know."

The guard gently reproved him, accepting a cigarette.

"Chief, can't argue with you. After all, money is for living, right?"

To conceal his feelings, Changyu kept up with the small talk.

"Sure, sure. I like you because you catch on right away to what an old man like me says."

The guard smiled contentedly and savored the smoke. Changyu took a deep drag and sat back down in his seat.

"Chief, that VIP a while ago, what kind of business is he in?"

"Him? Why do you ask? They're all loaded, money piled high, they live in a different world."

"The hell with money, what can you do with money? He was nothing but wrinkles."

Changyu was getting impatient but tried not to hurry the chief guard.

"Right you are, if there's one thing neither our president nor President Hwang of Manmul Industrial can't control, it's old age. However rich you are, money can't buy youth. If there's one thing fair in this world, that's it, I say."

The guard's laughter didn't reach Changyu's ears. Manmul Industrial Company, Hwang . . . he was confused. The last name was not Bae, but Hwang. Could he have been mistaken? He resisted an unwelcome disappointment.

"What line of business is he in to make so much money?"

"Machine tools or something like that."

Machine . . . inside Changyu's head "machine" was set side by side with "blacksmith."

"Where's the company?"

"Why, plan to try opening a new channel to that company, too?"

The guard feigned a dirty look, then grinned knowingly.

"Sure, I would if I could."

Changyu responded in the same mood.

"Talking's thirsty business."

"All right, I'll buy you a drink."

"Just kidding. I heard it's somewhere on Toegyero, maybe the fourth block."

Changyu was about to ask for the full name but thought twice. He'd find that out soon enough in any case. He left Sun Corporation after slipping the guard more than the usual amount. From there he went straight to Manmul Industrial. The building was easily found, but he had to wait three hours to get a closer look at the president's face when he left the office. It certainly was the blacksmith Bae Jomsu.

That night, Changyu barely slept at all. After ten years of fruitless searching, now that he had Bae Jomsu right under his nose, he felt strangely confused. Somehow he had known Bae was still alive through all those years of pursuit, but now, confronted with his irrefutable existence, Changyu was unable to come to grips with it. Perhaps it was because Bae Jomsu had turned out to be a successful businessman of such formidable status. This perplexed him to no end.

It was not so much that the man's astronomical wealth scared him, but he was puzzled at how someone with a past like Bae's not only survived but achieved such enviable success. In other words, he felt terror at the cunning resourcefulness of a man capable of such things. The fear provoked in him a sense of foreboding that this was no one to be dealt with rashly. Thus, the manner of confronting Bae presented Changyu with a complicated problem. As he wandered in search of the man, he had never gone so far as to contrive any specific plan for dealing with him. He had just been sure that once he tracked him he would, by whatever means, assure that he did not survive.

Changyu passed the night reflecting on his father's absurd death, on his mother's awful memories and her unslaked thirst for revenge, and on the exhausting past ten years of his own life.

He had started selling books on the installment plan back in his college days. Without his mother's knowledge, he was attending night classes. To attend a university on the pittance his mother earned from the small farm was out of the question, and anyway, for one who had always found life empty, a university education bore no special meaning for Changyu. At first he had only been curious to find out what "university studies" were all about, so he'd had no misgivings about settling for night school. During the days, he sold books.

As a source of income, the job was not so bad. After all, earning money usually forces one to give up being squeamish, so there is no need to exaggerate the hardship. The money was never abundant but it covered his tuition and living expenses. Once his mother died, that part-time work took on an added significance by furnishing the means of fulfilling her last request. What other job would've given him better opportunities to meet people from all walks of life?

Book sales helped him get a college diploma and fed him through all those years. After four years of selling day in and day out, Changyu became a veteran salesman. Right after graduation, he moved down to Pusan to join a sales team. Until then he had been scouring Seoul looking for Bae Jomsu without any success. Innumerable times he'd felt his heart sink at the sight of someone who looked like Bae but turned out not to be him.

The reason he went to Pusan was not because it's the second biggest city in Korea. He was aiming to take the psychology of the criminal into account. He thought it unlikely that with his past and need for anonymity, Bae would remain near his home in Cholla province. It seemed likely that he would have headed to the opposite end of the country, such as to Kyongsang or Kangwon provinces.

So, Changyu spent the next six months in Pusan and its environs, another six months in Taegu, six more months in Kangneung and Sokcho up in Kangwon province, and a year in Kwangju and Chonju back down in Cholla. He spent another year around Chungch'ong province, but Bae Jomsu could not be found.

After four years of roaming the country he returned to Seoul. Bae Jomsu had not been found, but during this period he had managed to save up a tidy sum of money. Changyu always felt a late autumn chill in life itself, and he had never fancied the mundane pleasures of drinking, gambling or womanizing. His acquaintances looked on him as a boring conformist, but his style of life allowed him to save quite a bit.

From the very next day, Changyu started working on the guards at Manmul Industrial. He planned to expedite the fall of the guards into his confidence by throwing around more money than usual. So quickly and effortlessly did they succumb to his blandishments that he found himself bemoaning how integrity never withstands the onslaught of money. Before ten days had passed, he was freely mixing with the guards, and a fortnight later he could mine information in as much detail as he needed.

The president's home address, his family relations, the scale of the business, his personality, the atmosphere in his office, and even the women he flirted with soon were disclosed. Still, there was one thing the guards didn't know—the past of Bae Jomsu, or rather Hwang Bokman. As far as they knew, their president was a descendant of noble ancestors and had come South from Hwanghae province during the Korean War. To them he was the most venerable man on the whole planet.

Even on the family register, a copy of which Changyu got from the district office, the man had listed Hwanghae province as his birthplace. His real name had evaporated into thin air, just like the mole under his left eye. The metamorphosis had been perfect. Discovering this impeccability in Bae Jomsu's nature, Changyu felt fear and bewilderment. The man's resourcefulness had something in common with the mercilessness of the murders he had committed. Here was a person who, after killing so many, could calmly engineer such a total transformation to survive. Perhaps the mass slaughter had been possible precisely because he felt nothing outside of his own existence.

Finally, Changyu began to plan step by step how he would dispose of Bae Jomsu.

He was a traitor and killer of thirty-eight men, and now he lived under a false identity. Those were his crimes. Changyu decided to ignore the forged identification and the treason, focusing on the murders instead. He settled on the simple idea that Bae Jomsu had already lived too long.

He had lived on almost thirty years since murdering those thirty-eight people. His depriving thirty-eight people of thirty years each meant he had extinguished one thousand one hundred and forty years of life. Even if their life expectancy was only twenty years on average, it still came to seven hundred and sixty years of human life. There was no denying that he had shamelessly survived them. How could he protest being sent before the thirty-eight wronged, vengeful spirits awaiting his atonement? In their presence, he had no right to request that his own life be spared.

Changyu resolved to dispatch him to the other world as quickly as possible, to unshoulder his own heavy burden. Perhaps, he told himself, all these years he'd been living someone else's life. Until the age of thirty, he'd lived in the shadow of the war, but he meant to escape that cold, damp darkness. He would live a life of his own, in the new light, creating his own memories and tracing the path of his own life.

Changyu resolved that the matter definitely would be handled from a distance, by remote control. A hasty confrontation or reckless accusation might bungle it. A clumsy investigator exposes himself to being murdered by the fugitive under pursuit.

The preparations were in place once he learned all he needed about Bae's eldest son. Changyu had mixed feelings at discovering that the son had become a university lecturer at an early age. A blacksmith guilty of treason has a son who is a scholar, but the son of the teacher murdered at the traitor's hands has turned out to be a peddler of books. If the object of communism is to indiscriminately liquidate all the rich and the privileged, the blacksmith's position had been completely upturned. What would Bae Jomsu say now if fanatics went after him with knives in the name of communism? Bae Jomsu's communism had been just a spontaneous urge to kill, only senseless barbarity wrapped in a glossy package.

Such superficiality and simple-mindedness was dangerous and degrading. Changyu despised Bae's brazenness and the perfection of his metamorphosis, but he felt no envy at the vast wealth he had amassed. Neither did he feel any antagonism at the ironic twist of fate that presented Bae's son as an university lecturer and himself as a mere peddler. His sentiments, it's true, were not free of a tension, but it was of a kind that could be contained strictly between Bae Jomsu and himself. Bae's eldest son was not at fault and in no way responsible. If contact between the son and himself was necessary, it would be just destiny, nothing more. Each of them were merely playing out the preordained roles into which they had been born.

Of course, Changyu thought over and over again what he would do to Bae Jomsu. He felt no guilt about such plotting. He thought of Bae's children as well. The three of them would lose their father—but how many children had been deprived of their fathers by Bae? Bae's children were already grown, anyway, unlike some of the children left alone thanks to him.

He considered collecting all the evidence and relying on the law for help. But that would mean starting a new war. Apart from entangling himself, what would happen to Bae's children after their father's ruin? Witnessing the exhumation of their father's past in all its corrupt details . . . Changyu really had no desire to see that happen. It all had taken place before their birth. It should be resolved among those directly involved.

Finally, Changyu made a decision to send Bae Jomsu alone to meet the spirits. And he decided to reveal everything only to his eldest son, not to other relatives. Though the son was a Hwang and not a Bae, still he felt the son ought to know the truth about his father.

Changyu planned to execute everything over the telephone. It was the only way to deal with Bae without confronting him in person. After hearing of his chronic high blood pressure and affliction with diabetes, the telephone seemed enough to send him on his way to the other world.

The plan was slowly and steadily to drive Bae toward death by nightly phone calls. Facing prosecution for treason, murder and forgery, what choice did he have but to listen to the calls? Could he complain to the police? That'd be like leaping into a fire holding a gasoline canister. Help from his family was also impossible. He could only fight in solitude, a tiger awakened to find himself already trapped in a cage. It would be a slow struggle. It had taken ten years to find him. He would allow ten months for a leisurely demise.

Changyu made his first call to President Bae Jomsu, or rather President Hwang Bokman of Manmul Industrial, at the close of office hours. As though to buttress his will to fight, as he dialed he said aloud, "Bae Jomsu, you've lived too long."

The ringing registered, he delivered the prepared lies to the secretary, and instantly the gruff voice of President Hwang Bokman flowed into his ear. He quickly drew a deep breath. Then, trying to control his feelings, he slowly opened his mouth and said, "How do you do, Mr. Bae Jomsu?"

Human Pagoda

1

As soon as he arrived at the hospital Hyongmin was escorted to the Emergency Room. Upon seeing the bright red "Emergency" sign against a cold white acrylic background, his nose was filled with the stench of death. It was more riveting than the gloomy chill one feels in passing a mortician's shop with coffins stacked up high in anticipation of this and that death. It was no surprise that his father had ended up in the emergency room. That much he had foreseen, and now, he had a premonition of having to send his father down the road of no return.

Now, his father seemed like a tiny sparrow with a pellet in its heart. The chances of recovery were almost nil. This was something apart from the prognosis of the physician. A doctor could observe only physical symptoms, but Hyongmin could see within his father's soul. To call what his father had experienced a "shock" was hardly adequate. Not even prefacing it with emphatic adjectives such as "great" or "enormous" could begin to capture it. The incident had been like being struck by a bullet that pierced deep into his heart. No matter how strong his father's will, never again would he breathe easily after this mortal blow.

"Don't be too alarmed. This is how unconscious patients usually look," said Father's doctor, Dr. Chun, pushing open the door to the Emergency Room. Hyongmin answered with a glance. Inside the spacious emergency ward, there were many patients' beds scattered about, separated by portable green canvas screens. His father was lying in a corner opposite the entrance, away from the area of most hectic traffic.

All Hyongmin could do was stare down at him. His lifeless form evoked in Hyongmin a despairing compassion for the vulnerability of human life. Tubes were stuck in his nostrils and the needles in his arms looked awful. Two large intravenous solution bottles hanging upside down over the bed, an oxygen tank the size of a man, and a strangely emaciated appearance that had quickly surfaced in the past several days—all these plainly bespoke the serious nature of his father's condition.

Hyongmin locked his eyes shut, opened them again, then strenuously closed his eyes and squinted once more. His father's body seemed to be sinking into the bed, never before had he seemed so diminutive. Even if the form was utterly limp because of unconsciousness, what he witnessed seemed unbelievable. From the time he was a boy until only a few days before, his father had always been an image of power and strength. But now, he told himself, Father may leave us forever without emerging from his present state.

"Let's go now," said Dr. Chun, bringing Hyongmin back to reality.

Ominous presentiments again engulfed Hyongmin. Thirty-eight vindictive spirits, crying out for revenge. Those ghosts already might be dragging his father's soul into the other world. This chilling notion gave Hyongmin goosebumps all over.

Even granting it had happened long ago at a time when many boiled with rage, Hyongmin still found it hard to identify this pathetic old man already slipping under the dense shadow of death with the murderer of thirty-eight people. But it was a fact, and the agonized face of his comatose father proved it was true.

"Now, let's go."

Dr. Chun tugged at Hyongmin's sleeve. Hyongmin let his head hang and shut his eyes. Turning away from his father he exhaled, his breath rushing out in choppy waves. It was less a breath than a sob, a vomiting of the bile of sorrow.

"No need to abandon all hope yet."

Dr. Chun had already rehearsed the condolences. But to Hyongmin the remark was hollow. His father's soul had been mortified before his body began to collapse. As long as Dr. Chun knew nothing of the real cause, his treatment could never succeed. And, even if he was told of the cause, what could he do? He was merely a physician trained to cure bodily ills, he had no miraculous power to undo past crimes.

Dr. Chun probably thought the sudden breakdown was the culmination of slowly developing symptoms. If he knew the real origin of Father's affliction—the brutal massacre thirty years ago when he was an ardent communist, then the rise to his present status based on a metamorphosis of identity and history—how could he admonish Father to stop worrying so much? Maybe he would just confess his incapacity to be of any help.

"We've taken more X-rays, so let's wait for the results. Your father is basically a healthy man, and awfully strong-willed, so don't worry yourself too much."

Hyongmin had not inquired about his father's condition, but Dr. Chun, seemingly impatient to be consulted, offered his opinion as they walked along the hospital corridor. He had spoken not only as a medical doctor but to demonstrate human concern, but Hyongmin had nothing to say, no matter how hard he tried to open his mouth. He was no longer like those naive patients who desperately want to keep faith in the omnipotence of their doctors. The thought haunted him that his father may already have surrendered the last thread of his will to live and soon would embark on the journey of no return without further ado. That was why Dr. Chun's genuine concern elicited no gratitude, and why he could not blindly rely on the physician.

"These past few days, your father's shown signs of suffering from some mental anguish. Do you, by any chance, know what it's all about?"

Hyongmin, as if by reflex, glared straight into Dr. Chun's eyes. At the same time, he tried to collect his wits in the wake of the great shock that had fractured them. Upon hearing Dr. Chun's opening phrases, his mind had instantly started shattering into thousands of pieces. In panic, he wondered how the doctor could have found out. Then, however, the last part of the doctor's question, asking whether Hyongmin knew the source, offered a miraculous escape.

"If I'd forced him to enter the hospital sooner, his condition might not have deteriorated this far. For your family's sake, I'm sorry I gave in to his stubbornness."

Dr. Chun, who had been their family doctor for more than ten years, really did feel sorry about the situation. Hyongmin was genuinely grateful for his sense of responsibility and his well-meaning concern.

"You really have no reason to apologize . . ." was all Hyongmin could manage to say, releasing a lengthy sigh as he spoke. Due to the tension he felt a moment before, his heart was still oppressed. He was surprised at himself, reflecting upon his hypersensitivity at the prospect of a disclosure of the facts. It was instinctual, like something brushing against a bug's antennae, a defensive response totally unrelated to his rational capacities. He realized his dread was far graver than he thought.

In actuality, it was all too dreadful to bear. Since his father's history had become crystal clear, he had been terrified of the stranger whose unseen presence seemed to keep every move he made under close surveillance. That strange fellow who had with three nocturnal calls put his father into a coma, and who had dispatched him to his father's birthplace to excavate his father's past crimes in minute detail, Hyongmin dreaded what he might do next. Inevitably night would fall, and without fail he would be calling again. Hyongmin feared that call, and feared to think what turns his father's condition might take. And what would happen to his family when the crimes eventually were all brought to light, of that he dared not allow himself to think.

"How did he look to you?" asked his mother as he walked into the relatives' waiting room adjoining the emergency ward. She sought his opinion as if he could somehow help. He looked silently into his mother's eyes. They were tearful, clouded with a thick grey fog of anguish and uneasiness. From her emanated the loneliness of a woman forced to confront her own helplessness in the face of the imminent loss of her husband. The agonizing grief of his mother's soul passed directly into Hyongmin's heart. He could say nothing. Maybe she didn't expect any remark from him. Then, her eyes suddenly burned with hatred and she said,

"Dear, you may not know it, but somebody's driven your father into this state. We've got to find out who the bastard is who's been phoning your father every night."

"That's not what matters now, Father's recovery is the important thing," Hyongmin said hurriedly, trying to block her from proceeding further. She wanted to tell her eldest son everything that had happened. First, she wanted to report what had precipitated his father's decline, which she thought he couldn't know about since he no longer lived in the same house. Thus she hoped to lighten her burden of anguish by sharing with her son what she had been shouldering alone.

In fact, however, it was she who knew nothing about the matter. All she could reveal, all she knew, was that some stranger had been torturing her husband with nightly phone calls. She had not the slightest idea who he was or why he was telephoning. She had never imagined that the stranger had followed each call with another to Hyongmin.

"No, dear. Each night that bastard threatened your father with some kind of blackmail. I'm sure that was it. We've got to find him and have the police arrest him for blackmail."

Amazingly, his mother was already leaning in the direction of revenge. He silently reminded himself that the police would not be likely to end up on his family's side.

"Settle down, Mother. At this point, what's more important, do you think? To track down somebody who hasn't left a clue, or to care for Father? Which side are you on, anyway?"

Hyongmin spoke coldly in a measured voice, despite the sympathy he felt for his mother.

On the verge of weeping, she said, "God, what can we do now?" Then she collapsed back into her chair, drained and pathetic looking. His mother looked more vulnerable than he had ever seen her, just as debilitated as his father had become, sinking into his bed. Like a deadly cancer slowly spreading, the stranger's assault had already struck deep inside his family and started its disintegration.

As time passed, the fissures would widen until the decomposition was complete. Watching his family fall to pieces, collapsing a bit at a time,

Hyongmin felt completely frustrated, again and again, without recourse in the face of undefiable attacks. For about an hour he waited in a vacant state of mind. Only when a nurse brought a message that Dr. Chun wanted to speak with him did he regain alertness.

"What now?" Mother asked the nurse in a rush, her expression exhibiting a mixture of fright and stress.

"I don't know the details," said the nurse dryly as she exited from the room. Hyongmin felt his mother's glance on his cheek, but disregarded it and followed the nurse.

"Nothing wrong with his brain!" said Dr. Chun brightly, like someone about to shake your hand.

"Thank God!" Mother exclaimed with a heartfelt cry, pressing both hands to her breast.

"At first we suspected the x-ray wasn't exposed right. But the second picture came out the same. Looks like his coma is only temporary, a result of shock. You can stop worrying for now." Dr. Chun spoke confidently.

"Thank you, doctor. Thank you, doctor."

As if praying to Buddha, his mother pressed her hands together and bowed deeply again and again.

"Oh, no, it's uncalled for. It's not my doing, it's entirely good fortune in favor of the president."

So protested Dr. Chun, but he seemed to relish being appreciated by his patient's family as a capable doctor.

Hyongmin stood silently. He couldn't help being dubious about the recovery anticipated by the physician. Inside, he was tormented by the thought that even if his father recovered, he would soon suffer another stroke and be dragged again into a coma. The man's nightly calls would resume, and Father again would be strangled by an unseen noose.

"Don't you think your father has lived too long?"

That was what the stranger had said, as if to underscore his goal. Those sluggish yet crisp syllables issuing from that sterile monotonous voice had become a wire garrote around his father's throat. Unless the stranger loosened the garrote, it would be no use for Father even if his condition temporarily took an unexpected turn for the better. But to count on the stranger loosening the noose would be like expecting rain on a cloudless day. When he obeyed the man's order to visit Father's hometown, he had entertained vague hopes of solving the problem with a large sum of money. But after unearthing the details of the deeds, on his way back home he realized it was not the kind of problem that could be solved by cash.

"When he recovers, I'll use whatever means necessary to have him retire from the chairmanship of the company."

Mother was so relieved she was rambling in a tearful voice about her plans after Father's discharge from the hospital.

"You really ought to. What's business after all, health comes first. Business and money are for living, aren't they?"

Dr. Chun concurred with Mother, in words that would have been more fitting for a decrepit old real estate broker with smoke-yellowed teeth.

"Dear, don't just stand there like that, say something to the doctor."

His mother's rejuvenated energy was as pronounced as her pained exhaustion had been shortly before, and she had recovered sufficiently to chastise her son for his breach of etiquette.

"Oh, please don't . . . Professor Hwang, come on over and sit down. Looks like you needn't be overly worried."

Dr. Chun looked almost light-hearted, very different than when he had first accompanied Hyongmin into the emergency room.

"Oh, well . . . I think I'll take a short walk and then come back."

Hyongmin sped out of Dr. Chun's office as if under pursuit. He could not bear to linger with these people who were totally ignorant of the actual situation. He walked along the corridor, soon reaching the emergency room. He looked about. Nobody. His heart was still pounding. Half-consciously he had been checking to see if any suspicious characters were hanging around. It was automatic behavior—he was preoccupied with the stranger on the other end of the phone. He made his way back through the corridor to the waiting room.

"How's your father now?" asked his wife, rushing up to him. She'd been silent all this time, perhaps because of his mother's presence.

"Well, his brain is undamaged, and the doctor said he's temporarily unconscious from shock," said he, forcing a smile.

"Really? That's good news, dear. Very lucky, indeed."

Almost jumping with joy, his wife clutched his arm. Her face, not long before hardened with tension, beamed with a radiant smile. Despite his wife's relief, Hyongmin felt the situation remained dreadful. The conditions of bliss his father possessed were almost complete—solid wealth, a prosperous business, a devoted wife, three children all conscientiously fulfilling their promise, and even this daughter-in-law delighted at his improved condition—all these were proof of it. Nevertheless, his father was floundering in an unconscious state on a dangerous precipice where he might soon plunge down and lose everything.

"Please, smile a little. Are you tired out from your journey down to the countryside, is that it?"

His wife's attention quickly shifted and was now focused upon him. He felt this was not a topic on which to linger.

"His condition hasn't improved enough to smile, yet. The x-ray results were better than expected, that's all. I'm no doctor, but don't forget the human body is not so simple that all its afflictions are clearly revealed in x-rays."

Hyongmin's voice was diffident, as though he sought to reproach his wife's relaxed attitude.

"Why, what do you mean?" she quickly responded.

It was necessary to acknowledge her rejoinder, a simple expression of the tension rebuilding in her mind. As he expected, his wife fell into a gloomy silence, and he smoked a cigarette to distract himself from the unabated stress.

The x-ray results revealing no brain damage had evoked real hope for the moment.

This good news permitted him, once evening rolled around, to send his mother, wife and two younger siblings home without much protest from them. If the x-rays had revealed anything ominous, on top of the bad portent for Father, they all would have stayed overnight in the waiting room. Then, he would have faced an imminent risk of the secret leaking out to the other family members. He was sure the stranger would call the waiting room late that night, at an hour chosen by him alone. However well Hyongmin succeeded in disguising things, it might be impossible to deceive four people who would be all ears. Besides, his mother already knew the late night calls were responsible for his father's afflicted state.

After the family left the hospital with raised spirits, Hyongmin collapsed into a chair in the waiting room. The fatigue weighed heavily on him, giving a sensation of being sucked down into some subterranean realm.

He could not be sure how long the secret would remain a secret. To delay its disclosure as long as possible was his priority. For his father, it was a time bomb about to explode after ticking for twenty-nine years. How much longer could it be held back, try as he might? The bomb sooner or later would go off in the family's face—what would happen then to his mother . . . to his younger brother and sister . . . and to his wife? He laid his head on the chair, closed his eyes, and moaned.

It must have been only a few seconds after he dozed off.

"Mr. Hwang Hyongmin, telephone call."

He sprang up and snatched the receiver from a fortyish man standing by the phone. Already his heart was violently pounding and he gulped loudly without being aware of it.

"Hello, Hwang Hyongmin here."

"How do you do, Professor Bae Hyongmin?"

Hyongmin shuddered as the slow, icy voice coiled around his neck. He kept trying to imprison Hyongmin in a common guilt by using "Bae" in place of "Hwang."

"Fine. . . ."

Again he gulped, looking quickly about.

"I heard your father, Mr. Bae Jomsu, is hospitalized?"

"That's right. . . ."

"Fainted and in the hospital after only four calls, not at all like the Bae Jomsu who once killed thirty-eight people, wouldn't you say?"

Hyongmin clenched his teeth. His heart was about to burst from indignation. This man was enjoying a leisurely sport over the phone. He was a sadistic and cunning cat, toying with a mouse that was mortally wounded, playing in a spacious yard and enjoying the final agony of the bleeding prey. The mouse, gasping for air, collects all its remaining strength to attempt an escape. Bloody, staggering, the mouse flees desperately while the cat, forelegs extended and back arched, observes the snail-paced movements of the mouse. Just when the mouse reaches the threshold of safety, the cat springs, flailing its forepaws. Pinned between razor claws, the mouse is tossed into the air and falls to the earth. At first the mouse is motionless as though it is dead, but then it once more collects its energies and attempts another escape. But the sequel is the same. After repeating this a few times the cat tires of the game. Then he sinks his teeth into the prey and saunters off to retire to some shady place.

"This is inevitable, after all, but it's disappointing to me that it came so soon. It takes all the excitement away. Don't you think so?"

"Well, I uh . . ."

"Please, don't try to change the subject."

Hyongmin felt his knees buckle. He was being treated like a criminal with no right to speak freely.

"I know you've been to your father's hometown."

" . . . ."

"Did you verify the number thirty-eight?"

"Yes . . ."

"Good. What else have you confirmed?"

He was forcing Hyongmin to speak. He seemed to be intending to cross-examine him like a witness to convince him of his father's guilt. Hyongmin didn't know how to begin. Never in his life had he felt so humiliated. Being forced to enumerate his father's deeds one by one was like a son being forced to lash his own father for theft in front of a crowd.

"What are you waiting for? Tell me, now."

The slow, emotionless voice was driving Hyongmin into a corner.

"I've confirmed all you told me," replied Hyongmin, feeling almost suicidal despair.

"Professor Bae Hyongmin, it's useless trying to outjuggle me. Your agony, I do understand it. But has it ever once occurred to you, even for a moment, that your suffering is utterly trivial compared to what I've endured from the day I was born into this world? Don't try to deceive me. If I wanted revenge against your father because of my emotions, I never would have chosen this method of calling as I am now. There are plenty of other ways, swifter and more aggressive. Remember, this is no threat or blackmail. I'm trying not to become emotionally involved. I thought you would at least be capable of seeing that much, well, was I wrong?"

"I'm sorry. . . ."

The words just sprang from his lips. Listening to him, Hyongmin understood what he meant only too well, and he actually did feel suddenly compassionate and apologetic toward him. The man's words were not to be contradicted. His father in fact had been murdered by Hyongmin's own father. That alone would suffice to justify irrationality on his part. And he'd said that after thirty years, his mother had died and left him a last request. How could Hyongmin's pain be compared with the suffering he has endured? What's more, if he had wildly chosen to inflict revenge, Hyongmin's whole family would be devastated by now. Long before the law descended to prosecute the treason and murder, the family would have been annihilated at the hands of the victims' survivors themselves. Hyongmin had seen that vindictiveness in the flesh when he visited his father's hometown.

"Plenty of time has passed, but the rancor of those days remains alive and fresh. As for me, I don't know."

Those were the parting words of Shin Jungol, who told the story of his father's crimes, words from one who himself had barely escaped death at his father's hands. The old man guessed Father was no longer among the living, but his lust for revenge still lived on. And surely he was not the only one with such hatred toward his father. The man on the phone could not be ignorant of such sentiments throughout the Shin clan. But his unmasking of Hyongmin's father had not been divulged even to his own relatives. One word, and Hyongmin's family even now would be in ruins from the vengeance of Shin Jungol and the others. Just as he said, he clearly had been trying to avoid emotional involvement. Each word he said was neither threat nor blackmail, only the simple truth. Hyongmin wondered whether he should feel grateful for his rational conduct up to then.

"I heard every single crime my father committed from Mr. Shin Jungol who owns a restaurant there. That he not only killed people but buried them in graves he forced them to dig themselves on the slope of *Sambongsan*, the ancestral shrine of the Shin clan."

"Do you know what that means?"

He interrupted Hyongmin with this pointed question.

"Yes, . . . it was to sever the vein of *Sambongsan* at the same time the tombs were dug . . ."

He couldn't go on.

"And then?"

"My father made iron spears at his smithy . . ."

"And then?"

"Mr. Shin Jungol was dragged away . . ."

"And then?"

Sweat was streaming down Hyongmin's forehead. The noose of "and then" and "and then" was closing around his throat.

"I heard of the death of my father's first wife."

"Where?"

"Well . . . under the dangsan tree . . ."

"How?"

"Stoned to death . . ."

"All right. And then?"

"I learned I had a half-brother still living."

"How?"

"He's an idiot . . ."

"You heard about it, and that's all?"

The stranger's voice sounded hotter. It was the very first trace of emotion revealed.

"No, I met him."

"Good. You're a worthy professor, after all. How did you feel?"

That grinning face, gaping mouth, peering up at the sky. He could imagine his half-brother, tall, perfect build, but totally dull face, glazed eyes. Waves of sadness washed over Hyongmin's spirit. Then he felt a revival of that guilt he had experienced.

"Tell me frankly, what did you feel?"

"I felt guilt, knowing he had done nothing to deserve it."

"Can I trust what you tell me?"

"Well, how can I respond to that?"

"Fine. Having encountered him, what did you think about your father's relation to this son of his?"

Hyongmin was momentarily at a complete loss for words. He had been shocked beyond telling when Shin Jungol had described how, the day after his father vanished from the village, his wife had been bound to the dangsan tree and stoned to death in front of the five year-old boy, and how his half-brother had been reduced to imbecility by the trauma and had lived like that ever since. When he had gone to the inn to sleep that night, his half-brother had been prominent among many thoughts torturing him.

His first thought had been that his father must have known absolutely nothing about his son being alive. Then he had recognized that his father, for his personal safety, had run away, leaving his wife and son in an extremely perilous place to suffer for his crimes, and he had never returned for them. It was an unforgivable thing for a man to do. Later, he had considered that his father might have come back, but after learning of his wife's death and discovering the boy was no longer normal, he may have abandoned the child. That would have been more unpardonable still. Other than these two accounts, Hyongmin had been unable to come up with any plausible explanation for his half-brother's abandonment.

"Why don't you answer me?"

The voice coldly demanded a response.

"Well, I've thought about it, but I can't come up with any answer," replied Hyongmin haltingly.

"Thought about it . . . what do you mean?"

"Either my father knows nothing about him, or else he knows but has ignored him because of his abnormalities."

Hyongmin used "abnormality" because he lacked the heart to call him an "idiot" or "retard." Similarly, he chose "ignored" in place of "abandoned."

"Well, which do you think it was in this case?"

Hyongmin was overcome by a cold, stifling feeling. For reasons unknown, he found himself instinctively leaning towards the worst case. At the same time, he couldn't say in so many words that his father had evidently abandoned his own son. He said in agony, "You already know all about it, don't you?"

"I'm glad you're not slow. Your father abandoned his own son!"

Heaving a long sigh, Hyongmin nodded imperceptibly to himself.

"And not even a normal child at that."

In those times, his father might have had no choice but to leave his son there because he was an idiot, but now he appeared to be a diabolical character who abandoned a blood relation, a totally vulnerable idiot utterly in need of protection. And this tended to support the other side of it, that a man like that would also be capable of treason and of slaughtering thirty-eight people.

"Professor Bae Hyongmin!"

Hyongmin grew alert. Changing directions completely, the voice on the phone assumed an entirely different tone and said,

"Do you expect your father to die in his present condition, or are you hoping for his recovery?"

Hyongmin shivered. The trembling was not from fear. Presented with this cul-de-sac of a question, Hyongmin felt a sudden loathing at the human species' wretched desire for life.

"You needn't answer. You're the son of Bae Jomsu. But take your time, don't get excited, and try to decide rationally. If you do, you'll realize soon enough which way would be easier."

It was a declaration of his resolve that, whatever happened, he would never allow Hyongmin's father to survive.

"Did you verify any other facts?"

The stranger on the phone again changed his tone.

"Well, not really . . ."

Hyongmin was exhausted.

"You've now learned as much as there is to know, except for one thing that remains."

He stopped abruptly. Hyongmin reflexively grew tense.

"You know nothing about me."

True. He had hidden himself at the far end of that line, and all he had said was that he was the son of one of the thirty-eight.

"Not only did your father kill my father, he . . ."

Again he paused. Hyongmin felt a hot wind blasting his face.

". . . raped my mother. She was pregnant with me at the time."

Hyongmin's head reeled and the people and chairs around him began spinning before his eyes. He groped for the corner of the desk to support himself.

"It's getting late. That's all for today."

Click. He hung up.

2

Hyongmin was to take turns waiting with his wife, who had returned to the hospital early the next morning.

"You were up all night, weren't you, dear?"

As soon as she saw her husband, she expressed an exaggerated concern.

"Um, I'm a little tired."

He was impatient to leave the waiting room and so tried to minimize the time spent chattering with his wife.

"Well, what did I tell you? Didn't I say I should stay? Go on home now and rest. Don't go to school today, please. If you don't take care, you too might . . ."

She went on talking at his back as he left.

Hyongmin trotted down the corridor to the Emergency Room. A night shift nurse turned a blank stare his way, looking like a withered flower.

"Mr. Hwang Bokman is my father. Just one minute . . ."

The nurse pointed the way with her chin, then turned around. Father did not seem to have improved at all since the day before. It was a continued coma suggestive of death. What rancor could he have felt to commit such . . . Hyongmin was sunk in thought as he looked down at his father, whose face now exhibited irreversible signs of his advancing age.

"Do you expect your father to die in his present condition, or are you hoping for his recovery?"

The stranger had asked but he really did not expect any response. He was a disciplined man, to be sure, and his reason was as cold-blooded as a serpent. Hyongmin turned away from the bed. He thought his father had to regain his lucidity even if he was doomed to collapse again with the next tug at the noose. There were too many secret problems and unanswered questions.

"My mother, who lived her whole life in resentment and rancor, never forgave your father even on her deathbed. She became the thirty-ninth spirit."

These words obsessed Hyongmin as he took a taxi home. The same words had plagued him all through the night. He had not paid any special attention when the stranger first said that, he only had surmised the woman must have hated his father for murdering her husband and still wanted revenge even as she lay dying. But the words had taken on a new significance after the latest call.

Hyongmin's despair had deepened overnight. His father was sinking deeper and deeper into death's quicksand. "My mother was pregnant with me at the time." Next to these words, his father's life became a scrap of paper tossed in a fire, and that was why Hyongmin's despair was boundless. Even before entering the world, the stranger had suffered the double trauma of his father's death and his mother being raped. Was he the boy old Shin Jungol had in mind when he told of a posthumous child bowing at the sacrificial altar to a father whose face he had never seen? So he had grown up fatherless, then his mother left this world full of rancorous vindictiveness, and now he had surfaced as an adult to confront the foe who murdered his father and raped his mother. To a man like that, how much would the life of Bae Jomsu be worth? Hyongmin could find no room at all for beseeching the caller to let his father live.

Hyongmin took a shower and drank a glass of milk. He was so dizzy from exhaustion that he couldn't even stand up straight. So that he wouldn't be late for school, he took a nap sitting on the sofa.

The place was like a cave. But it was not cold and bare, this place was warm and cozy. Then, all of a sudden, there was turbulence and the atmosphere grew stifling. As time passed, it grew worse. Something was slowly pushing in from the entrance. He backed up farther and farther as it closed in on him, but then there was no way to back up any farther. The suffocation was unbearable, and still it kept building, pushing forward. Unable to stand it any longer, he screamed out loud. No, no . . .

He awoke with a start. A dream. He moaned and nervously rubbed his face repeatedly. It was a weird, incredible dream. The screams obviously came from the stranger as a fetus, and the intruding object was nothing else but his father's sex organ. Physically and mentally, he was in no condition to go to school. But he had already missed two days of lectures during his trip south, so he had to go.

His lectures all came out vapid and disorganized that day. The classrooms and the students were the same, but two days had brought a sense of remoteness and alienation he had never felt before. Am I really qualified to be standing up here, is there such a thing as plebeian blood? If Father dies now, how will things unfold? What kinds of lives did my grandfather and his father before him lead? If war had not come, what would Father's fate have been?

Thoughts like these kept popping into his head as he tried to lecture, and each time he became muddled and distracted.

After barely making it through his morning lectures, he returned to his office to find a note waiting on his desk.

"Father regained consciousness."

As soon as he saw the note, the reflex of joy was instantly knotted with fear. He sat down. It was impossible to bear the gloomy prospect that his father's recovery would meet with an immediate resumption of torment. He felt miserable and realized that his initial impulse to rush to the hospital was cooling off. He decided to phone Dr. Chun first.

"Ah, Professor Hwang, have you heard the news?"

"Yes, we are grateful, indeed. You've worked awfully hard."

Despite his ambivalence, Hyongmin's voice expressed only relief, perhaps because it was the doctor on the phone.

"But there's still a problem that makes your thanking me premature," said Dr. Chun in a sober tone with a businesslike air. Hyongmin at once felt that something was seriously wrong.

"The thing is, and it's not clear what caused it, he regained consciousness, but there are symptoms of global paralysis and aphasia."

"Aphasia . . ."

Hyongmin mumbled the word, and the concept of "human vegetable" flashed through his mind.

"Don't lose hope yet. It's only been a few hours since he awoke, and his condition may yet improve if we just wait a while."

Hyongmin started to ask whether the paralysis and aphasia were caused by brain malfunction, but he didn't. Instead, he thought of a more important question.

"With aphasia, can he still hear even if he can't talk?"

"It's a neurological syndrome, and without the capacity to speak he may also have serious difficulties in understanding what he hears."

"What about telephone rings, for instance?"

"No problem recognizing such simple sounds."

"Where's my father now?"

"As soon as he woke up, he was moved to another ward."

"Is there a phone in his room?"

"Sure, it's a private suite."

"I'd appreciate it if you'd have the phone disconnected."

"But why? Won't it be inconvenient for the family?"

"When my father is not well, the ringing of clocks or phones always irritates him a lot," Hyongmin said without hesitation.

"I see. That's something I didn't know. Your idea is a good one."

Dr. Chun readily concurred with him.

After hanging up the phone, Hyongmin sat at his desk for a long time. Into his blank mind came a depressed reflection that life could be just too exhausting. His father had escaped the crisis for the present. He had heard of people sometimes living for years as vegetables. Unless the paralysis and aphasia could be overcome, his father would be like them, little more than a vegetable. It would be a state of semi-death. If that happened, how would the stranger respond? Would he be satisfied with his goal only half accomplished? Or would he seek some other way to fulfill his aim? Hyongmin rose heavily from his chair for his last lecture of the day.

Although his father had recovered consciousness, there seemed to be no great improvement in his condition. Tubes were still stuck in his nose and the IV needle was still in his arm. His eyes were no longer closed, but they seemed not to be focusing on anything in particular. They were glazed and expressionless, with fixed pupils that seemed unable to function. The instant Hyongmin saw his father's eyes, he was reminded of his half-brother's eyes. The resemblance between the dull stares of the two men seemed to confirm a chilling curse of fate.

"Don't just stand there like that, say something to him," said his mother anxiously, pulling at Hyongmin's sleeve. He approached closer to his father.

"Father, do you know me? It's Hyongmin, Hyongmin!" Lowering his face close to his father's eyes, he unconsciously raised his voice. But there was no response. The pupils were immobile, oblivious.

"Louder, say one word at a time."

His mother advised Hyongmin how to communicate; she had already tried.

"Fa-ther, this-is-Hyong-min, Hyong-min!"

His eyes fluttered slightly, and the pupils moved a bit. Then the eyes slowly closed. There was no way to know if he had recognized him. Then, he saw tears flowing from his father's closed eyes. At the sight of the tiny tears issuing like drops of dew condensing, Hyongmin felt a deep pity.

"He recognized you, recognized you." His mother was moved almost to weeping.

The tears of his father's eyes were the first Hyongmin had seen in his entire life. Under no circumstances would his father allow a man to cry. Hyongmin and his younger brother had been "men" since they were four or five, so crying had been forbidden even when they were hurt, wronged or sad. Not even when Father himself whipped his sons on the calves with a thin switch were they allowed to shed tears. Now, what was the meaning of tears from such a father? Hyongmin thought the manliness of his father was deteriorating. Was it advancing age or was he surrendering all in the face of inevitable defeat?

"Son, why did you have them disconnect the phone? The only public phone is down at the main entrance. And what about incoming calls?"

His mother insensitively complained about the telephone.

"Father's not suffering from just any ordinary illness. From now on no visitors, even from our family, except you and me. He needs total rest or he'll be in real peril. Understand?"

Hyongmin overruled his mother in a single sentence. He chose a tone of such exaggerated coldness that it was too cruel to even be taken seriously. Mother instantly turned white as a sheet, her lips twitching though she was speechless. Hyongmin was well aware of how his standing as the eldest son and a university lecturer weighed upon his mother as well as his father. His strong words must have shocked his mother.

"Remember, no relatives visiting, either."

Hyongmin drove the command home once more, and she just nodded with a hardened expression like that of a surprised statue.

"You stay here tonight, Mother."

Since the phone had been taken out of his father's room, Hyongmin intended to wait for the call at home. He had taken thorough precautions to protect his father, but was anxious because such steps could provoke the suspicion of Dr. Chun. He could easily be rid of his wife by persuading her to spend the night at his parent's home. Guarding her in-law's house during their absence was a fitting duty for the wife of an eldest son. The pretext for him staying home alone had already been laid; he had an urgent paper to write. His wife believed his visit to his father's hometown had been to collect data for that project.

President Hwang Bokman's mind was wandering through an expanse of dense fog. Before him was an interminable, shapeless, cloudy field. No matter how loud he screamed, not a sound could be heard. Everything was indistinct and constantly swaying.

Where on earth am I? How did I get here? Got to get away. With such thoughts, President Hwang continuously thrust the fog aside, but it kept flowing back in. No matter how hard he struggled, he couldn't move, and his desperate cries for help were suppressed by the thick blankets of fog. He couldn't tell whether he was dreaming or awake.

All at once some whitish forms appeared beyond the fog. They were approaching his way at a sort of trotting gait. Each step was accompanied by a whooshing noise, followed by a gust of wind, and President Hwang was overcome with terror. He wanted to flee but his feet were nailed to the ground.

In the midst of his struggle, he found himself in the center of a maelstrom of uncanny winds.

"You bastard, Bae Jomsu, listen closely!"

A sudden, thundering voice almost ruptured his eardrums. Startled, he turned towards the direction whence the voice came. President Hwang was horrorstruck. Those whitish things were already right beside him, and they were now discernible as none other than the Shins he had killed with his own hands. Each one of them looked just as they had at the hour of their deaths. Their hair wildly tangled, their bodies gashed and punctured, blood streaming, they were slowly converging on him.

"You, bastard, we've been waiting too long for you. Now, it's time to go. Yeah, we'll cut you into thirty-eight pieces. With your petty tricks behind our backs, you've been thinking you'd live forever, weren't you?"

As they closed in, each said something different. Unable to stir, he quaked like a leaf.

"You bastard, come over here!" shouted one of them at the top of his voice, clutching him by the throat. The touch was like ice. The frigid hand was throttling him. Suffocating, he struggled and struggled in vain.

Haunted by these phantoms, President Hwang was in reality submerging slowly into unconsciousness. But because there were no external signs of these torments such as screaming or writhing, the people watching him had no way of knowing what he was experiencing inside. When he closed his eyes, they thought him asleep, when his eyes were open, they assumed he was awake.

Wandering thus on the borderline of consciousness and total oblivion, President Hwang met random memories, and was plagued by horrifying phantoms.

For Jomsu, the pointless death of Chairman Pang, who had indoctrinated him with communist ideology and cast his ideas into iron molds, meant despair, the collapse of the heavens onto his head. Only because of Pang's presence, and not out of any belief that those free, lost times would soon return, had he been able to endure the hardships of endless flight in the mountains, of living a life with day and night reversed. He had sensed a strangeness in Pang's behavior but never had dreamt he would kill himself that very night.

Pang's dangerous advice, that Jomsu should leave the mountains because no hope remained, was in effect his last will and testament. Jomsu decided to heed Pang's last words. On their next nocturnal raid for food, he had managed to escape. As he fled in the darkness on a line leading away from his hometown, Jomsu realized the gravity of his past deeds in a new light. His birthplace had become a place to which he could never return as long as he lived. The little son he had left behind in that place brought him heart-shattering pain. The image of little Chilsung kept appearing before his eyes. Jomsu ran for three days and nights. He moved stealthily so that nobody would catch sight of him. He was now a fugitive pursued by both sides.

At a small village he reached on the fourth day, he immediately noticed the change in dialect. It was Kyongsang province, the southeastern region. He was relieved he at least had made it somewhere far from his hometown. Cautiously, he took on odd chores, whatever turned up, anything to feed himself three times a day. He spoke as little as possible and pretended to be dim-witted. He knew people everywhere are charitable to the handicapped, and nobody with a sharp mind pays any attention to the past of a half-wit. His tactic was well-chosen. Nobody suspected him or thought twice about his presence. They treated him as a strong and healthy imbecile, wandering around oblivious to the war raging about him.

As time went on, Jomsu realized how hideously absurd his life in the mountains had been. They had been defeated and were no match for this side, but the militia officer still barked about the coming day of People's Liberation. He felt boundless pity for those who believed such nonsense as they constantly tried to evade capture and went on perilous nightly forays just to put food in their mouths. At the same time, Jomsu felt a profound guilt. He was mortified at his killing of so many people, and tortured by recurrent nightmares in which the dead returned. Most unbearable of all was the way his sister, Sunwol, had killed Shin Byongchul and his wife.

The couple had been butchered by Sunwol, their bodies slowly hacked into pieces. They had been imprisoned separately in a cave, and tortured there by Sunwol. They were fed a bowl of barley each day, and little by little bled to death from their wounds. Sunwol came every day to the cave where they were strung up stark naked, and she went mad, slicing the skin off their bodies.

"You bastard! You're my mortal enemy! You're the reason I was driven from my husband's house. You ruined my life, and thought you could go on living happily ever after, dropping your own whelps, eh? Nope, no way, can't be!"

By this time Sunwol had become a shaman sorceress practicing exorcism. Madness glowing in her eyes, she would scratch a long line in Shin Byongchul's flesh with her knife and then do the same on his wife's body. The cave echoed with agonized shrieks, and crimson blood spurted along the path of the knife, streaming over the dark clots that had dried elsewhere from the days before.

"You think the almighty mountain spirit's on your side, eh? No way, you scum. That dear spirit's fair, so he took you from the sun into this dark place. Now, the sunny place is mine, you know that? You're my enemies, know that?!"

And once more the knife would slice their flesh. Nobody could stop Sunwol's atrocities. Jomsu tried a few times but gave up.

"What does that old story got to do with your husband kicking you out for not having a child?" Jomsu asked.

"Brother, how can you say something so cruel to me? If you, who know all about it, say such things with no sympathy, what can I do?"

"It's a lame excuse to blame your barrenness on that incident. Not bearing children is your lot. Yours."

"Brother, can you really be on their side? If that's how you're going to be I'll stick this knife in myself right now!"

Sunwol moved the knife to her breast, and her insane look screamed she was ready to do it.

"No, no, I don't mean it," Jomsu could only relent.

That same ancient episode that had led to Jomsu becoming a black-smith—Ha Kuchon's son and Byongchul poking Sunwol between the legs with a stick—because of that incident the couple were dying these horrible deaths. Sunwol had married at twenty and her husband abandoned her five years later because she couldn't bear children. Sunwol returned to her family utterly downcast. Neither her father nor Jomsu had been able to console her.

Though Sunwol seemed to have no interest in life, she had poured her heart into any work that came her way, to distract herself from her sorrows, apparently. She rarely spoke to outsiders and seldom smiled. When she heard her husband had remarried, Sunwol showed no outward reaction. Then, after about a year, there was word that her husband had been blessed with a son. At that news, she took no food for three days. The family feared for her life. However, slowly she regained her strength and worked harder than ever before. Father used to sigh deeply whenever he watched his daughter from a distance. She looked much older than her years. After six years of living that destitute life, the world turned upside down in one night. Sunwol welcomed the change with far greater delight than Jomsu. Her excitement was astonishing.

"Brother, that bastard Shin Byongchul and his wife, you leave them to me."

When she first said that, Jomsu agreed without knowing her intentions. She was firmly convinced her inability to bear children was caused by Byongchul's poking that stick into her womb when they were kids. Even if the lack of connection had been medically explained, no soul on earth would ever be able to convince Sunwol otherwise.

Screaming, begging, the couple survived with incredible tenacity for almost a month and then died in the most atrocious shape. Byongchul's dying words were a curse upon Jomsu and Sunwol:

"You bastard and bitch! My spirit'll chase you as long as you live and revenge'll be mine!"

From then on, Jomsu was repelled by Sunwol. A woman's wrath can bring frost in mid-summer, but he had never imagined any woman could be that vile and sadistic. His notions of women were as fruitful mothers and diligent housekeepers, capable of bringing beauty into the world. But he realized that women can unexpectedly turn into the most frightening of beasts.

In those days, Shin Byongchul and his wife haunted Jomsu's nightmares. Perhaps, their ghosts really were following him everywhere. Sometimes, full moon overhead, Jomsu would sit awake transfixed, oblivious of sleep. The past came alive again in his contrite mind. They say the life of a man is like the blink of an eye, yet this is not equally true for everyone. For those leading a soft life with full bellies, time rolls away, and for some monks, chanting a prayer to Amitabha and gorging themselves on donated rice, this earthly life may well appear as ethereal as the clouds overhead. But to those who can barely afford greens and who endure the constant gnawing of hunger, every single day is like a tough strand of hemp that must be stretched taut.

"No matter how great your rancor, it can't be as great as your father's. In spite of the pain and sorrow, I sent you to the smith so you wouldn't be growing up with rancor in your heart. And now, what's all this? They're no mortal enemies of yours. Those feelings come from rich and poor living mixed together. So where the hell did you learn to treat human beings like dogs? With the smith's skill you could of been making fine tools for farmers, but, you bastard, you made spears for killing people. And Sunwol's gone crazy as hell, too. It's wrong. You'll never sleep easy after killing so many people like they were mutts."

Those had been his father's breathless words as he lay there sick, pounding the floor weakly. Like someone poisoned by snake venom, Jomsu had ignored those words as the ravings of a senile old man. But now those very words had returned, rattling his heart.

They say one pays for sins and is rewarded for good deeds. But why is one born into a rich, noble family and another born as the child of a peasant farmer? Still, Father always said the world was a lot better than in the old days.

"How can you talk about the old days, when you yourself lived your whole life under the heel of those rich bloodsuckers?" Jomsu had asked his father.

"Listen, son, you don't know what you're talking about. Even in your grandfather's time slave documents were bought and sold. You can't imagine what it was like to have your life bound up with slave documents."

"Anyway you go, there's only one life to live, so I'm going to shake things up, all over. A blacksmith can't even fill his own belly."

"Hear me, better watch what you say. So this fate's too much to live with?"

In the end his father was always enraged. But then he would calm himself and say quietly,

"True, at times the world looks fair, but then again it looks unfair. That's just what living is like. Look at the stars at night. If you look real close, every star's a different size. But they never fight, do they? Living in this world works the same way. Everybody lives their own lives, shining in their own ways. If you let your young spirit take revenge on innocent souls, vengeance'll come back to you. So stick to your own work. That's for the best, you hear me?"

Jomsu reluctantly used to nod agreement, but in the end his father's warning went unheeded. Now his father's words came alive once more in his heart, shining like those stars in the dark sky.

Jomsu's father never observed the ancestral rites for his own father or grandfather. The most he ever did was bow twice at a sacrificial altar he set up on Chusok, the Harvest Full Moon Festival, for all the dead. For some time Jomsu used to think their poverty was what kept Father from celebrating the feasts for the ancestors. But families even poorer than they were always held ancestor rituals, and on the day after those rites, their children may not have had fancy rice cakes, but at least they came out to show off the squash cakes from their feast. Jomsu was confused. He finally asked his mother about it one day.

She answered, "You see, well, to follow the ancestors' rites, we'd need to know when they passed away."

"Is Father some kind of fool, then? He doesn't even know when his own father died?"

"No, he's no fool, he just plays the fool because your grandfather was so odd."

"What do you mean?"

Great-grandfather had been a faithful follower of Tonghak, the Eastern Learning movement. When the Tonghak peasant rebellion came, great-grandfather joined in, needless to say. And he didn't join alone, but brought his son along with him. With the passage of time the Tonghak power waned and in the end they were suppressed and hounded by the government. Hundreds of rebels were slain at a time.

Then news reached home that great-grandfather had died in a battle on some hillside far away. The family traveled there to retrieve his body but it was in vain. On the way back home, great-grandmother and grandmother were forced to flee for their lives. It turned out the rebels' families were also being tracked down to be executed. On that very day they had trudged twenty miles. And from then on they lived the life of outlaws.

One night, about three years after the insurrection, grandfather, long given up for dead, suddenly appeared. But he was no longer the same man. He had been crippled and his mind was twisted. Only four days later he ran off to become a gong player with a *namsadang* troupe, traveling actors. Every few years grandfather would appear and then vanish again like the wind. People said he lost his mind at the sight of his own father's death, and that the *namsadang* players had saved his life. After a few visits like that, the family never heard of grandfather again. He probably died on the road somewhere.

"For your descendants to prosper you got to be buried in good ground. All your ancestors became ghosts on the road. So even if we wanted to do the rites for them, we can't because we don't know when they left for the other side."

Hearing this story made Jomsu feel he was even worse off then before. In spite of the humiliation he endured, Father lived his whole life working himself to death on Shin lands. And he died in his own room so there was no obstacle to performing the ancestral rites. But now, Jomsu, the man whose duty it was to keep the grave decent and to observe the feasts, had become an outlaw and was doing his best to steer clear of his hometown.

Both his great-grandfather and his grandfather, like Jomsu himself, must have fervently believed the world had to be changed. What could have passed through great-grandfather's mind as he died, trapped by government soldiers? What could grandfather have thought as he dragged his lame body down the road with the *namsadang*, a troupe blowing about the country like gypsies? As a boy, Jomsu spent sleepless winter nights pondering such things. Winter was long.

Since late autumn, Jomsu had been collecting firewood for a village inn at the request of the widow who owned it. The widow was in her early thirties, and seemed to have a good heart. She gave Jomsu plenty of hot rice and offered him brimming cups of wine. When he had stacked a big pile of wood out back, she slipped some money into his hand to buy winter clothes.

When Jomsu peered into the burning fire, he saw the image of his son, Chilsung, in the shadows of the flickering flames. Was his son still alive? Jomsu's mind constantly ran back to his home village. His plaintive heart was bursting with mournful regrets and compassion for his own flesh and blood.

"Hey, Jomsu, it's freezing tonight, how about a drink?" the widow shouted out from the main room. Jomsu leapt up. The way he felt now not even a barrel of wine could make him drunk. Stepping inside, Jomsu made a broad oafish smile.

"Sit yourself down. You know, I kind of like the fact that you're a bit of a dimwit."

The widow smiled back at him as she poured some liquor into a big bowl. Her cheeks were plump and her bosom was full. Jomsu hastily looked away.

"Hurry, drink up, now. What you're waiting on?"

Jomsu drained it in one gulp.

"You really got some style. Care for another?"

"Yes."

Jomsu picked up a pickled radish and loudly chewed it.

"I say, with your face and body, it's a waste. I mean, how'd you get to be a dimwit? You catch the measles or typhoid or what?"

The widow grumbled this idle lament as she poured another drink. Hiding a bitter grin, Jomsu took the bowl and emptied it again.

"What's today? You been saving all your drinking for a special day, uh? Another?"

"Ya."

"Look, you idiot, even if you're a dimwit, don't just belch 'ya, ya,' at least be polite enough to offer a glass to your partner."

"Wanna drink, too?"

"So I told you. Come on, fill her up for me."

Jomsu handed over the empty bowl and filled it. A number of exchanges were made this way. Jomsu felt the alcohol flowing through him and the widow at last looked over at Jomsu with a hazy glance and said, "It's a waste, indeed. Such a grand body for a dimwit. Wonder if downstairs on this dimwit is as slow as upstairs."

She must have thought Jomsu was too dense to understand. He felt an energy building in his groin, a power shooting from inside to light a flame down there. It had been ages since he felt such hunger for a woman.

"Look, after the drinking and all, might as well find out what's what once and for all."

The widow sprang up and moved next to Jomsu. She softly took his hand and he felt the woman's ripe breasts heavy on his arm.

"Now, you're shaped like a man, so damn it, let's let your thing do what a man's thing is for. The thirst's killing me."

She murmured torridly and her hand steadily crawled in between Jomsu's legs.

"What's this? What in the world is it doing?"

The instant her hand touched his groin, she cried out with surprise and delight.

"Can't fool a grand body, right? You're a fine dimwit. God only knows why I didn't check this out sooner."

The widow trembled, holding Jomsu close in her arms.

"Jomsu, let's go on in the room. Hurry, come on, get up now."

She tugged at his arm and he, feigning reluctance, got up slowly, smiling like an imbecile.

As if stripping burning clothes from herself, she was naked in an instant and then began disrobing Jomsu as he stood there pretending to be bewildered. Then the woman tumbled down with Jomsu in her embrace. She was on fire, and for the first time in months, Jomsu poured himself into female flesh. The dam rapidly burst. The widow induced Jomsu to stay at the inn for good. The food on the table improved day by day and he drank whenever he pleased. He was spared menial work.

One night, as he fell asleep, he thought he heard something in his dream. It wasn't the sound of wind, but a human voice. He hastened to check the bed next to him. She was gone. Instantly, he was wide awake.

"Sure you didn't fuck around with that bastard?"

It was a man's bass voice.

"What kind of nonsense you talking? That thing is a dimwit, body and mind. You know too well, the village men bother me because I'm alone. I just took that dimwit in to make sure nothing happens."

"Is that the truth?"

"Why in the world should I lie? Shall we wake up that thing and ask him?"

"You crazy?"

Silence.

"What's the situation with you?"

"Awful mess."

"Then, what you gonna do?"

"Nothing. Got to stay put as long as we can. They say the North Army will soon be counterattacking."

"This ain't the first time they said that. How's about you change your plans now?"

"Oh, shut up. Is everything ready like I told you last time?"

"Yeah . . ."

"So, you really haven't been doing anything with that bastard, uh?"

"You're really an odd one. Didn't I say to wake him and ask him yourself?"

"All right, but if there's anything at all, I'm gonna shoot you and the bastard both, on the spot."

"Why don't you worry instead about the sky caving in? It'll be dawn soon, so let's have a go before you leave."

"All right, off with your clothes then, and lie down."

As he listened to the loud, heated sounds of the two tangling, Jomsu felt weak in the knees. She was no widow, and her husband was a fugitive in the mountains. Jomsu made up his mind to disappear the next day, leaving no trace behind in that village. He'd been sleeping on a volcano, and if he left the inn he had to leave the village. Staying would mean to them that he might know their secret, and that would put his life in their hands.

3

Rrring.

At the first ring Hyongmin picked up the receiver. He was so overwrought and tense he could not bear waiting for the phone to ring a second time.

"Hello . . ."

Hyongmin spoke glumly, expecting to be assailed by the slow sterile voice of the stranger.

Silence. It was not a pause between spoken words, but a deliberate silence. Thus, in a sense, it was a mode of expression.

"Hello!"

Hyongmin anxiously spoke again.

More silence. The message was terrifying. Worse than anything the man had said to Hyongmin up to then, this silence was a voice filling his heart with dread.

"Hello, this is Hwang Hyongmin."

"Professor Bae Hyongmin, so, you totally ignored my favor."

The stranger's voice was even colder than before. In that frigid atmosphere, Hyongmin sensed violence.

"What favor . . . ?"

"I asked you not to be in a hurry or to get excited, to stay cool. Just last night."

Hyongmin soon realized what he meant. He was upset at Hyongmin's removing the phone from the hospital room. But taking that decision had been a cool, calculated act. It was precisely intended to place an impediment in the way of the stranger's achievement of his purpose. But Hyongmin himself had resolved to confront him directly. Father had regained consciousness, but the aphasia and paralysis made it clear how his state would remain. Even though Father could not decipher complex communications, he would recognize a sound as simple as a telephone ringing.

Hyongmin himself had become neurotic about the rings, and their effect on Father would be beyond description. To allow the phone to ring in his room would literally drive him into the arms of death. The remnants of mind Father had left kept him precariously clinging to life as if ten fingers were holding the full weight of a man dangling from a precipice. To leave the phone in his room would have been like murdering Father. Whether Hyongmin could endure these confrontations with the stranger was beside the point. Getting rid of the phone had been the only thing to do. The wrongs his father had committed could not be considered. Only removing the phone would fulfill a son's duty to his parents.

"Why don't you say something?"

Like a prosecutor conducting an interrogation, he would not permit Hyongmin to keep silent. Hyongmin's lips twitched convulsively for a while, but he didn't speak. He knew he had to say something without antagonizing him even more, but he couldn't think of anything suitable.

"If you have taken up silence as your weapon from now on, so be it. I'll no longer deal with you on the phone."

"That's not it, hello, that's not it at all."

Hyongmin spoke hurriedly in the confusion of the moment, clutching at the receiver with both hands.

"Hello, hello?"

"Go on."

"As you may already know, my father regained consciousness, but he's still . . . What am I supposed to do as his son in a position like this?"

Raising such a rhetorical question, Hyongmin felt as powerless as a scarecrow. Yet he wanted to be frank and thought that would be his only weapon in dealing with the stranger.

"I have nothing to say if you meant to execute your obligations as a son by removing the phone, but . . ."

Silence. Hyongmin breathed deeply. Each of his words were impressed on his mind with the force of printed inscriptions.

". . . but, you knew that such conduct would directly block my purpose, didn't you?"

His words were homing in like an arrow to the bull's eye, and Hyongmin had no response.

"Judging from your silence, I gather you don't disagree with what I said. There's just one more thing, then, that I must make clear. Your intervention in my work doesn't end with that one block, but should mean that you are prepared to confront me on behalf of your father . . . well, are you ready for that?"

Hyongmin shut his eyes and listened to the sound of his whole being crumbling to dust. The battle against him wouldn't last even five minutes before coming to a preordained conclusion. The stranger's tone was still devoid of emotion, but his annoyance had been clearly conveyed, which was exactly what Hyongmin had feared even before confrontation was mentioned.

"No, that was never my intention. It's just that I was truly . . ."

Hyongmin's pride prevented him from continuing. To fight with the man would be useless, like a mouse fighting a cat.

"You were just truly what?"

He cruelly forced Hyongmin to spit out words he already knew. Hyongmin felt the redoubled humiliation of a kneeling man being trampled.

"You were just truly what?"

"Hoping to protect my father."

"Protect? Protect . . . I would like to hear what you planned to do next."

Again Hyongmin was at a loss for words. In fact, there was nothing specific he had intended to do next.

"Listen, Professor Bae Hyongmin, has it not occurred to you that your dutiful behavior as a pious son might bring even more pain to your father?"

With a pain as if his head had been split open with a sharp wedge, Hyongmin dizzily realized the meaning of those words.

"All right, in professional boxing there's a rule allowing unlimited knockdowns. It's no miracle for a fighter to win even after being down two, three or four times. It's fine with me if you want to play by that rule."

He was triumphantly revealing his confidence in his strategy for the future, like a pro boxer who has floored his opponent, or rather like a peerless boxer fully relishing his secure victory even as he repeatedly knocks down a challenger through measured applications of his power. He planned to drive Hyongmin's father into the corner of death three or four times running if he wished.

"Listen, please, let us meet. We'll meet to talk this out. When I see you . . ."

"Professor Bae Hyongmin, learn to keep cool as a professor should."

Hyongmin felt as though he'd been slapped across the face.

"At the outset you asked me to meet you. What do you suppose we would do if we met? Please, don't forget that this is not something you and I can solve. It's a matter between your father and thirty-eight people, including my father. They're people of an earlier generation, and only they can solve it. I trust you won't commit the hideous blunder of asking me if that's the case when why the hell am I ranting and raving about it. I've been unfortunate enough to be chosen as an agent to act for those vengeful spirits. All I want is to break free of that bond as soon as I can."

Hyongmin had a queer, somewhat hazy impression that the stranger's sole objective was to prevent his father from living any longer and nothing beyond that. But Hyongmin couldn't linger on that thought.

"I understand fully how you feel. But it all happened so long . . ."

"Wait, don't delude yourself into thinking you can persuade me. It's a stupid notion. Don't you understand what rancor is? Inside that stone, you won't find any half-baked sentimentality."

"Then, you mean to . . ."

"Now, Professor Bae Hyongmin, let's come to today's conclusion."

Hyongmin involuntarily took a deep breath.

"Put the phone back in the room tomorrow without fail!" he said coldly and firmly.

"My father is still in no condition to answer the phone."

"Put it back. He can't talk, but he can hear the ring."

Hyongmin was in a dismal dilemma. He knew he had to resist somehow, but he couldn't open his mouth.

"It's for you to decide whether to surrender your father alone, or to bring everything to ruin along with him."

The phone was dead. Receiver in hand, Hyongmin sat listlessly as though his soul had evaporated away. Confusion and chaos filled his skull.

Rrring. Rrring.

An expanse of dense fog stretched endlessly before him, so he could not see an inch from his nose. From somewhere, there was the incessant sound of a telephone ringing. If he turned left, the sound came from the right, and if he turned about, it came from the front. President Hwang, shuddering at the sound, staggered all over in search of the phone but it was useless. Then the ringing abruptly stopped and there was a sudden bellowing,

"Mr. Bae Jomsu, don't you think you've lived too long?"

An oppressively humid wind blew from nowhere, raising an eerie wail. President Hwang backed up, pushed by fear and loathing. Then something blocked his retreat from behind. As he turned to look, he felt an icy touch on his neck. Petrified, he tried to shake it off. In vain. The more he struggled, the tighter the freezing grip squeezed his throat. As he threw his head back to gasp for air, President Hwang turned deathly pale.

The thing throttling him was the wife of Shin Byongmo. Her body was four times bigger than a man's, and she was naked. She was pinching his throat between her thumb and finger. Suddenly, she lifted up her hand, and President Hwang was dangling by his neck high up in the air. He struggled to free himself from her grip, to breathe, but her fingers would not budge. Then the thing shouted, "You, son of a bitch, how did you dare touch my body, you, worse than any beast, not once but four times! Come to think of it, it was for the best, because now your own seed'll take revenge for your wrongs. Whatever you do, you bastard, you're doomed to die at the hands of your own son. You, son of a bitch, want to see how your filth dirtied my body? You gotta see!"

The woman suddenly loosened her grip. President Hwang tumbled down to the ground like a rock. When he came to his senses, he could not believe what he saw. Blood was pouring out of the woman's huge, gaping vagina, several times bigger than a cow's. The blood, God only knows how long it had been bleeding, was everywhere, his feet were soaked in it. He backed away, but the blood kept spreading, as if pursuing him. President Hwang took bigger steps backwards. The blood chased him faster. He was so terrified that he turned and ran. He didn't know how long he'd been running when his body was all of a sudden suspended in the air.

"Where do you think you can run to, bastard? You, son of a bitch, you're gonna die imprisoned in the place you liked so much."

With those words from the woman, the president writhed, but his body was already transported to the mouth of that enormous, bleeding womb, which slowly opened like the doors of a great gate. President Hwang wriggled and twisted with all his might, but he couldn't resist the gigantic hands. At last his head touched the vagina. Then, propelled by an uncontrollable force, his head was pushed inside. In the obscure darkness he was suffocating. He kept shouting and shrieking for help, but his body was pushed deeper into the dark, suffocating hole.

Breathless, President Hwang was slowly submerging into unconsciousness. His wife, standing vigil at his bedside, thought her husband was asleep.

The grounds for arrest of Shin Byongchul's brother, Shin Byongmo, had been clearer than for the others. As a high school teacher, he had long been known for his opposition to the leftists. In short, he was an unpardonable counterrevolutionary.

"Arrest Shin Byongmo first. That man is the most dangerous kind, fully equipped with reactionary ideology."

Chairman Pang had given that special order. His arrest had been easier than expected. They had anticipated at least a little resistance, but he had walked out of his room on his own. As Jomsu forced Shin Byongmo, his pants beltless, to walk up front, he had found the whole business too dull and flat. Then, Shin's wife, left all alone back in that room, flashed into his mind.

She was known as the most beautiful of all the daughters-in-law in the Shin clan. The most beautiful woman . . . it was a sudden impulse. He ordered his men to lead Shin away and turned back, saying he had something else to take care of. She wouldn't give in easily, of course. Her relation to the Shins, the beautiful face, and the prospect of feeble feminine resistance all combined to heat up Jomsu's male urge. In receiving him, her body wasn't half as pleasurable as her beautiful face. It was hard as a wooden board or a cold slab of stone.

Naturally, Jomsu hadn't expected her to share the pleasure. The mere fact that he was touching her naked skin with his, that he was inside her inner flesh, gave him more pleasure than any physical climax. Twice, three, four times it was repeated, but still she remained cold as ice. Jomsu felt rage swelling in his soul. He thought, we'll see how long you'll act this way as you receive a man's flesh deep into your own, we'll see how long before you relax yourself. Jomsu was lusting after a burning mutual love between them, but he quit after the fourth time.

It happened that two of his men, sent to imprison Shin Jungol after his arrest, blundered by losing their prisoner. Not only did Shin Jungol escape, but both of Jomsu's men were hacked to death with their own spears. He couldn't understand how in hell two armed men could have been killed by one empty-handed prisoner, but the incident was caused by his own irresponsibility. He had prevaricated when explaining the matter to the Chairman, but after that he lost all desire for the woman.

Even much later, his back turned to his birthplace, the memories of that time often reemerged in grotesque manifestations to torture him. He did his best to suppress those recollections, to struggle free from the web of memory, but it was fruitless. Perhaps those memories would forever course in his blood. However, of all those images, the memory of raping Byongmo's wife was not one that had surfaced. Possibly it had been buried under the more blatantly atrocious incidents. On the third day after the phone started ringing, the stranger had finally revealed his identity.

"Shin Byongmo was my father."

At that instant, president Hwang was so shocked he thought his head would explode, and as he desperately tried to cling to consciousness he had been simultaneously driven to a dreadful conclusion.

"You must be my own bastard, no doubt, you gotta be my own son."

And then, in utter despair at his accursed fate, with his life under attack from his own flesh and blood because of his evil deeds, President Hwang sank into a coma.

After sneaking away from the widow's inn after finding out she was no widow, Jomsu left behind the village where he had stayed for several months. Still impersonating a half-wit, he probed his way through unfamiliar villages. The war seemed to push and pull back in turn, and the villagers, pinched by poverty and careworn by insecurity, were panic-stricken. Jomsu tried his best to reach somewhere as far as possible from the mountains.

Villages near the mountains suffered from frequent incursions of partisans. By bad luck, he might be taken back to one of their sanctuaries, and there was no guarantee one of his old comrades would not recognize him. Due to this evasion of the highlands, he ended up in a large city. Compared to villages, cities provided almost no hospitality. There wasn't enough work for a half-wit to do to earn three meals a day. It would have been easiest for him to return to working metal at a forge, but that was the last thing he could do as he feared the prospect of being identified. Once he picked up a hammer his skill would be noticed at once and a half-wit trained as a blacksmith would hardly be credible.

When he arrived at the city of Masan, he was reduced to begging in the street. The larger the city, the thicker the clusters of refugees from up above the DMZ. Every single one of them, eyes revealing their ravenous hunger, was desperately seeking a way to earn some food. Jomsu realized at last that among these masses he could not survive by impersonating an idiot. He knew as well that Masan was far from the mountains and remote enough from his hometown. People were too preoccupied with their own lives to be nosing into the affairs of others. It was an environment different from that of a small village. Jomsu decided to drop the role of an imbecile and made up his mind to earn a living with the skills he already possessed. He began a serious search for a foundry. Once he made this decision, he felt like an entirely different person, and a strange energy emerged from the recesses of his body. Only later did he realize that his body had withered during the interval of impersonating a half-wit.

"What'd you say? You wanna work as a blacksmith, you say?"

The owner responded reluctantly, sizing up Jomsu, who looked like a beggar, from head to toe.

"Yeah, that's what I asked."

"Look here, are you asking me to teach you the trade, or are you saying you already have the skills and can work as a smith right now, which is it?"

"I can start right away."

"Really?"

The owner took another look at Jomsu's pitiful appearance. He craned his neck around and asked in a slighting tone, "If you say you can, how good are you?"

"I once had my own forge, sir."

"Huh, is that a fact?"

By then, the owner had retracted his neck to its normal position and was standing rigidly erect.

"Why should I lie? It can't help me. I can't fake it if I pick up a hammer, can I?"

Jomsu said this haughtily, feeling his biceps surge with strength.

"You have a Cholla dialect, don't you? Cholla smiths are famous for their skill. I'm just wondering how you sank to this sorry state, uh?"

The owner wore a puzzled look.

"Yeah, I get you. The red bastards done in my father, so I killed a couple of them to get revenge before running away. I knew they'd catch me if I stayed down in Cholla like a dunce, so I crossed over the mountains to Kyongsang."

Jomsu calmly dispensed these lies he'd concocted in advance for just such an occasion.

"Ain't that something? Now, then, you're a good son and a patriot, huh? Well, well, sit yourself down here. Sorry, I didn't recognize a real man at first sight."

The owner brushed the dust off a log chair beside him and offered Jomsu a seat.

"Sitting can wait, first I need to know if you'll hire me or not."

Jomsu knew the job was already his, but he wanted to hear it for sure.

"That goes without saying. All the decent smiths have either been killed in the war or drafted into the army. These days, you know, skilled hands are few and far between, so I'll count myself lucky to have a Cholla blacksmith," said the owner brightly.

No wages were settled, no benefits promised. For three meals a day Jomsu absorbed himself in work. Handling the red-hot iron, hammering with all his might, Jomsu felt the fulfillment of having something precious to him restored. Blacksmiths, like peasant farmers and butchers, for generations these occupations were scorned. He had leapt into a tumultuous fray hoping to turn that life of insult and injury into a new world. Now, haunted by both sides, he picked up the hammer once more to fill his stomach. And to be reborn. Yet, Jomsu still suffered from pangs of guilt.

What if the world had turned into a paradise for peasants and workers as Mr. Pang had promised, what then would he, who knew nothing except ironwork, have done? A mayor or a district chief? Could he even have worked as a lowly clerk in a district office? There would have been no such place for a barely literate man like him. After all, the only thing he could do with pride and integrity was blacksmith's work. No matter how completely the world might change, a blacksmith would never be as respectable as a mayor or a police chief. But back then, he had never heard these things. His vindictive urges had felt like heavy stones pressing on his heart, making it bloat up like a raked haystack. And once it caught fire, the flames erupted out of control until only ash remained.

Those Shins should not have been hacked up like sardines on a string. If only he had not raved so insanely, his father need not have died in despair, his good-hearted wife would have been spared that agonizing death, and his son would not have been abandoned, with his father uncertain whether he was dead or alive.

Whenever thoughts like these came over Jomsu, he would start swinging the heaviest sledge hammer like a madman. Oblivious of Jomsu's motives, on such occasions the owner would stop him from flailing with that huge hammer, pleading, "Easy now, easy. A knight of the hammer shouldn't be bothered with the heavy sledge. Leave that to the apprentices, what're you saving them for? Stop that, now. Stop."

Gazing at a lump of iron reddening amidst the tall flames of the furnace, Jomsu felt the mindless emptiness of life. Mr. Pang, whose father died accused of a murder committed by his master's son, had concealed the awful flame of resentful rancor when he taught Jomsu. And his hopeless life had ended in a vain suicide after he caught one small bullet. What was that all about? In the end, the whole universe depended on your own life. The world looks good or evil depending on how you see it.

If only Pang had not had such a bitterly spiteful attitude, he could have lived a quiet and calm life, receiving the respect due to a teacher. But his heart took him elsewhere, and so his short life ended on a nameless mountain. The same was true of Jomsu himself. If only he had heeded his father's words. But then, such thoughts were futile.

He was so swamped with work at the forge that he needed more than two hands. Unlike back in the village, he seldom made farm implements anymore. Most of the work was to fabricate commodities for daily use, things like kitchen utensils. The owner was earning fairly good profits. Cartridge casings bought dirt cheap were made into pots and pans which could be marketed at good prices. Cartridge casings were good quality brass and during the war they were everywhere.

After another year or so, the war was subsiding. People didn't seem to pay much attention to the war, partly because the front line was far from Masan. Only the occasional sound of weeping from a family notified of a battle death served as a reminder that the war was still underway. Maybe people were just too worn out from everyday poverty to pay constant attention to the war as it dragged on interminably near the 38th parallel.

Jomsu decided to move to Pusan, a place he had only heard about until that time. He had no special plan. It was simply that Pusan was a much bigger city than Masan. That Jomsu found himself drawn to a big city stemmed from a wish he had vaguely entertained since he was a small boy. When he was very young, he had a secret yearning to see big places. He was fed up with the idea of spending his whole life in a tiny hamlet where everyone knew everyone else, and where the high and low were separated by a line as clear and hard as a stone wall. He had dreamed of living in a huge city full of strange faces.

"What's this nonsense you're talking now? I haven't told you, because I thought it'd sound like I was flattering myself, but for some time now I've been putting aside a share for you, and I've been secretly looking for a bride so you can have a grand wedding and all. You rascal, cut this talk about leaving right now. No more of that. I almost choked at what you said."

The owner tried to ignore Jomsu's plan from the start. But Jomsu didn't change his mind.

"Um, what the devil is this? All right, if you're so sure you wanna leave, there must be a reason. Well, let me hear it."

Jomsu couldn't say why in so many words. No matter how well he explained, he didn't think the owner would understand.

"Well, once you made up your mind, not much I can do about it. So, what you gonna do once you get to Pusan?"

"Ain't decided yet."

"What's to decide? Gotta keep on with what you been doing. That's the surest thing, isn't it? Listen to me, you should open up a smithy. With your skill, you'll be seeing bright times ahead."

The owner handed him an unexpectedly large sum of money.

"Add a bit more to that, and no reason why you can't have your own smithy."

Pusan was indeed a big city crowded with people and full of noise. Jomsu couldn't have been happier that among so many faces not a single one was familiar. He didn't consider saving more money to add to what he had. Instead, he planned to open his own smithy right away. The scale of the forge could be adjusted to the money he had, and he no longer had the patience to go on working under somebody else just to save money.

He opened a small smithy on the outskirts of the city. Without any greed driving him to hoard money, he still poured body and soul into his work in hopes of forgetting his former life for good. But a strange thing happened. As time passed, orders piled up and so did the money. The wholesalers found that his products were well-made and easy to sell. Still, it brought no satisfaction to Jomsu. His mind was always vacant, and he felt self-pity at the nightmares that kept on tormenting him almost nightly.

About this time there were widespread rumors that the war would soon end. Jomsu was the subject of an unsolicited proposal for an arranged marriage that one of his buyers had cooked up. At first he was unenthusiastic, but once he saw the woman, his mind changed. His heart racing, he surprised himself by feeling the sensation of a new life budding somewhere in his hardened body. It was a change he had not even dreamt of, and he was a mystery to himself.

After divining Jomsu's mind, the matchmaker hurried the marriage along. It happened that this matchmaker, a well-known trader, was none other than the bride's maternal uncle. He had had Jomsu in mind for his niece for a long time.

For several nights, Jomsu racked his brain over a problem he faced. If he married, the law required making a report on his family register, which would necessitate a visit to his hometown. Hometown . . . Jomsu buried his head in the corner of the room. Then, one day, a solution flashed into his head. Just then many refugees from the North were obtaining what they called "interim registrations." His problem could be solved simply by making an interim registration.

Still, to carry out the idea was not so simple. It pained him that he had to make up a fictional birthplace for a new family registration when he knew his real home too well. He passed several days in bitter agony. The matchmaker, not knowing what was going on, aggravated matters with daily visits. Even apart from the marriage, Jomsu could not go on living with his true identity left behind in a home to which he could never return. He decided to proceed with the interim registration. As long as he was changing his birthplace to the North . . . the idea dawned on him that he could change his name as well. Then, what he had done wrong in the past could perhaps be buried forever. That was it. To bury Bae Jomsu for good in this world. Like a man possessed, Jomsu followed this line of thought in unexpected directions. Get a plastic surgeon to remove the bean-sized mole under his eye, wear a pair of glasses, get rid of his dialect . . . Jomsu was totally absorbed in this plan he had hatched, trembling with the joy of rebirth.

4

"No ordinary case, this."

Without being indiscreet, Dr. Chun started with the conclusion first. Hyongmin was troubled, but thanks to Dr. Chun's tact, he was able to control his emotions. With a glance, Hyongmin urged the doctor to go on.

"His condition is not improving at all, and why is beyond me. Your father seems to be under some unrelenting stress. It's as if he's plagued with constant nightmares, even when awake. He floats in and out of consciousness, and his blood pressure fluctuates badly. I know it sounds irresponsible, but a doctor can't do much for a man in such an unstable state."

Dr. Chun was slowly shaking his head. Hyongmin found this gesture more telling than anything he had been told. Regaining and losing consciousness, his blood pressure out of control . . . and in the end, Father would die, such seemed to be the prognosis.

Dr. Chun was a fine, honest man. He made it clear that unless Father could somehow break out of his unstable state, there was nothing more a physician could do. That meant Father was already caught in death's trap. The nightmares tormenting him were no mystery. They had not left him even after he changed his name, his birthplace, his face, and his manner of speech.

Like a virus dormant over a long period of incubation, they had slept in his blood and then, with the appearance of the stranger on the phone, they all at once launched their assault. Nobody could drive those nightmares from Father's exhausted mind, weakened by aphasia and paralysis—not famous doctors and not exorcists. Nobody but Father could save himself.

Hyongmin almost spoke but then had second thoughts. What if Father received another shock in this state? That was the question on the tip of his tongue. But to such an idiotic question a doctor could only answer, "Well, you know . . ." with barely concealed contempt. To ask that would have been no more intelligent than to ask how long a naked infant would survive in the scalding sun, or how long an eighty-year-old man would last in an icy river.

"Does my mother know?"

"Not yet. When your father is unconscious, she seems to think he's asleep."

"Don't tell my mother about this, please. Nor any of the others in the family."

Hyongmin's low voice was wrapped in a frigid solitude.

"That probably would be better for the patient, too, for the time being."

Hyongmin felt a black vertigo at Dr. Chun's remark. His initial "no ordinary case" had already become "for the time being." "For the time being" never meant any lengthy period of time, and it suggested Father's life was now just "a matter of time" in the doctor's opinion.

Hyongmin thought he had to ask how long it would be. It was his duty, his obligation as a son. Still, he couldn't bring himself to say it. "Parents . . ." the word seems trite, yet for children it means everything. The value is absolute. To realize that the time is at hand for the one who gave you life to leave you forever, to confirm the moment when you will be losing that beloved person, that is a heart-rending pain.

"Doctor, how long will my father . . . ?"

His throat was too constricted to go on.

"Well . . . three days at the most."

Hyongmin ground his teeth together so hard it was audible. Even now, if only he could . . . but Hyongmin coldly suppressed such primeval desire. He got up to leave. Dr. Chun also stood and silently opened the door for Hyongmin. He slowly walked down the corridor.

Three days . . . barring a miracle, there was no hope for father. Three days might be overly optimistic. As a professional, if the happiest thing for a doctor is the recovery of a patient, the most unpleasant must be informing the patient's family of his death. In that delicate situation, a doctor would use his best judgment. When he told the family how long he thought the patient had left, instinctively he would stretch the period beyond his real prognosis. Not for the family's sake so much, but to protect himself. It's odd how most people seem far more sensitive to bad things than to good. Perhaps doctors seldom err in their final prognoses for dying patients. Three days . . . it might have been extended from two days, a day and a half, or even a single day. One day . . . Hyongmin sighed mournfully.

"It's for you to decide whether to surrender just your father, or to let everything be ruined when he departs."

Hyongmin stopped. He thought over the same thing he had mulled over the night before. The meaning was simple enough if he just took the man's words at face value. But, once he regarded them skeptically, they became extremely dangerous. He lit a cigarette and inhaled deeply. He felt an instant dizziness and his mind wavered. Ah, in all of life does the thirst for living ever provide the pleasure, the hypnotically comforting peace, that a smoke can give? He continued to inhale deeply as he walked along the corridor.

"Son, just before you came in, your father showed a bit of smile," said his mother in a sentimental tone as soon as she saw Hyongmin. On her care-worn face, a glimpse of morning light lingered for a fleeting instant. The kind of new morning Mother longed for—never again would it shine down on her.

"Sure . . . he'll soon recover. Father's always been so healthy, you know."

Hyongmin forced a smile as he tried to shut off the tears welling up from the depths of his soul, and the odor of blood was thick in his head.

"Son, did you get some sleep?"

Even in such circumstances, Mother did not neglect her maternal con-cerns. If the sorrow of losing a parent was like the agony of having one's own flesh torn, how much worse would the sorrow be at losing one's lifelong mate? The pain of having one's body cut in two. . . . No matter how sincere and profound the grief of a son, it could never compare with the bereavement of a wife.

Soon Mother would have to endure that agony like having an arm and a leg amputated. But now, oblivious to what awaited her, here she was dream-ing of mornings they would share, overjoyed at a faint smile on Father's face. It couldn't have been a smile, more likely a grimace. Mother had mis-taken for a smile a grimace expressing the torment of nightmares she could never imagine, just as she had mistaken his lapses of consciousness as mo-ments of restful sleep.

Hyongmin stood over his father's bed. He certainly looked much worse than in the emergency room, and it was not only because of what the doctor said. Hyongmin was obsessed by a realization that the aphasia and paralysis represented zones death already had conquered. And now the last citadel was under siege. It was only a matter of time before Father was utterly vanquished by death.

"Put the phone back in the room by tomorrow!"

Hyongmin closed his eyes tightly, clenching his teeth with all his strength. From his nose a soft but deep sigh emanated with a sniffle reminis-cent of weeping. He felt for his father's hand. Those huge rough hands were unseemly on a man of fabulous wealth, and the warmth that Hyongmin used to find in them was no longer there. Only the inanimate feel of matter, like when you touch a piece of plaster. Father . . . slowly Hyongmin's cold ratio-nality was returning.

"Mother, you feel cooped up here, don't you? Shall we have the phone back?" Hyongmin said as he stood there.

"Could we? Then I'll feel less stifled."

She responded instantly.

"All right. I'll have it reinstalled, just wait a little while."

Hyongmin's voice was clear, but tears ran down from his closed eyes.

It was so dark you couldn't see your own feet. After bowing for the second time, Jomsu kept kneeling, unable to stand.

"Father, thinking over all of it, I've been out of my mind, stark raving mad. Just like you told me, it was nothing but rancor built up over a lifetime. Your grave's so poorly looked after because I've been chased all over for my crimes. And, Father, what can I do with Chilsung? Why in the world's he been turned into an idiot who can't even recognize his own father? While I was out ranting about, what god-awful sickness did he get to make him like that? What can I do, his mind's gone and he don't even know me, his own father?"

His head on the ground, Jomsu didn't move for a long time.

Before remarrying, Jomsu wanted to find out whether Chilsung was still alive. If so, he intended to reclaim his son and enter his name on the family register. Jomsu had the mole removed from under his eye and got a pair of glasses. For the first time in his life he bought a Western-style suit. The man in the mirror was a stranger even to himself. In this disguise he was not afraid to visit his hometown. But as he got closer to that place, he tensed up so badly he could barely stretch his knees out straight. Finally, he got off the bus three miles from the village. Then he waited until sundown. He walked the three miles to his home village. As he came closer, terror and panic gripped his soul. If anyone saw through his disguise, he'd never leave the place alive.

Except for scattered patches of light from lamps, the streets were dark. Nothing had changed. Chinese medicine shop, clothing store, general market, dye shop, they were all still there. Jomsu's head boiled with one thought. The town had to be the safest place to gather some word on Chilsung's whereabouts. The villages of Hoejongri, Chungokri and Dongchonri were each about a mile from the town, and going straight to Hoejongri would be like jumping from the frying pan into the fire.

As he passed by a store, Jomsu had an eerie premonition. He had just passed by a boy squatting and eating in the dim light, and the child suddenly captured his attention. Indecisively, Jomsu turned back. Then he took a few quick steps.

"Chil, Chil . . ."

Jomsu froze and then ran towards the boy. Despite the dim light, there was no doubt he was Chilsung. Jomsu almost wept with joy. His son was still alive; he thanked the boy's unknown protector. He wanted to know if it was the storeowner who had so lovingly cared for his son. But Jomsu lacked the courage to expose himself so recklessly. From his dark hiding place, he watched the boy for a long while.

A man came out from the store. Jomsu ducked further into the shadows.

"Hey, Chilsung, you idiot, get on up now and be on your way to find a place to sleep tonight. I gotta close the store now. I say, get up, hurry now!"

The man spoke in a loud voice, almost shouting, and waved his arms like he was shooing flies away. Jomsu was stung by the words "Chilsung" and "idiot."

Chilsung wobbled to his feet and began walking off into the dark. "Chilsung," "idiot," repeating those words, Jomsu followed as if pulled by a magnet. The boy walked fearlessly through the dark night toward the marketplace. After crossing through the unlit market, his son stepped into a pen beside a cowshed. Jomsu stood for a long time in front of the pen, his sense of guilt overwhelming. His son was a beggar.

"Chilsung!" Like a howling animal, Jomsu raced into the pen.

But the boy was an imbecile. Jomsu gagged and bound his struggling son to sneak out of town, then rested until dawn, pressing his face against his son's, anxiously repeating, "I'm your father."

But the boy stared vacantly about with glazed eyes and kept yelling "Mama! Mama!" in a tongue-tied voice.

"It's all your papa's fault. We'll be going now, from now on I'll make up for the wrongs I done to you. Come on now with papa."

But the boy was persistent. "Mama! Mama!" he screamed pathetically as he wriggled to his feet. Bowing to an uncanny feeling, Jomsu released him. His son ran for his life back towards the town, shrieking "Mama! Mama!"

Watching sadly, Jomsu had the tortuous realization that he was abandoned even by his idiot son. And he realized he could not take his son. Leaving his hometown empty and alone, Jomsu wept for his son, and for himself.

Jomsu was stranded in his longing and sorrow for Chilsung. But his new surroundings did not permit him to stay in such a state forever. He went ahead with the interim registration and then remarried.

The war had ended and the world was restless in the post-war atmosphere. People felt good, and the general mood was that of a carnival where all was possible. Meanwhile, Jomsu's smithy had grown and acquired a new name. It was no longer a smithy but an iron works, and Jomsu went from a forge owner to a company president.

As life settled down gradually, the demand for everyday consumer goods mushroomed, and Jomsu's iron works prospered more and more. There was nothing his mill could not manufacture, and Jomsu was a shrewd business-man well on his way to becoming a big-time entrepreneur.

Jomsu labored hard without sparing himself. Since he lacked educa-tion, he made up for his ignorance with sheer physical work, solving prob-lems through will instead of intellect. He had resolved to make as much money as his ability would allow and to go as far as his luck would take him. The abominable poverty of his past, he told himself that maybe that poverty had been responsible for all the horrible things that had happened. His growing wealth gave him much more pleasure in living, and in turn, his success gave him the courage and incentive to work even harder. His absorption in work freed him from remembering the past.

Behind all this hovered his inseparable shadow, his wife. She was a clever and thrifty woman, taking good care of money and equipped with the cunning and foresight needed for making more. Though she had only a pri-mary school education, her natural intelligence was a great help to Jomsu's business decisions. It was she who taught Jomsu how to keep accounts and to calculate with an abacus. She had an uncommon talent of transferring every-thing she knew to her husband for his use. At the same time, she was an obedient wife.

Jomsu's gravitation to the metropolis of Seoul began six years after the war ended. His works by then had grown into quite a business, and a separate company was formed to manage the manufacturing side. He decided to move to Seoul to make more money.

In Seoul, his business prospered even more. Rarely did he encounter any failure. Then, with the arrival of a government policy to promote indus-trialization, his company grew by leaps and bounds to its present size.

As twilight deepened, Hyongmin plugged in the telephone cord. Then he considered trying to persuade his mother to go home for some rest, but gave up on the idea. He could not separate her from his father now. How could he face her resentment if he were to pass away during her absence? But he feared the stranger's call might come while she was in the room. Still, since the important matters had already been settled, he might be able to manage the situation without arousing her suspicion.

"Son, what do you think about Father's condition now?" his mother asked, looking blankly into the air.

Hyongmin felt compassion at the extreme anxiety she must be suf-fering.

"He'll soon recover. Don't worry, please," he replied in a confident tone, but he could not bear to add the mundane phrase "in the doctor's opinion."

"You still have no intention of handling the business?"

Hyongmin didn't answer. It had been a much debated issue back when he was offered a position at the university. Hyongmin knew only too well that he was not cut out for the world of business, and it had been silently understood that Father's successor in the company would be Hyongmin's younger brother.

"Your father's a great man. How hard he worked. The company is not only a business, it's his life. Wouldn't it be wonderful if you could carry it on for him?"

"Mother, because the company is Father's life is precisely why I shouldn't be his successor. Soon I would make it sick and in the end I would wreck it."

Hyongmin spoke in an unpleasant tone, causing his mother to clam up with a deep sigh.

It was clear that Mother was fully expecting Father's recovery and was planning further steps. Hyongmin knew the reason she wanted him to take care of the company was not because she distrusted his younger brother, but because he was the eldest son. However, if the second son was not yet ready, there were plenty of people in the company capable of managing things.

The phone then rang an hour earlier than usual. On the first ring, Hyongmin picked up the phone.

"Hello?"

"Professor Bae Hyongmin, you needn't be in such a rush to answer the phone, do you?"

The syncopated voice, slow and expressionless, instantly divined Hyongmin's thinking.

"Put your father on the phone."

"His condition . . . is the same as yesterday."

"Can I trust you?"

"What am I supposed to say to that?"

"All right. Then, I'll try again. But next time, don't pick up the phone until it rings at least five times."

Hyongmin shuddered. The stranger was intending to deliver the coup-de-grace. He must have had this in mind when he demanded that the phone be reinstalled.

"Look, I understand your thinking very well. But you needn't do such a thing."

Conscious of his mother's presence, Hyongmin had used "thinking" instead of "intention" and omitted "cruel" from "such a cruel thing."

"I guess you mean to say his condition has deteriorated. How is it?"

In the course of six calls over the past six days, this was the first time the stranger asked a question the answer to which he did not know.

"It's such as to make it unnecessary."

"Professor Bae Hyongmin, I've no intention of playing word games with you."

The voice was somewhat incensed.

"Neither do I. I'm not alone now."

The stranger was silent for a while.

"Professor Bae Hyongmin, since your father snatched thirty years each from the lives of thirty-eight persons, it amounts to one thousand one hundred and forty lost years for them. Or, even if you reduce thirty to twenty years each, it would still be seven hundred and sixty years. Don't you think that's enough? You will not be correcting my calculations, will you?"

Silence.

"I do not forgive your father. Nor do I have any hatred for him. I do understand the circumstances your father found himself in. This means I admit the tyranny of the Shin clan to have been unjust. All the same, what your father did was unpardonable. By your father's own logic, you do understand that he, with his vast wealth, has to be stabbed to death and by whom? Precisely by a poor man like me. The logic is that absurd."

Hyongmin remained silent.

"Several times you asked to meet me. In a state of anxiety and urgency you said it was to save your father and your family. Even if we met, the kind of solution you wished for was never possible. Because I would have agreed to no conditions. I just wanted your father's life. No more. Neither his wealth nor your present status have anything to do with the crimes he once committed. All I want is to leave your father to the thirty-eight spirits, and to shake off my own yoke. I had no wish to extend this matter into something between us, so that's another reason why I refused to meet you. Once all this ends, you'll go your way and I mine. You, in the end, as Hwang Hyongmin."

After the stranger hung up the phone, Hyongmin sat absent-mindedly for a while. The faceless voice swept through Hyongmin's heart like a cold wind. Once again, he felt the icy, serpentine logic of the stranger.

Then Hyongmin heard his mother's scream. He sprang up to the bed. As if howling, his father had opened his mouth as wide as he could, and on his face was a terrible grimace. But no sound issued from his mouth.

The thick fog suddenly dispersed and President Hwang saw clearly the faces of his wife and his eldest son. Then he saw the fog approaching again in the distance. He began to scream with all his might.

"Go to Hoejongri in Cholla province, you'll find your grandfather's grave there. And you've got a half-brother who's an idiot. Take good care of him, understand, Hyongmin? That's your father's home . . ."

"Dear! Dear, dear . . ."

Mother's cries echoed through the ward. Hyongmin reached out to shut his father's wide open eyes.

It was two o'clock in the morning.

Disregarding various conflicting recommendations, Hyongmin decided to hold a three-day family funeral. Many people seemed puzzled by Hyongmin's decision, but he remained silent. There was talk about a tomb plot of fifty or seventy square meters, but Hyongmin settled for the normal size of twelve square meters.

They were busy preparing a sacrificial altar before the hearse left.

"What? The chief mourner? Who's speaking? He's busy now, if you leave your name . . ."

Hyongmin quickly turned around. He had a strange hunch.

"Give me the phone."

He almost snatched the receiver.

"Hello, this is Hwang Hyongmin."

Nothing. Hyongmin knew instinctively who the other party was.

The silence persisted on the other end of the line and Hyongmin, too, kept silent. He thought he heard a prolonged, deep breath and then the line was cut. Hyongmin slowly replaced the receiver.

CORNELL EAST ASIA SERIES

FORTHCOMING

Principles of Poetry (Shi no genri), by Hagiwara Sakutarō, translated by Chester Wang

Realistic Noh, translated by Mae Smethurst

Troubled Souls from Realistic Noh Dramas, by Chifumi Shimazaki

To order, please contact the Cornell East Asia Series, East Asia Program, Cornell University, 140 Uris Hall, Ithaca, NY 14853-7601, USA; phone (607) 255-6222, fax (607) 255-1388, internet: kks3@cornell.edu.

Playing With Fire

CHO CHONG-RAE

TRANSLATED BY CHUN KYUNG-JA

CHO CHONG-RAE is among the most popular contemporary Korean writers, dealing in his fiction with the personal trials and social agonies of Korea's division into North and South. In this suspenseful tale, a former communist partisan guilty of atrocities during the Korean War hides his past by assuming a new identity, but decades later is tracked down by a descendant of one of his victims, who exacts a terrible revenge. *Playing With Fire* was awarded the prestigious Korean National Literature Prize upon its publication in 1982.

CHUN KYUNG-JA holds a Ph.D. from the University of Texas at Austin and is currently director of the Korean Language Program at Harvard University. She has published many translations of modern Korean prose and poetry, including such novels as *Peace Under Heaven* by Ch'ae Man-Sik (M.E. Sharpe, 1991) and *The Shadow of Arms* by Hwang Suk-Young (Cornell East Asia Program, 1994).

1-97/1.6M paper/.4M cloth/TS